# Mercy Row Retribution

Book 3 of the Mercy Row Series

# Harry Hallman

Octane Interactive, LLC
Publishing

Mercy Row Retribution Book 3
by Harry Hallman
www.mercyrow.com

This book is dedicated to my wife Duoc, my son Bill, my daughter Nancy, my granddaughter
Ava and all of my family, past, present and future.
I would also like to thank Bill Hallman, my brother, and Dave Carr, my
brother-in-law, for being there when I called checking on some memory or another.
A special thank you to all the men and women who served during the Vietnam War, and those
who served our country before and after.

Published by
Octane Interactive, LLC - Publishing

ISBN- 1519290926
ISBN 13: 9781519290922

# Part One

# Chapter One

The C123 Provider aircraft, traveling over 200 miles per hour, suddenly dropped from the sky and nose-dived towards the dense Vietnamese jungle. When the plummeting plane reached 400 feet, co-pilot Lieutenant First Class Gerry Byrne Amato flawlessly executed a maneuver that leveled the plane at just 100 feet above the treetops. Amato felt exhilarated as the green expanse sped by. He loved the feeling of flying so close to the ground. It was dangerous and it took a high level of skill. One small error, one misjudgment would mean a fiery death. Fuck! I love this, Amato thought.

Gerry Amato joined the Air Force in 1963, just after finishing college. He wanted to be part of the war everyone expected would break out between the Soviet Union and the United States. In 1961 the Soviets had the East Germans build a wall between East and West Berlin effectively imprisoning their own people.  In addition, in 1961 a failed attempt from U.S.-backed Cuban counter revolutionaries against Fidel Castro's communist regime, heightened tensions.

In 1962 an American U2 spy plane flying 50,000 feet over Cuba discovered Soviet-made missiles directed at various U.S. east coast cities. This caused the U.S. to blockade ships from arriving in Cuban ports thus creating a larger rift between the U.S. and Russia. For a few weeks, many government officials and the people of the United States believed a war with the Soviet Union was imminent. The Soviets blinked first and had the missiles removed from Cuba, and the world avoided a conflict no one could win. Gerry fearing he would miss the war accelerated his course load, attended summer school, and was able to graduate college with a degree in business one year early.  He immediately joined the United States Air Force.

By the time Gerry finished flight school in early 1964, President Kennedy was dead, things had settled down with the Soviets, and he had found the love of his life; flying. His first main assignment was at an airbase called Tan Son Nhat in Saigon, South Vietnam. He had never heard of Vietnam before this assignment and had to go to the public library to look up where it was located.

When he learned that the U.S. had thousands of military advisors in the country to help the South Vietnamese people fight a war against communist rebels supported by the North Vietnamese, he was excited. He wanted to be part of the effort and do his part to save the world from communism.

At first, Gerry co-piloted a C-123 cargo plane delivering goods to various bases where there were large numbers of U.S. military advisors. Within three months, he was reassigned to Captain Al Watson's C-123 aircraft as Co-pilot. Watson was a seasoned pilot who had first seen action during the last year of the Korean conflict. Gerry and Watson became part of a top-secret special missions group shuttling unprocessed reconnaissance film shot by U2 spy aircraft in North Vietnam and the Ho Chi Minh trail in Laos and Cambodia. Occasionally the cargo included film from unmanned flights over Southern China.

Their normal flight route was to leave Saigon, travel to a special landing strip in Cambodia near the border with Laos. The crew would pick up film that needed transport and then they flew it to another secret landing strip near the coastal town of Kampong Seila, Cambodia, close to the boarder of Thailand. Once there, they transferred the film to CIA agents who transported it to Thailand and on to Washington. The whole flight was approximately 1000 miles and they did this four, sometimes five times a month. The C-123 aircraft was unmarked because of political sensitivities of the Laotian and Cambodian governments.

During the flight to deliver the film to the CIA agents, Gerry and Watson always made a special stop at a plantation owned by a French expatriate with ties to the Marseille Mob. They would load up the C-123 with 10,000 lbs of Cambodian marijuana and deliver it to a cargo barge that took it to a ship waiting in the Gulf of Siam. When the ship had received a minimum of 30,000 lbs of marijuana, they delivered it to Gerry's Uncle Jake Byrne in Philadelphia. From off the coast of Cape May, New Jersey transport boats would travel it up the Delaware River to warehouses in the Port Richmond section of the city.

The street value of a single shipment was approximately nine million dollars. The profit was split between the Marseille Mob and the North Philly Irish mob established by Gerry's Grandfather Jacob Byrne and his Uncle Franklin Garrett in the early 1920s. The locals called them the K&A Gang.

Gerry Amato devised the marijuana smuggling plan after his first few months in Vietnam. He realized the drug was plentiful and had become very popular with American youth. It was easy to find a grower and when he was assigned to be part of the special missions group, the plan fell into place. The route they flew was far from the U.S. military establishment and no one really wanted to talk about what they were doing. It was the ideal situation to piggyback a smuggling operation.

When he told Watson and the two other crew members how much money they would make by working with him, they were more than happy to assist. Each delivery meant a cash deposit of $50,000 would be placed in each of the two crew member's special bank accounts. Captain Watson received $100,000. When these men finally left Vietnam to return to the States, they would be wealthy.

Gerry operated the smuggling ring for over two years and his time in Vietnam was ending. A couple more flights and then he would rotate out of Vietnam. He missed his Mother and the rest of the family. It was time to go home.

Gerry arranged to have a new crew take over the smuggling operation and his Uncle Jake would, hopefully, continue to get shipments as long as the war lasted and beyond. Having done his duty, Gerry was excited to resign his commission and start developing the marijuana business at home. He was convinced marijuana sales had unlimited potential. Just as his grandfather Jacob did with booze during Prohibition, Gerry was ready to take advantage of people's appetite to get high and feel good.

"Watch that tree, Watson yelled.

Gerry banked the plane left missing the tree by just a few feet and said," Take it easy, Al. I saw it."

"You're too fucking low," Watson said.

"What's the matter, Al? Losing your balls?" Gerry said laughing as he pulled the C-123 up to 250 feet.

Gerry had become good friends with Al Watson and his other two crew mates, Jim Johnston and Theodor Raymond Edwards III who they nicknamed Tripp. Watson was from a small town near Atlanta, Georgia called Decatur. Jim Johnson hailed from Louisville, Kentucky and Tripp was born and raised in Manhattan. Watson had fifteen years in the Air Force and planned to resign a rich man when he cycled back to the States a month after Gerry. Johnson and Tripp both were enlisted men and had another year in-service before they there discharged.

"Better take her up to a thousand. The trail's coming up," Watson said.

Gerry pulled the plane up and said, "Tell me again why we have to take pictures of the Cong strolling down the fucking Ho Chi Minh Trail?"

The brass decided that since Watson was flying over the trail anyway, his aircraft could do double duty by taking some recon photos. It was bullshit and everyone knew it. The jet jockeys did a much better job of recon then a C-123 could do. Some colonel or general was trying to make brownie points by showing how brilliant he was. The problem was it put Watson's plane and crew in danger.

Their C-123 had no armaments other than several AR15s the crew members were issued when they arrived in Vietnam. Each man also carried a military-issued .45 Automatic. Gerry had a leather double shoulder holster and two older model .45s that were a gift from his Uncle Frank. Frank told him it belonged to his Grandma Rose's long dead husband George Graham. Gerry had never met Graham as he was murdered before Gerry was born, but he had heard all of the stories and was proud to be wearing his guns.

A few months after he joined Watson's crew, Gerry traded a grunt some weed for a couple of cases of hand grenades. They had never had to use them, but it gave Gerry and the others a false sense that they were well armed.

"Jesus Christ, Gerry you know why. Now get us up to a thousand," Watson said.

"Yes sir, Captain," Gerry said mockingly and saluted.

"Tripp, you awake back there?" Watson asked into the microphone.

"Yes sir," Tripp answered.

"Get the camera ready and turn them on when I tell you," Watson ordered.

"There it is," Gerry said and banked to the north. As the plane righted Gerry yelled out, "Holy shit, there's Cong on the trail."

It was unusual to see the enemy on the Ho Chi Minh trail. As soon as they heard an airplane engine, they melted into the jungle.

"Bring her down to 800, Gerry. Tripp, turn the cameras on," Watson ordered.

"Done," Tripp answered.

"Hold her steady, Gerry," Watson said.

"What the hell are they doing down there," Gerry asked seeing several of the Cong pointing at their plane.

"I don't know. We've done this so many times, maybe they know we don't have any weapons. They're not afraid of us," Watson said.

"They..." Gerry was about to say something when he heard a metal on metal sound and something hit the bottom of his chair. "What the hell was that?"

Gerry reached under his seat, felt around and found a warm piece of metal. He held it in the palm of his hand to show Watson and said, "Son of a bitch. How'd they do that?"

Gerry made a hard bank to the left, did a u-turn, and came back up the rail.

"What the hell are you doing?" Watson yelled.

"Teaching those fucks what happens when you shoot at us. Tripp, you and Jim grab a few grenades and open the side doors. When I tell you, pull the pins and drop them on those bastards. Tell me when you're ready."

A minute later Jim Johnson's voiced cracked over the communications system, "Ready."

Gerry put the plane into a dive and leveled out just 150 feet above the trail. The Viet Cong soldiers who shot at the C-123 rushed to the cover of the jungle.

"Toss those bad boys in the trees. Now," Gerry yelled.

Tripp and Jim pulled the pins on four grenades and threw them into the jungle as far as they could. Several seconds later, there were four explosions. Gerry pulled the plane up and then banked left on a course for the secret airstrip on the Cambodia Laos border.

"Did we get them, Tripp?" Gerry asked

"Nah. The grenades exploded before they reached the treetops," Tripp said.

"Too fucking bad," Gerry said.

Watson stared at Gerry for a moment and said, "You are one crazy son of a bitch."

"I know," Gerry replied.

# Chapter Two

The rest of the flight was uneventful. They made their pickups, dropped them off and returned to Tan Son Nhat Air Base near Saigon that evening. The next morning Gerry put on his civilian clothes, walked to the commissary and purchased twenty cans of spam, a large box of chocolate bars and a bottle of Johnny Walker Black. Then he walked to the gate and got into one of the many tiny Renault taxies waiting to take GIs into the City of Saigon.

Gerry lightly slapped the sleeping driver's head and said, "Wake up, Hung. You can't make any money sleeping all day."

Hung rubbed the sleep from his eyes and said, "Mr. Gerry, I wait for you."

"How'd you know I'd need you today?" Gerry asked.

"I not know. Just wait," Hung said.

Gerry met Hung on his first trip into the city of Saigon. He and two of his fellow pilots had been drinking at the officers club and decided to continue the party on Tudo Street. Tudo Street was well known for its American style cafes, bars and the beautiful women who worked in them. During the trip to Tudo Street in Hung's cab, his fellow pilots started yelling, "Di di Mau" and threw hundred Dong bills at Hung. It didn't take Hung long before he understood that the faster he went the more hundred Dong bills he got.

The small car sped through the streets of Saigon dangerously twisting and turning through traffic and pedestrians. Everyone in the car was laughing, until Hung lost control of the vehicle, spun around four times, hit the curb and ended up on the sidewalk. Gerry told his friends to go on and he stayed to help Hung. The next morning he bought Hung a new taxi and gave him money to make up for his lost fares.

"How's the family, Hung?" Gerry asked. Hung was married and had three children of various ages from ten years old to nineteen.

"They good. My Mai, she get married one month. You come, Mr. Gerry?" Hung said.

"I'm sorry, Hung. I got my orders this morning. I go home in three days," Gerry said.

"I happy for you, but sad for me," Hung said.

"I'll miss you, Hung. You've been a good friend," Gerry said. "Listen, Mr. Tripp will take care of you after I leave."

"He give me pot?" Hung asked.

"Yes, same deal. You pay him. If you have any trouble, you let me know," Gerry said and handed Hung a large envelope. "My address and phone number are in there and some cash for your family. I got a going away present for you." Gerry handed Hung the bottle of whiskey.

"Thank you, Mr. Gerry. I hide this. My wife, she like Johnny too much," Hung said and laughed.

When Gerry began smuggling marijuana, he started giving Hung four kilos a month to sell to other taxi drivers, who in turn sold it to GIs. Now Hung was selling twenty kilos a month and became wealthy, by Vietnamese standards, and was able to buy a small Villa.

"You number one, Mr. Gerry," Hung said as he started to drive away and quickly stalled the vehicle.

"And you're a number ten driver," Gerry said and laughed.

Hung laughed, restarted the car and drove off.

"Same, same place?" Hung asked.

"Yeah, Hoi Duc Anh Orphanage.

Thirty minutes later Hung pulled up in front of the orphanage. It had been over a year and a half since Gerry began volunteering at the orphanage. He helped take care of the children and provided money for their health and welfare. Twice a week, sometimes more Gerry would visit and bring food, candy and items for the Catholic nuns and locals who ran the orphanage. In recent months, the number of children at the facility had doubled and resources were running thin.

"Hung, take your money home and you can meet me back here in one hour," Gerry said.

"Okay, Mr. Gerry. I take home, give wife. Be back soon. I park outside bar," Hung said and pointed to a bar across the street from the orphanage.

Gerry patted Hung on the shoulder and walked into the courtyard of the orphanage. As soon as Gerry appeared through the double doors, twenty or so children starting screaming and rushed him. They grabbed his arm and walked him across the yard to the stairway leading to the children's rooms on the second floor.

"Cam, take this, and share it with the other kids," Gerry said and handed the box of chocolate to a twelve-year-old girl who was carrying a baby on her hip."You promise?"

"You betcha, Mr. Gerry," Cam replied.

Gerry walked up the stairs and halfway there he stopped, turned around and asked, "Where's Ho today?"

All the children answered together making it impossible to understand them. Their gesturing indicated that Ho was in the playroom. Nguyen Van Ho was a two-year-old boy whose parents the Viet Cong murdered when he was just six months old. He arrived at the orphanage at about the same time Gerry started volunteering. Gerry made it a point to take care of Ho personally and over the months both Gerry and Ho had grown close to each other. Gerry thought about adopting Ho, but he wasn't married and he didn't think his lifestyle was suitable for a toddler. Fortunately, a well off Vietnamese couple with no children adopted Ho and he was leaving the orphanage in a week. Gerry knew this was the last time he would see him.

"Good morning, Sister Kim," Gerry said as he approached the nun who was cleaning up a mess an infant had made. "Sister, why don't you let me buy you some diapers?"

The nun turned, shook her head and said, "Vietnam too hot. Make bottom sore. No diaper better."

"Sister Kim, I have my orders and I am going home very soon. This will be my last visit," Gerry said.

Sister Kim looked down at the floor and said, "We will miss you, Mr. Gerry." A tear fell down her face.

"Don't cry, Sister, I'm still going to take care of the children. My mother runs a charitable group called the Mercy Row Foundation. I talked to her and she promised she would send money on a regular basis," Gerry said touching the Sister's chin and bringing her head up to face him.

Sister Kim leaned over and kissed Gerry on the cheek and said, "You number one man, Mr. Gerry. You make children happy. You take care of us. We miss you."

Gerry hugged Sister Kim and said, "I'll miss all of you too. Now where's Ho? I want to spend some time with him and the other children before I leave."

"I take you," Sister Kim said.

"Oh Sister here," Gerry said and handed Sister Kim the bag of Spam, and then a thick envelope.

The sister opened the bag, saw the Spam and her eyes lit up. It was her favorite American delicacy. Then she opened the envelope and she looked up at Gerry, her eyes wide and her mouth open. In the envelope was a large stack of American $100 bills.

"I put the name and address of an Indian money changer in the envelope. He won't cheat you. He'll give you the best black market rate for the U.S. dollars."

Sister Kim just stared at Gerry in stunned silence.

"Okay, Sister. You go put that away. I'll find Ho," Gerry said.

Gerry found Ho playing with other children in the large open playroom for toddlers. He spent forty minutes with them, said his goodbyes and walked to the window to see if Hung had returned with his taxi. He was there, parked in front of the bar as he said he would.

Sister Kim walked up to Gerry, took him by the arm and started walking him to a room across from the large window he had just been looking out. "Please, Mr. Gerry. You say goodbye to other Sisters?"

"Of course I will, Sis..." Gerry was interrupted when the window behind him exploded inward. He felt the concussion before he heard the explosion. Gerry grabbed the nun, threw her to the floor and covered her body with his. She tried to get up. "Stay down, Sister," Gerry screamed just as a second lesser explosion shook the building.

After a minute of so, Gerry got up from the floor, walked to the window, and looked across the street. There were large black plumes of smoke coming from the bar doors and windows making it difficult to see. When the smoke began to clear, Gerry could see torn and broken bodies, including several children, lying just outside of the bar doors. One had a missing leg; another's upper portion of the body was gone. It was a bloody mess.

Then he saw Hung's cab upside down in the middle of the street. Gerry ran down the steps, out into the chaos and over to the cab. He pulled at the door but it wouldn't open. Gerry bent down to see how Hung was and a bloody shocked face looked back.

Hung said, "This number 10, Mr. Gerry," and then he died.

The bottle of Johnny Walker Gerry had given Hung was laying next to Hung's body miraculously unbroken. Gerry sat staring at the bottle for a minute and then picked it up, opened it, poured some on the street for Hung, and took a long swig from the bottle. He said a prayer for Hung, hoping his catechism teachers were wrong about non-Catholics not being able to enter heaven. He then walked over to the curb by the orphanage door and sat down. Gerry was stunned. Hung was gone. He couldn't believe it. *The fucking Viet Cong murderers. The fucking bastards,* Gerry screamed inside his head. He threw the bottle of Johnny Walker to the street smashing it.

The Viet Cong had pulled one of their classic terrorist moves. They planted one bomb in the back of the bar and when it went off, everyone still alive ran towards the door to get out. Just as they were leaving the second bomb, usually a Claymore mine directed at the doorway, exploded killing those who thought they were running to safety.

The nuns ran out of the orphanage to see if they could help. Sister Kim saw Gerry sitting on the curb, came up behind him and said,"Mr. Gerry, Mr. Gerry, you hurt."

Gerry, still reeling from Hung's death just shook his head no.

"You hurt, you hurt," Sister Kim insisted. "Glass in back."

He didn't feel anything, how could that be? Clearing his mind he said, "Pull it out, Sister. Please pull it out."

Sister Kim took the first chard in her fingers and gently pulled. Gerry instantly stiffened and said, "Oh, now that hurts." The Sister stopped pulling. "Keep going, Sister." Gerry insisted.

Sister Kim pulled the glass free and dropped it to the sidewalk. She then took the Secord chard in her fingers and quickly pulled it out, then the third. Gerry tensed and looked up. "How many more?"

"That all, Mr. Gerry. Now I go help," the Sister said and began to run off to the bar.

"Sister Kim, wait," Gerry yelled. "How are the children?"

"They good. No one hurt," Sister Kim responded as she started running again.

Gerry watched her go into the bar and he could hardly imagine the carnage the Sister would see. He put his hands on his face, leaned over and cried for Hung and his family.

# Chapter Three

Jake Byrne and Mike Kelly entered the well-appointed offices of the Wolinski Brick and Tile Company. Both men were wearing impeccably tailored suits. Jake's was a three-button dark gray suit with the new narrow lapel style. Mike's suit was a black double-breasted style with the older wide lapels. Both men wore white shirts. Jake's tie was a solid gray thin style while Mike wore a colorful hand painted wide silk tie favored in the 1940s.

The secretary saw them, took a job application from the desk drawer, and handed it to Jake. She looked at Mike and said," I'm sorry, sir but the sales position is for a younger man."

Mike glared at the secretary for a moment and said nothing. "We're not here for a job, Miss. Is Wolinski in?" Jake asked and gently placed the application on the desk.

"Oh, I'm so sorry, sir. Do you have an appointment?" the secretary asked.

"No, but he'll see us," Jake said as he and Mike started walking to Wolinski's office door.

The secretary stood up and said, "Sir you can't just…" Mike interrupted her by looking at her and putting his finger to his lips, suggesting that she be quiet. The secretary, sensing Mike was not a man to disobey, quickly sat down.

Wolinski, seeing the men enter his office got up from his chair, put his hand out across the desk and said, "Jake, how are you? I didn't know we had a meeting today."

Jake brought his hand up, leaned across the desk and punched Wolinski in the face. Woliniski fell back into his chair and grabbed his nose. Blood ran from between his fingers dripping onto the desk.

Mike pulled out a fine linen handkerchief and tossed on the desk. Wolinski picked it up, held it to his nose and looked wide-eyed at the two men.

"I told you. Did I not tell you? If another single brick was stolen from a Byrne Construction site I would visit you. And I believe I warned you that it would not be a pleasant visit," Jake said in a low deliberate voice.

"Jake..." Wolinski tried to plead.

"Shut the fuck up." Mike yelled.

"Yesterday your men delivered forty pallets of red bricks to the Byrne's Knights Road project. This morning fifteen of those pallets were missing," Jake said.

"I did..." Wolinski started to say but was interrupted by Mike.

"I told you to shut up," Mike said as he moved around the desk and put the point of a ten-inch stiletto switchblade to Wolinski's neck.

"We know it's you. Doesn't matter. You're responsible to deliver the bricks. You're also responsible make sure they stay where they are supposed to stay. Now listen closely, Wolinski. If one more brick is missing from any Byrne's Construction site, we'll hold you personally responsible for the loss. My associate and I will visit again and we won't be so nice," Jake explained.

"Should I cut the tip of his nose off so he remembers next time," Mike said as he moved the knife to Wolinski's nose. Wolinski tensed. "Nah, that's a bit much. How about you take off an ear?" Jake said. Mike moved the knife to Wolinski's ear. Wolinksi's eyes widened and he started breathing hard.

"Nah, too much blood. You got your good suit on. Don't want you to ruin it. How about we just give him a good beating?" Jake suggested.

"Okay. Good. You do it. I got arthritis in my hands. It hurts when I punch someone," Mike said.

"Shit, I hurt my hand when I hit him. I can't do it either," Jake said, paused, thought for a minute and continued, "Say, I saw a movie where these Jap gangsters cut off the pinky finger of a guy who screwed up. Why don't we do that?"

Wolinski began to say something so Mike moved the knife back to his throat and he stopped.

"Okay, that's good with me," Mike said and handed the knife to Jake, then wrapped the already-bloody handkerchief around the tip of Wolinski's pinky finger. Mike then put his hand over Wolinski's month and said, "It'll be a lot worse if you make any noise."

Jake placed the knife on Wolinski's finger and quickly cut just above the first joint. Tears ran out of Wolinski's eyes and mixed with the blood from his nose. He remained silent.

Jake wrapped Wolinski's finger with the handkerchief, then wiped the blood from the knife on Wolinski's white shirt. He took Wolinski by the chin, pulled his head up so he was looking into his eyes and said, "Next time I'll cut off your pecker."

Jake and Mike walked out of the office leaving Wolinski sobbing and holding the handkerchief to his finger to stop the bleeding. Jake seeing the secretary's wide-eyed expression, pulled out a business card and dropped it on the desk. Then he said, "I think you're going to get fired. If you do, come to this address and we'll get you a new job. Better go find a towel for your boss. He had a small accident."

In the mid 1950s Jake's father Jacob Byrne and Franklin Garrett decided to reorganize the Irish K&A Gang they had started back in the 1920s during Prohibition. In the 1930s they created separate crews of ten men each. Now these crews were operating autonomously. The idea was similar to creating franchise owners, but instead of hamburger joints these franchisees would head their own criminal organizations. The crews managed themselves and were responsible to kick up a fee based on the amount of money they made to Jacob and Franklin. In return, the criminal franchisees received protection in terms of political connections and heavy work if needed. Jake Byrne and Mike Kelly provided the heavy work.

The crews were also supplied quantities of pot from Jacob's grandson, Gerry Amato's smuggling racket. They sold it on the street, nightclubs and bars. Jake Byrne was also in charge of marijuana distribution.

Many of the K&A Gang crews also did second story work. Their main targets were the northern Philadelphia suburbs, the Main Line and sometimes cities in New Jersey, Maryland, Virginia and North Carolina. A rule established many years before, forbade crews from stealing from anyone in North Philadelphia or in the territory held by the Italian Mob, mostly in South Philadelphia.

The second story work netted jewelry, art and antiques. These were fenced through a small group of experts managed by Mercy Byrne Amato who is CEO of the Mercy Row Foundation. All profits derived from the sale of the fenced goods are funneled into her foundation and then used for charitable work.

Jacob Byrne, Mercy's father, created the Mercy Row Foundation in the 1930s when as a child, Mercy suggested they make some empty homes they owned available to the homeless. While Mercy recovered from a gunshot wound she received in an attack on her father by the Chicago Mob, Byrne remodeled the homes and placed his then housekeeper Rose Reilly Graham in charge. In later years, Rose retired and Mercy took over the management of the foundation. The family also received money from a network of bookies spread throughout North, Northeast Philadelphia and suburban towns. The bookmaking locations ran numbers, horse race betting and sports gambling. Charlie Byrne, Jacob's son, was in charge of the gambling business.

Jacob Byrne turned over control of the legitimate family business, Byrne Construction, to his adopted son Jimmy Byrne. The construction business, originally founded by Jacob's father Charles Byrne in 1905, was responsible for building many of the homes, churches and factories in North Philadelphia. After World War II the firm was contracted to build several projects to house the families of returning soldiers. Byrne Construction located an office on the northeast corner of a housing project they built near Grant Avenue and Roosevelt Boulevard. They moved their headquarters to Northeast Philly when Byrne Construction began building row homes in and around Woodhaven Road.

As Mike Kelly and Jake Byrne were leaving the Wolinski Brick and Tile building, Mike asked, "What time's the party?"

"Six," Jake answered.

"Why so early," Mike asked.

"Rose likes to eat early, so Mercy is taking her to church at four and then Rose thinks she's having a small family dinner to celebrate her birthday at my Mom and Dad's place. They want the guests there before Rose gets there so they can surprise her," Jake said.

"You think it's okay to surprise an 87- year-old woman," Mike said.

Rose Riley Graham started her association with the Byrne family in the 1920s when she took a position as housekeeper for Jacob Byrne and Franklin Garrett. Through the years, she became a surrogate mother to Jacob and Molly Byrne, a grandmother to Jimmy, Mercy, Charlie, Jake and Georgie Byrne and a great grandmother to Gerry Amato and Jimmy, Charlie and Jake's children. They loved her as if she was from their own blood, and she loved them.

"Nobody's going to jump out and yell surprise. We'll just be there for her when she arrives. Molly invited a couple of her old friends who are still kicking. Frank, Catherine, Grady, Jerome, you and your family will be there. Everyone will be there. Should be a fun time," Jake said.

# Chapter Four

Mercy Byrne Amato finished brushing her hair then opened the diamond-encrusted locket she always wore around her neck. She studied the photos inside. On the left was a picture of her Grandfather Charles Byrne and on the right a photo of her namesake and Grandmother Mercy Byrne. She had never met her Grandmother Byrne. She died long before Mercy was born.

Mercy prayed her Grandfather and Grandmother were looking down from heaven with pride for all their family had achieved. She closed the locket and tucked it safely under her dress.

Looking in her mirror, Mercy inspected her reflection. What she saw was a still beautiful 43- year-old woman, with just a few wrinkles that gave her character, she thought. Her body was trim, her auburn hair was shoulder length and her green eyes sparkled.

Mercy picked up the necklace Gerry had given her when he graduated from flight school. It was a miniature pair of wings on a silver chain, very similar to the one Gerry wore on his uniform. She kissed the wings, put her fingers to her lips, and placed them on the framed photo of Tony Amato she kept on her dresser. Tony, Gerry's father and Mercy were married in 1943. Not long after Tony, who was a sailor in WW2, was killed in action off the coast of Sicily. He had never seen his son Gerry.

Rising from her chair, Mercy walked down the carpeted stairs and knocked on Rose's bedroom door. When the original Mercy Row Foundation homes ceased to be available for military families in 1947, Mercy had the homes redone to their previous state and sold them. She used the proceeds for her foundation's work. She kept two homes of the four homes her father had combined in the 1920s for his use. She wanted to bring up Gerry in the neighborhood she loved so she refused to move.

Mercy, Rose and Gerry lived together until Gerry joined the Air Force. Several years before, Mercy had one of the lower floor rooms converted to a bedroom with a bath for Rose so she didn't have to climb the stairs.

Mercy knocked on the door. Rose didn't answer so Mercy knocked again. Still no answer. Mercy slowly opened the door and walked into Rose's room. Rose was sitting in her overstuffed chair. Her head was leaning to one side and her eyes were closed. A stab of fear rippled through Mercy. She quickly walked to the chair and put her hand on Rose's shoulder and shook her gently and said, "Rose, wake up. Time to go." Rose didn't answer.

Mercy shook her again and said, "Time to wake up, Rose."

Rose slowly opened her eyes, looked around and said, "I wasn't asleep."

"I think maybe you were," Mercy said smiling.

"No, no. I just closed my eyes. I felt a little dizzy so I sat down and closed my eyes. I wasn't asleep," Rose said.

"No matter. Are you okay now? Can you get up?" Mercy asked.

"Of course," Rose replied and started to get up from the chair. Mercy assisted her.

"Have you asked the doctor about these dizzy spells?" Mercy asked.

"Yes. He says it is nothing to worry about. My blood pressure's fine," Rose lied.

Mercy helped Rose put her coat on and buttoned it for her. "It's getting nippy outside," Mercy said. They left the house and Mercy had to help Rose into the front seat of her 1966 cherry-red Mustang.

"This infernal car will be the death of me yet. Why are the seats so low," Rose complained.

"I'm sorry, Rose. I should have borrowed one of dad's cars," Mercy said. "Here, let me help you put on your seat belt."

"That's another thing. We didn't have seat belts when I was young and we're all fine. They're too tight," Rose complained.

"It's the latest in safety for cars and remember what my dad always says," Mercy said then cocked her head and looked at Rose.

"Oh my dear God! If I hear that one more time, I'll faint. Better safe than sorry, indeed. He needs a new saying," Rose said and giggled.

"Well, we don't want to lose you, Rose. You got a lot more years to go," Mercy said and clicked the seat belt into the fastener.

Mercy drove Rose to St. Hugh's Church on Tioga Street. Rose wanted to get to the church early so she could light candles for her departed husband George Graham, and her son Sean, who was killed by the Italian Mob in the 1920s. She also wanted to say a prayer for Gerry who was fighting in Vietnam.

Mercy guided Rose to the candles. Rose put a donation in the box and lit the two candles. Mercy lit three candles, one for her grandfather Charles Byrne, one for Tony and the other for her grandmother Mercy Byrne. She also said a prayer for her son, Gerry.

The mass was shorter than Mercy expected and she had to kill time before they drove to her mother and father's house for the surprise party for Rose.

"Rose, we have some time before dinner. Do you mind if we drive by the old house on Broad Street."

"No. It would be good to see it again."

Charles Byrne, Mercy's Grandfather, had purchased the Broad Street mansion not long after the turn of the century. He modernized the house and when he passed, Jacob Byrne, Mercy's Father, moved the family into the large home. By 1960 the area on Broad Street where the mansion was located started to deteriorate so Jacob sold the home and moved to a 6,000 square foot ranch home in Lower Moreland Township, a northeast suburb of Philadelphia. Several years after Jacob moved, a house next to him went on sale. Franklin Garrett, Jacob's partner and friend, and his wife Catherine bought the house.

Mercy took Mascher Street to Allegheny Avenue, then west to Broad Street. She drove south on Broad Street, past Fairmont Avenue and then pulled up in front of her parents' old home. Mercy sat there for a moment reflecting on all the great times she had in this old house. She looked over at Rose and noticed that she was staring at Franklin Garrett's old home.

"You okay, Rose?" Mercy asked.

"Yes, I'm fine," Rose replied as she wiped a tear from her eye. She had been thinking about the day when the Johnson gang from Oxford, Pennsylvania murdered her husband George in Franklin's house.

*The longer you live the more sadness you see*, Rose thought. Her first husband had died young leaving her with a house full of children. When the South Philly Italians killed her son Sean, she felt as if life was not worth living any longer. Then George Graham came into her life, and gave her hope. In what seemed like a wink of the eye he was gone.

*Oh, you old biddy. Stop feeling sorry for yourself. You have lots to be grateful about. You have Jacob's family, their children, and your two daughters,* Rose thought. *Buck up, woman,* Rose said to herself. To Mercy she said, "Let's get to your Papa's house. I'm getting hungry."

With traffic, it took about twenty-five minutes to drive to Mercy's parents' house. She parked the car in the circular driveway and helped Rose out. When Rose opened the front door to the house, a host of family and friends greeted her. She acted surprised, but she had known about the so-called surprise party for a couple of weeks. One of Charlie's kids had slipped and made a comment about going to a party on this date. Rose put the pieces together and realized it was a party for her.

After all the kisses, hugs and happy birthdays from the partygoers, Rose took a seat in the center of the large couch. The Byrne family children rushed to sit next to her. To them Rose was their great grandmother. She had been part of the Byrne family their entire lives and they adored her. Jake and Maria's daughter Alicia, who was sixteen, sat on her right; Bella, Charlie and Janet's daughter age fifteen was on the left. Mark, Charlie's son, was the youngest and sat next to Alicia. He had just turned eleven. Joey Byrne, Jake and Maria's Son, and Jeff Byrne, Charlie and Janet's son, both thirteen years old, stood in front of Rose.

Joey handed Rose a small box decorated with green and white striped paper and a bright orange bow and said, "Happy birthday, Grandma. It's from all of us."

Rose took the present and opened the paper, taking care not to damage it so it could be used again. "Oh my. I wonder what's in this box," Rose said.

"It's a picture of all of us," Mark blurted out.

"Mark," Alicia said and lightly punched Mark on the arm. Bella rolled her eyes in disgust.

Rose opened the box and took out the gold plated ornate picture frame, looked at the photo and said, "I love it!" She held her arms out and each child hugged and kissed her.

"Where did you children get this beautiful frame? It looks so familiar," Rose asked.

"Grandpa Jacob gave it to us. He said it was his father's," Alicia said.

"Ahhh. You know children, I must have picked this up and dusted it a thousand times, back in the day. I love it and I love the photo of all of you. Now I have a present for you."

Rose opened her large pocketbook and took out two bags of homemade chocolates she bought at Emily's candy shop on Front Street and handed them to Alicia. "Alicia, take these and share them with all the children, please," Rose said.

"Thank you, Grandma," Alicia said and kissed Rose on the cheek. She walked off with the candy and the children followed her.

When the children left, Jerome Washington walked up to Rose and said, "Happy birthday, Rose," and kissed her on the cheek.

"Jerome, oh it's so good to see you. Where have you been keeping yourself?" Rose asked.

"Well, I've been traveling a lot. Helping with Gerry's business, you know," Jerome said.

"I've missed you, Jerome. I miss your dad too. I'm sorry you lost him. Nate was a good, god-fearing man. You know we knew each other for almost 35 years," Rose said.

"I know, Miss Rose. I miss him too," Jerome said. "You know Willy Williams, Miss Rose," he continued and pulled Willy to be in front of Rose.

"Of course, Willy and me are old friends."

When Nate Washington died of a heart attack in 1964, Willy Williams took over management of the gambling business in the African American neighborhoods of North Philly. Like all of the crews, his organization was independent from Jacob and Garrett, but they paid a portion of their proceeds for protection.

"Happy birthday, Miss Rose," Willy said and kissed Rose on the cheek.

"Thank you, Willy. By the way, I think you owe me a little something. My numbers came in today," Rose said.

"They did that. You want to let it ride on tomorrow's numbers?" Willy asked.

"Okay, Willy. You do that."

"Ms. Rose you look a little peaked. Can I get you something to eat? Or maybe a drink," Jerome asked.

"Oh, I'm fine, Jerome. Just the excitement, I guess," Rose said. "You go enjoy yourselves and get yourself something to eat."

Jerome and Willy kissed Rose on the cheek again and wished her a happy birthday.

Mary Byrne, Jimmy and Sally's daughter, pulled her car up in front of her grandparents' house, her tires screeching and rushed through the door. "Am I late? Is Grandmom Rose here yet?"

Joey, who was standing near the door, his mouth full of Rose's candy, just pointed to Rose sitting on the sofa. Mary rushed over to Rose, kissed her and said," I'm so sorry I'm late, Grand mom."

"Oh, don't be silly, Mary. I know you're busy with school," Rose said. Mary was in her first year of medical school at the University of Pennsylvania.

"I didn't have time to wrap this. Happy birthday," Mary said as she handed Rose a record album featuring various songs sung by several Irish tenors. "I know you like the old Irish songs."

"Thank you Mary. You are always so thoughtful," Rose said. "I love you, Mary, you know that, but I don't like those dresses you wear. Too short. Too short." Mary was wearing a floral pattern dress with the hem five inches above the knee.

"It's the style, Grandmom. I almost got you a dress just like this one," Mary joked.

"Oh, nobody wants to see my old legs anymore," Rose said. You go say hello to your mom and dad. And get something to eat. You're getting too skinny."

Mary kissed Rose and started to walk off to find her mother. Rose called after her, "Mary, I see Grady over by the food table. Can you ask him to come over here?" Mary waved to indicate she heard her.

A few minutes later Grady Hanlon walked over and kissed Rose on the cheek and said, "Happy birthday, Rose.'

"I saw you limping over here. Are you okay," Rose asked.

"Bum knee," Grady said.

"Sit down then," Rose said and patted the seat next to her. After Grady sat, Rose asked, "How do you like retirement, Grady?"

"I'm still getting used to Florida. It's hot there. But I like the winters," Grady answered.

"What do you do with yourself all day?" Rose asked.

"I fish a lot. Bought a twenty-four foot cruiser and I take a little book from my neighbors, mostly for Jai Alai and dog racing. It helps me keep busy," Grady said.

Mercy brought Rose a plate with a roast beef sandwich, potato salad, Rose's own recipe, and potato chips and said, "Okay, Grandmom time to eat."

"Rose took the plate and said, "How am I going to eat all this?"

"Do what you can," Mercy said. "I have to go see my father for a few minutes and I'll be back."

"Send over one of the children to get Grady something to eat. He's got a bad knee," Rose said.

Mercy saw Bella and asked her to make Grady a plate and take it to him, and then she opened Jacob's office door and walked in the room. Jacob Byrne was sitting at the head of the large oak conference table. Franklin Garrett was sitting to Jacob's right and Mike Kelly was on his left side. Jimmy, Charlie and Jake Byrne were standing in the corner of the room talking.

When they saw Mercy, each of her brothers hugged and kissed her and took their seats at the table. Mercy walked to her father, kissed him on the cheek, and then did the same with Mike and Franklin.

"Happy birthday, Uncle Frank," Mercy said and handed him a small box wrapped in gold paper. "Sorry I couldn't make dinner yesterday. I had a little trouble to take care of."

"I missed you but it is no big deal. When you turn seventy-one you really don't do a lot of celebrating," Franklin said.

At seventy-one Franklin was the oldest person on the council. Mercy couldn't help being impressed at how young he looked. His hair was still black with just the right amount of gray on the side. He had kept himself fit and trim. More likely, his wife Catherine had kept him in shape. Over the years, Catherine had become a fitness freak, running everyday and eating only wholesome foods. She had even convinced Franklin to stop smoking cigars. Catherine was forty-nine years old and looked thirty.

Jacob, Mercy's father, also looked younger than his sixty-four years. He still smoked the occasional cigar and drank Irish whiskey moderately, but he watched his diet. Jacob even joined Frank and Catherine on their morning runs, several times a week. Jacob's blond hair had turned white, but it suited him well. He was still a handsome man.

"Okay. I'm sorry to have this meeting during Rose's celebration, but it's like pulling teeth to get you all together. So Mike, tell us how you're doing?" Jacob asked.

"Jimmy, you won't be missing any bricks no more," Mike said. "Other than that Jake and I took care of a couple problems between crews last week. Nothing big."

"Jake," Jacob asked as he turned his head and looked at his son. "What's the latest with Gerry?"

"We just got a present from him yesterday. It's in storage. We'll sort it out tomorrow. You all know Gerry's getting out of the Air Force in a couple weeks. He'll be home soon. I know that makes you happy, Mercy," Jake said.

Mercy smiled, sighed, and said, "It can't happen too soon."

"He made arrangements to have Jerome Washington find and buy two airplanes. I think the same kind he flies in Vietnam. He wants to start a freight company when he gets back, so he can ship our special cargo from Mexico," Jake said.

"Jake, is this a good idea? This pot stuff," Jacob asked.

"Pop, it's no worse than booze. It's not the hard stuff like heroin or coke. People want it," Jake said. "We give it to them."

Jacob nodded and said, "Ok. What else?"

"Mickey Callahan wants us to supply him in California. Says it's a big thing there and we could all do very well. I told him to wait till Gerry got home and we would work something out."

Mickey Callahan was one of the crew that had tried to take over the K&A Gang in 1944. He was just seventeen and his father forced him to be part of the failed attack on Jacob and Franklin. The leaders of the revolt were killed and several others, including Mickey's father, were banished to Los Angeles where they set up a small branch of the K&A Gang and paid tax to Jacob and Franklin. Mickey was taken to the recruiting office and signed up for the Army. After basic training, he fought in Europe where he distinguished himself and won the Silver Star for valor. After the war, Mickey contacted Franklin and worked as an enforcer for the gang. Two years later he was sent by Jacob and Franklin to oversee the Los Angeles crews.

"The only other problem we have is supply. We need more. Gerry's working on that," Jake said.

"Jimmy," Jacob said.

"The pallets of bricks that had been stolen showed up at the work site late this afternoon. Thank you, Mike and Jake. Other than that, we're still building in the Northeast and I have a proposal out to build several shopping centers," Jimmy said.

"Need any help greasing the way?" Mike asked.

"Not yet, Uncle Mike, but I know where to go if I do," Jimmy said smiling. Mike smiled back and nodded in the affirmative.

"Charlie, you have anything?" Jake asked.

"Not much, Pop. Everything's running smooth. People bet, some win, most lose, we win."

"How's Willy doing?" Franklin asked.

"He's good. Done a great job of taking over for Nate. Willy brings in one of the larger chunks of cash in our network," Jimmy answered.

"Mercy," Jacob said looking at is daughter.

"We've stepped up our support of several childrens hospitals, as well as an outreach program for veterans. Gerry asked if we could send funds to an orphanage he volunteers at in Saigon and I agreed. And our Feed the Hungry programs throughout North and Northeast Philly are going very well," Mercy said.

"How about funds? Do you have enough?" Franklin asked.

"Yes, Uncle Frank, we're okay. The trust fund brings in a good amount, and we do get donations. Most comes from the," Mercy hesitated and then said," Well, special operations. Speaking of which, I do have an issue with one of our middlemen. Uncle Mike, Jake, can we talk about this when we're done here?" Mike and Jake nodded in the affirmative.

"Okay then. Just one more thing. Molly and I have decided to look for a home in Florida. By the end of next year, I'm hoping we can retire and move there. I'll be 65 and I promised Molly that if I made it to that age, we would retire." Everyone, except Franklin reacted with surprise.

"Catherine and I will also be moving to Florida. I can't let this old coot be alone down there," Franklin said as he put his hand over Jacob's.

Mercy got up from her chair, walked over to her father, kissed him on his cheek and said, "You deserve it, Papa. "You too, Uncle Frank," Mercy continued and kissed Franklin on the cheek.

Everyone in the room applauded.

"Okay, thank you. Now let's go help Rose celebrate her birthday," Jacob said.

As everyone left the office to resume the festivities, Mercy took Mike and Jake by the arm and guided them to a pair of French doors that led to an outside deck. Mercy opened one of the doors. The chilled autumn air engulfed her and Mercy shivered. Not from the cold, but because of what she was about to ask Mike and Jake to do.

# Chapter Five

Two days after his friend Hung was buried, Gerry Amato received notice that he was to leave Vietnam on October 10th via a chartered Continental Airlines 707. That same day Captain Al Watson told Gerry they had a mission the next morning at 0800. It would be Gerry's last mission in Vietnam and the Air Force.

"Where's Amato? I told him 0800 sharp. God damn it," Captain Watson said.

"I saw him around 0500. Said he'd be here and I was to have the back door lowered," Airman Tripp said.

"What? Why would he want the cargo door lowered? What's that son of a bitch up to?" Watson asked.

"Don't know, Cap. He didn't say why," Three answered.

Five minutes later, a disposable waste tanker sped down the road connecting to the runway. It was heading for Captain Watson's plane. The vehicle stopped in front of the loading ramp and Gerry Amato stuck his head out of the window.

"Morning, Boyos," Gerry yelled over the noise of the truck.

"You have to be fucking kidding me. What the hell is this and what's that smell?" Watson yelled pointing at the truck.

"It's a gift for Charlie, Cap. The shit of a thousand American soldiers," Gerry said as he pulled the truck into the plane.

Watson shook his head and he, Tripp and Jim Johnston followed the truck. Johnston pushed the lever that lifted the cargo door as Gerry jumped out of the truck.

"Are you out of your mind? How are we going to drop this on the dinks?" Watson asked.

"Easy. We come in low at around 100 feet, open the cargo door and drop this baby on the trail," Gerry explained.

"Then what?" Watson asked.

Gerry leaned in the truck and pulled out a box of C4 explosives and said, "Then we blow the shit out of them. Well," Gerry hesitated, "on them actually."

Watson looked at Gerry, put his hand to his head, made circles with his finger and said, "Dinky dau. Fucking Dinky dau."

"Yeah, what did you expect. I'm half Irish. Cap, we better get going before the APs catch up with me," Gerry said.

Forty-five minutes later, they were approaching the Ho Chi Minh Trail on the border of Cambodia and Vietnam.

"Cap, I'll be back," Gerry said and left to help Tripp and Jim set the C4 charges.

"Tripp, Jim set the detonators on the C4 for 20 minutes. We're 5 minutes out and another 5 to buzz the trail. That should do it. Drop some in the tanks and the rest in the cab," Gerry ordered.

"Thank the Lord Jesus. We are finally getting rid of this stink bucket," Tripp said as he and Jim set the detonators and placed the C4.

"After we drop this baby, keep the cargo door open for a few minutes and then open the side door. It should help clear out the stench. Don't forget your safety straps. We don't want to clear you out too," Gerry said and went back to the cockpit.

"There she is," Watson said as Gerry took his seat.

"Let me take her, Cap," Gerry said.

"She's yours. How much time?" Watson asked.

"Set them for twenty. Have fifteen left," Gerry said as he pushed forward for a rapid decent.

"I hope you know what you're doing?" Watson said.

"Cap, turn on the music, will you," Gerry asked.

Gerry bought a TEAC reel-to-reel tape recorder/player in the commissary a year before and rigged it to play in the plane. He liked all contemporary music but one song was his favorite when he flew dangerously close to the ground, which was often.

"Jesus, Gerry, do we have to? How about we play some Sinatra?" Watson suggested.

"No, you know everyone's talking about the bird," Gerry said and smiled

Watson leaned over and turned on the TEAC.

The plane descended and leveled at 100 feet above the ground as the lyrics to Gerry's favorite song started to play loudly in the background: *Well, everybody's heard about the bird. The bird's the word.*
The trail was very wide because much of the vegetation had been destroyed by the deployment of Agent Orange. The C-123 raced 180 miles an hour up the Ho Chi Minh Trail with 150 foot trees to each side flying by.

Gerry picked up the mic and said, "Tripp, Jim open the door and get the truck as close as you can to the back. I'll keep her level. Let me know when you're ready. Cap, time?"

"Twelve minutes," Watson replied. "I sincerely hope those timers are accurate."

"Guys, how are we doing?" Gerry asked into the mic. No answer. "Times a flying, guys." Still no answer.

Gerry looked at Watson and Watson undid his safety belt so he could go see what Tripp and Jim were doing.

"Done. We're ready," Tripp said.

Watson sat back into his seat as Gerry yelled, "Hang on, boys. Here we go."

Gerry abruptly pulled up the plane as Watson added power to the engines. The plane angled its nose high. The truck started to roll towards the door, then on the ramp and finally it dropped into the air. A few seconds later the truck hit the ground and billowing clouds of dust filled the air from the impact.

"Time," Gerry asked.

"Eight minutes," Watson replied.

Gerry leveled out at 2,000 feet and turned back towards where the truck had landed. He kept a distance from the trail so as not to scare any Viet Cong that might be nearby.

"Time?" Gerry asked.

"Four minutes. No VC yet," Watson said.

"There they are," Gerry said pointing to the jungle near the truck. Several small dark-clad figures started towards the truck, then several more. They were cautious, but also curious.

"Time?" Gerry asked.

"Two minutes. They look like ants circling a piece of bread. About ten of them now," Watson said.

"Tripp, Jim, you guys looking?" Gerry said into his mic.

"You bet."

"One minute," Watson said. "Thirty seconds. Fifteen. Five. Look at the fireworks kiddos," Watson yelled.

Nothing happened.

"Time?" Gerry asked.

"Minus one minute," Watson said.

"Son of a...." Gerry was interrupted when the truck erupted into a large ball of fire that engulfed the Viet Cong and created a large plume of smoke and fire. The feces from American soldiers fell back to the ground and left a coating of burnt brown sludge on the Ho Chi Minh Trail and what was left of the enemy.

Watson and Gerry slapped each other on the back and Gerry yelled, "Son of a bitch that was cool."

Tripp and Jim came to the cockpit to join the celebration, while Gerry positioned the plane for one more fly over the now disintegrated truck. As they passed over the destruction, Tripp held up his hand and made the peace sign. Then he slowly lowered his index finger, which presented a very different message.

"I'll take her," Watson said.

"You have her," Gerry said as he relinquished control of the plane to Watson.

Gerry sat back in his seat and a verse from the bible came to mind. *They will suffer the punishment of eternal destruction, away from the presence of the Lord and from the glory of his might.* Gerry nodded his head and said out loud, "Hung, you have your retribution."

"What?" Al asked.

"Nothing. Just mumbling," Gerry answered.

"Gerry, that is the last fucking time I'm going to listen to that song. It drives me crazy," Watson said.

"You have to be kidding, Cap, *Surfin' Bird* was the number one song when I was in flight school.

"Yeah, I can believe that. That crap your generation listens to be-fuddles me."

Gerry laughed and said, "Okay, old-timer."

Watson looked at Gerry, winked and then pointed the plane to the secret destination near the Cambodian Laotian border. They picked up the unprocessed film, endured a few wise cracks about how the plane smelled like someone took a crap in her, and took off towards Kampong Seila near the Thai border. Half way there, Watson landed the plane at the farm of Gabriel Barra, the cousin of Pierre Barra, the head of the Marseille Mob.

While Barra's men loaded ten tons of Cambodian marijuana in the C-123, Gerry and his crew had coffee with Barra. A handsome man, Barra looked to be in his early 50s, but someone had told Gerry he was actually 61. He had dark hair, slightly graying at the temples, and was slender, but also looked strong.

The rumor was that Barra had to leave Marseille in the 1930s after he killed the husband of his lover. He took up residence in Saigon, then a French protectorate and a city that was, at the time, considered the jewel of the orient. He quickly established a branch of the Marseille Mob. When the Japanese took over French Indochina, which included Vietnam, Laos and Cambodia, he moved to Quebec, Canada. When the war ended and the French took over again, he returned and started his illicit business for a second time and bought a dozen rubber plantations in Cambodia and Vietnam over the years.

"Gerry, we will miss you," Barra said.

"Mr. Barra, I'm going to miss our get-togethers. This is a wonderful, peaceful place. I really like the time we spend with you," Gerry said.

"Then don't leave. After you are discharged come back and work for me. I have no son to take over when I die. You could be my successor," Barra said.

"That's very tempting, Mr. Barra, but I have obligations to my family. Besides you'll be on this earth for a long time yet."

"I understand. How about you, Captain Watson? You want to fly for me? I will make you rich." Barra said.

"That would be an honor, Mr. Barra, but when I leave the Air Force I plan to retire and live a peaceful life. Thanks to Gerry here, I'll be able to do that in style," Watson said as he touched Gerry's arm.

My offer stays open for all of you," Barra said pointing first to Tripp and then to Jim Johnson. "I always need good men."

Jim Johnson nodded and Tripp said, "Thank you sir. We still have another year in the Air Force and right now, we're just interested in getting out alive. If we do I just might come calling on you."

"I hope you do," Barra said as a young boy came running up to the table and said something in the Cambodian language to Barra.

"Gentlemen, I am sorry to say your cargo has been loaded," Barra said and stood up. The others did the same.

Barra shook Gerry's hand then kissed him first on one cheek and then the other and said, "Au revoir, Gerry." He then shook each man's hand and said, "I bid you adieu," and walked off to the main house.

Gerry and the crew walked to the makeshift landing strip, checked the plane's cargo and took off to deliver the reconnaissance film and the Cambodian marijuana. The trip to Kampong Seila was uneventful and when they landed on the large dirt runway, two 1967 Chevy Impala sedans drove up to meet them. Six men with M16s took posts around the aircraft.

Tripp and Jim unloaded the film and put it in the trunks of both vehicles. Two other men handed Watson a clipboard and he signed a form, then handed it back to one of the men. The man signed the form, ripped off a copy and gave it to Watson. The men then got back in the Impalas and drove off.

"What the fuck is it with the CIA. They never talk. During all the deliveries they have never said a word," Gerry said.

"Bunch of tight asses," Watson said.

After the Impalas were out of sight, several trucks drove out from their hiding places in the jungle near the landing strip. A passenger in one of the trucks jumped out, walked over to Gerry and Watson, and shook their hands. The men in the other trucks started to unload the pot from the aircraft and load it in the trucks.

"Hello, Benny. How you doing?" Gerry asked.

Benny Breslin was sent to Thailand from Philadelphia when Gerry first started smuggling marijuana. Breslin had been an enforcer for several years, working with Jake Byrne. Benny married a Thai local and lived in Bangkok. He bought a used 1965 Bell 206 helicopter from a charter company that went bankrupt and used it to fly from Bangkok and Kampong Seila each time Gerry made a delivery. After he supervised the transfer to the ship waiting in the Gulf of Siam he returned to his family in Bangkok. The helicopter was hidden at the other end of the landing strip.

"Good, Gerry. I'm good," Benny replied.

"And the baby?" Gerry asked.

"Oh my. That baby is me pride and joy. She is the cutest thing and smart too," Benny said. "You know, when I came from Dublin to live in Philadelphia my wife left me and ran off with a fucking cop. I thought then that I might not have any kiddos. Now I do. Go figure," Benny said.

When the marijuana was loaded in the trucks, Benny said his good-byes and started walking to his vehicle. Tripp was finished refueling the plane and waved to Watson indicating they were ready to leave. Just as Benny got to his truck three jeeps with mounted machine guns burst out of the trees and headed for the plane. They were marked with Cambodian military insignias.

Watson and Gerry took off running toward the C-123 as fast as they could. Before they made it to the plane, one of the jeeps started shooting the machine gun into the air. One jeep took station in front of the plane while the other two blocked the trucks. Watson and Gerry put their hands in the air.

A black 1965 Citron sedan drove up to them and three men exited the car. Two were carrying automatic weapons. The third man walked up to Gerry and put his hand out. Gerry ignored him.

"Mr. Amato, my name is John Beaumont. I have a proposition for you," the man said.

"And you thought threatening us was a good way to meet our acquaintance?" Gerry said.

"I meant no offense, Mr. Amato, but Cambodia is a dangerous place and one cannot be too cautious. Wouldn't you say," Beaumont said.

"What is it you want?" Gerry asked.

"I, we want you to stop using the Barras and start buying from us," Beaumont said.

John Beaumont spoke English with a slight French accent. Gerry guessed that he was in his mid-30s.

"Why the theatrics," Gerry said pointing to the jeeps. "You could have just set up a meeting."

At that moment two of Beaumont's men brought Benny over and shoved him to the ground in front of Beaumont.

"We tried, but Mr. Breslin did not think you would be interested. My brother runs a business in Paris and he is an, shall we say, intense man. He does not take no for an answer. So you will start buying from us?" Beaumont said in a calm voice.

"The Barras have been good to us. They charge a fair price. Why would we change?" Gerry said.

"Let me show you why," Beaumont said as he pulled a Luger pistol from his pocket, pointed it at Benny's head and fired. Benny dropped to the ground in a heap. Gerry and Watson stepped back in surprise. "And you will pay us 15% more than you pay Barra."

# Chapter Six

Breslin's helicopter pilot saw Beaumont kill his boss and decided that it was in his best interest to get back to Thailand as fast as he could. He took off from the hiding place and began a wide turn past the C-123.

Beaumont, seeing the helicopter take off yelled, "Kill that fucking bastard," and pointed at the helicopter.

The men in the jeeps began shooting at the helicopter. In the confusion Tripp and Jim, who were still at the bottom of the C-123's loading ramp, came around the right side of the plane, and worked their way to the front where the driver of the jeep and operator of the machine gun were facing away from them, shooting at the chopper. Tripp unsheaved his government issued knife and slit the machine gunner's throat, while Jim smashed the jeep driver in the head with his fist. Jim pulled the unconscious driver out of the seat while Tripp took over the machine gun.

Jim drove the jeep from the front of the C-123 towards the jeep to the left of the plane and Tripp opened up on them. Both the driver and machine gun operator fell out of their jeep dead. Jim brought the jeep around towards the back of the airplane. As he did the jeep stationed at the rear of the plane opened fire on them.

Beaumont and his two bodyguards dropped to the ground. Gerry jumped on Beaumont, wrestled the Luger from him and emptied the clip into the two bodyguards. He then turned the gun on Beaumont and pulled the trigger. Nothing happened. The gun was empty. Beaumont kicked at

Gerry's legs knocking him to the ground. Meanwhile Tripp and Jim were able to kill the driver and machine gunner in the second jeep.

"Al, get to the plane. I'll take care of him," Gerry said pointing at Beaumont.

Watson took off to get the plane ready to fly and Gerry and Beaumont cautiously rose from the ground. At that moment, another Cambodian military jeep with a machine gun burst out of the small jungle trail Beaumont had used. They began shooting at Tripp and Jim. Then another jeep broke out of the same trail and began shooting,

Gerry took that moment of distraction to rush Beaumont and smashed him in the face. Beaumont went down in a heap. Jim slid his jeep to a stop in front of Gerry and said, "Get in."

Gerry picked up the unconscious Beaumont and put him into the jeep and yelled, "Go, go, go."

Jim floored the jeep leaving a cloud of dust behind him. Beaumont's two remaining jeeps were a few hundred yards away and still firing their machine guns. Watson began to move the plane forward as Jim drove the jeep up the ramp into the cargo area of the C-123, stopping just a few feet from the bulkhead.

The C-123 picked up speed and Gerry yelled, "Get out." Tripp began to pull Beaumont from the jeep. "Leave him," Gerry yelled over the roar of the C-123's engines. "Help me push this."

The three men pushed the jeep towards the door. Gerry set the parking brake and yelled, "Go hook up."

Watson pulled back on the yoke when the aircraft hit the proper speed, and with a groan, the plane started to rise. The cargo door made a loud noise as it scraped against the ground. Bullets from Beaumont's remaining jeeps peppered the plane as it gained altitude. At 200 feet, as the plane was still ascending, Gerry released the parking brake and held tight to a strap fastened to the bulkhead. The jeep slowly started to roll towards the door. Suddenly Watson increased the rate of ascent trying to get out of range of the machine gun fire and the jeep plummeted out of the plane with Beaumont still in the back seat. It smashed into the jungle trees below and disappeared in the dense vegetation.

Gerry pulled the lever to raise the freight door and then made his way back to the cockpit. He sat heavily in his seat, took a hanky from his flight suit and wiped the sweat from his face.

"Shit, that was close," Gerry said.

"It's not over yet. We're losing fuel. Must have been hit," Watson said.

"How much?" Gerry asked.

"Enough that we won't make it back to Saigon," Watson said.

Gerry pulled out a general map of the area and examined the route from Kampong Seila to Saigon. He said, "Do you think we can make it to the Mekong River?"

"Maybe, but maybe not. We're losing fuel fast. Why?" Watson asked.

"If we can get to Tan Chau, the river's pretty wide. We can ditch there," Gerry said.

There was no discussion of parachuting out of the plane over the dense jungle below. Chances of surviving the parachute landing were bad enough. Even if you did make it to the ground, the jungle was likely to kill you before help found you. Their best chance for survival was to bring the plane down with everyone in it. They also couldn't land anywhere in Cambodia because of the secrecy of their mission.

"That just might work if we can get there. The Navy runs boats up and down the Mekong. If we're lucky we'll find one quickly," Watson said.

"Tan Chau is small but we should be able to get some help there." Gerry paused, "If the VC aren't there."

Watson looked at Gerry, shrugged his shoulders and said, "Sounds like a plan. A suck ass plan but the only one we got."

Gerry informed Tripp and Jim what they were going to do and had them toss any loose items overboard. He told them to secure the half-empty box of grenades and the four remaining blocks of C4. Then he made his way back to the cockpit and asked, "How we doing on fuel?"

"Not good. Not good. We have about an hour to Tan Chau and I don't think we'll make it," Watson answered.

Gerry pulled the map again and studied it. "Looks like it's all jungle and rice paddies from here to Tan Chau. I don't see any place we can land," Gerry said.
"We can try to put it down in a rice paddy. Chances are we'll fucking upend her. Soil too soft," Watson said in frustration.

"If we can get close to Tan Chau we can try to bail. We'll be in Vietnam by then. Problem is the last I heard the VC were in this area," Gerry said.

"Shit!" Watson said, paused to think then said, "Gerry, my boy, you might want to say a prayer to your God that we make it to the Mekong River."

"Me? I haven't been to church in a few years," Gerry said.

"Been longer for me, so I think you might have a better chance being heard than me."

"Are you an atheist?" Gerry said in surprise.

"Kind of," Watson said.

"Fuck! I'm in a plane running out of fuel over the jungle and the captain doesn't believe in God," Gerry said.

Gerry picked up the mic and said, "Tripp. What religion are you?"

"Baptist," Tripp replied.

"Shit. Jim, how about you?"

"I don't know. My Mom's Jewish. So I guess I'm Jewish too," Jim said.

"We're fucked, Gerry said. "I'm the only one that's Catholic. I'm our last chance."

"Well, you better get with it. Pray for a miracle, because if it don't work I don't think they'll be making you a saint or anything," Watson said.

"Okay Okay," Gerry said then made the sign of the cross and said, "In the name of the Father, the Son and the Holy Ghost. Dear God I hope you're listening. I know I haven't been to church or confession in a very long time. I've eaten meat on Friday also and done a few other things you might not approve of. I also know that my crewmates are heathens, but if you see fit to allow us to reach Tan Chau and land safely in the Mekong

River, I swear I'll start going to church again. Watson also agrees to start going to a Catholic Church."

Gerry looked at Watson and Watson looked at Gerry, his eyes opened wide. Then Watson looked up and nodded yes. Gerry continued, "As for Tripp and Jim, I'll let them talk to their own Gods, but if you have any influence, I am sure they would appreciate it. Thank you, God for your time. Amen."

Gerry picked up the internal mic and said, "Tripp, Jim, we're trying to make it to Tan Chau and land in the Mekong. I'm ordering you to say a prayer to your God. Do it now. We're a half hour out. Buckle up."

Fifteen minutes later Watson said, "Gerry, we just passed over the border. We're in Vietnam now. Put out a distress call."

Gerry picked up the external microphone and dialed in the proper frequency on the radio. There was nothing.

"Radio's dead. Must have gotten hit," Gerry said.

"Dandy, just fucking dandy," Watson said. "Looks like we might make it to the river. It'll be close."

"There it is," Gerry said.

"I see it. Let's drop into that area just outside the town. It looks to be the widest and I'm hoping there's less traffic on it," Watson said.

"What about that island?" Gerry asked.

"We should stop before that."

"Okay, let's do'er," Gerry said.

Watson banked the plane to the port and started dropping altitude. He straightened the aircraft while continuing to drop.

Gerry picked up the internal mic and said, "Brace for crash landing."

The plan lurched to the starboard as the right side engine sputtered and stopped. Watson pulled her port and held it. Gerry grabbed his controls and helped to keep the plane on a straight path.

There were several small fishing boats in their path and Watson pulled up passing over them by 10 feet. They hit the water just 50 feet from the frightened but relieved fishermen. The plane skipped and continued up the Mekong and then hit the water again.

"Oh shit, we're not going to make it," Gerry said and did the sign of the cross.

"Fuck," Watson yelled as the plane hit the upward sloping soft river bottom of the island and the tail lifted out of the water and tipped the C-123 upside down onto the island.

# Chapter Seven

The walls of Saint Hugh of Cluny Catholic Church echoed the final words of the Song of Farewell. "…that you may enter into paradise."

Father George Byrne wiped the tears from his eyes and stepped to the pulpit. He cleared his throat and started to talk, "I will read a favorite prayer of the decea…" Father George's voice cracked. He coughed and continued, "deceased." George closed his eyes, bent his head and then opened his eyes and looked at the gathering and began the prayer."May the road rise to meet you. May the wind be always at your back. May the sun shine warm upon your face. May the rains fall soft upon your fields and until we meet again, may the Lord hold you in the palm of His hand."

George bent his head again, and the parishioners followed his lead. After a minute he said, "That concludes the mass, but if you will please keep your seats my father Jacob Byrne would like to say a few words."

Jacob rose from his seat in the first pew. He kissed Molly, then bent down and kissed Jimmy, Sally, Charlie, Janet, Jake, and Maria on the cheek. Mercy stood up and he embraced her tightly. She put her head on his shoulder and sobbed. "PaPa make the hurt go away. Oh, PaPa."

Jacob kissed Mercy's head and said nothing. There was nothing he could say. He couldn't make the hurt go away. Not this time. He sat Mercy back down in the pew and slowly walked to the pulpit forgetting to genuflect before the alter. He turned, wiped his eyes and began, "Many years ago God brought to me the most wonderful person one could hope to have in their life. An amazing person with a soul so energetic and bright that their glow is still with me and will be forever, even though she has gone to God's bosom," Jacob paused and looked at Mercy and the others and began again.

"My mother passed away when I was just a child, and when Rose Reilly Graham entered my life she became my mother. She became my children's grandmother. Now, like most Irish mothers Rose was bossy, snippy and a bit cranky now and then. But, she loved her children and she loved my children with all her heart. More than once she had to take Jake by the ear and teach him a lesson or two." There was laughter.

"I think she might have done that to Frank as well," Jacob said. More laughter.

"She readily welcomed Molly into our family and taught Jimmy the value of a good potato chip sandwich. Rose stayed up all night with Molly when Charlie had the whopping cough. And, when George struggled with his decision to take the cloth, Rose guided him to the right answer. When it came to her great grandchildren, she spoiled them rotten. She would hide candy from Emily's candy shop around the house just so the kids would have the joy searching it out and the reward of eating it." Jacob stopped for a second and looked at his grandchildren.

He continued, "Rose loved them all, but there was a special bond between her and Mercy. Rose taught Mercy the value of charity, the joy of working for a cause and the power one feels when they have helped others. What a teacher she was. Mercy runs the Mercy Row Foundation like General Patton ran his army. A little less cursing, of course." Some laughter.

"Mercy's son Gerry is serving in Vietnam and couldn't be here today. If he was I'm sure he would agree with me when I say that Rose's light will shine brightly on all of us for many, many years to come. We love you, Rose. And, we always will." Jacob left the pulpit.

George took his place and said, "After the burial you are all invited to Jacob and Molly Byrne's home to celebrate Rose's life. Please stay seated until we take Rose to the car and the family has left the church."

An Irish version of Amazing Grace began to play as the six pallbearers took their place by Rose's coffin. Mike Kelly was standing on the left front side and Grady Hanlon on the right side. Rose's two grandsons were in the rear and Willy Williams and Jerome Washington were in the middle. They rolled the casket to the door and then lifted it, walked down the steps and placed the coffin in the hearse. Rose Reilly Graham was buried next to her husband George Graham at Holy Sepulchre Cemetery. After the graveside ceremony, the family returned home to host the mourners.

Father George arrived at Molly and Jacob's house an hour after the family. He greeted his mother and father who praised him for the fine mass he had held for Rose.

"You okay, George? You look a bit out of it," Molly asked.

"No, I'm fine. It's just ...You know," George replied. But, George was not fine. He had a moral dilemma. He was about to take an action that, in his mind, could condemn his mortal soul to hell.

George saw Jake standing by the bar pouring whiskey for two of his friends. He excused himself and walked to the bar. As he approached Jake, George heard him say, "To Grandma Rose," and he clinked glasses with his friends and drank the whiskey.

Seeing George, Jake said, "Good job today. Grandma would have been proud. Guys, this is my brother George." Jake's friends shook George's hand and exchanged pleasantries.

"Excuse me, but can I borrow Jake for a minute," George asked. The two men nodded and left.

"Jake, can you find Mike and meet me in Dad's office in five minutes," George asked.

"Sure, kid. What's up," Jake asked.

"Just meet me and we'll talk about it," George said and walked off to his father's office. He sat at a small round conference table and lit a cigarette. When he finished it, he lit another. He took a deep drag on the cigarette and let the smoke out with a sigh. When Jake and Mike entered the office, George was sitting rapidly tapping a lighter on the table Gerry had sent him from Vietnam.

"George, those things will kill you. Didn't you hear about the surgeon general's report?" Jake said. Jake had never smoked. Not even as a kid. He found the habit disgusting.

"Sit down. Please," George said, avoiding the smoking issue.

Mike and Jake took seats at the table. "What's up, kid? You look like hell," Mike asked and pulled a hanky from his back pocket. "Here, wipe your face. You're sweating like a pig." George hesitated and Mike said, "Go ahead. It's clean."

George took the hanky patted his brow and cheeks and wiped his hands. He then folded the hanky, placed it on the table, and said, "I have a problem."

"Jesus Christ, George. Spit it out," Jake said.

"Somebody stealing from the collection box?" Mike asked and laughed.

"I wish that was the problem, Uncle Mike. It's much worse than that," George said. "I have a parishioner, a young mother with four children." George paused, picked up the hanky, wiped his brow and continued.

"God forgive me, you have to promise you will never tell anyone what I am about to say."

"Sure, George. You know we can keep a secret. You're not, uh involved with this woman are you?" Jake asked.

"God no! It's nothing like that. You know everything that's revealed during a confession is private. We call it the Seal of the Confessional. If a priest breaks this seal, he would be excommunicated. I am about to break the Seal of the Confessional," George said, then picked up a cigarette and lit it. "This woman's husband cheats on her."

"Ah, that's a pretty common sin, George," Jake said.

"It gets worse. Seems he is not very selective with his misconduct. Last year he caught Gonorrhea and gave it to his wife. She was pregnant and lost the baby. She tried not having sex with him, but he forces himself on her," George said.

"What's Gonorrhea?" Mike asked.

"Clap," Jake said.

"Oh!" Mike replied.

"She asked me to talk to him so I arranged to meet him in his home. I suggested that he seek some kind of professional help for the sake of his wife and children," George said.

"And?" Jake said.

"He told me it was none of my business and he could do anything he wanted with his own wife and children. Then he grabbed me, pushed me to the door and threw me down the front steps," George explained.

"The son of a bitch. I'll kill him," Jake yelled.

"A couple weeks later the woman came to confession again and told me that her husband had started looking strangely at their eleven year old daughter. She…" George was interrupted by Mike.

"That fucking bastard," Mike said,

"That's what I called him. God forgive me. The woman is so distraught she confessed that she wanted to kill her husband, and I believe her. I can't allow her to do that. She'll go to prison and the kids will be orphans."

"So what do you want us to do? Whack him?" Jake asked.

"No, of course not. I want you to talk to him. Scare him. Make him stop. I'm at my whit's end. I've been a priest for ten years and I've never seen anything like this. It's horrible," George said.

"Guys like that don't change, George," Mike said.

"We have to try, Mike. Can you help me out?" George pleaded.

"Write down his name, where he lives, where he works and places he goes," Jake said.

George complied and pushed the paper back to Jake. "Don't kill him, Jake."

Jake looked at the note and said, "Tom Gentry. Ok, give us a couple of weeks and we'll see what we can do."

# Chapter Eight

When Gerry Amato regained consciousness, he found himself upside down in the cockpit of the wrecked C-123. He tried to release the seat belt but it was stuck. He reached into his pocket, pulled out a knife, and cut the strap. He lowered himself to the ceiling of the cockpit and checked on Watson.

Watson was still unconscious but he was alive. Gerry gently slapped his face until Watson woke. When he was awake he released his seat belt and dropped.

"Holy shit. That was intense," Watson said.

"Grab the AR15s. I'll check on Tripp and Jim," Gerry said.

Watson picked up the AR15 rifles and crawled out the broken cockpit window, while Gerry made his way to the cargo area. When he got there Tripp was standing over Jim just staring at his lifeless body.

"No," Gerry said. "Is he...?"

"Yeah," Tripp said, tears in his eyes.

"Tripp, grab your weapon and let's get out of here."

"What about Jim?"

"Leave him. When we find help we'll come back for him," Gerry said.

"You're bleeding," Tripp said.

"What? Where?" Gerry asked as he ran his hands up and down his legs and torso.

"Top of your shoulder," Tripp said.

Gerry felt under his shirt and pulled out something that was stuck in the fleshy part of his shoulder. He held it out for Tripp to see.

"What the fuck is that?" Tripp asked and laughed.

"It's a damned Tiger's tooth from a necklace I bought downtown," Gerry said as he pulled the chain and broke it.

Gerry threw the tooth and necklace on the floor then picked up an emergency bag that had a first aid kit and several C-rations and slung it over his undamaged shoulder.

"Get your weapon and ammo, Tripp and let's get out of here," Gerry said.

Tripp picked up the tooth and necklace and put it in his pocket then grabbed two AR15s and a box of ammo.

Gerry kicked the half-opened door and he and Tripp jumped to the ground. The island they crashed on was dense with foliage and trees. The chem boys had not hit this area with Agent Orange, a strong herbicide designed to clear large areas of vegetation, yet.

Watson was standing towards the front of the aircraft holding two AR15 rifles and an ammo pack. Seeing Gerry and Tripp he ran back to them, handed Gerry a rifle and asked, "Where's Jim?"

Tripp looked at him and said, "Gone."

Watson shook his head and said, "Fuck!"

"We have to try to make it to Tan Chau. It's to the south," Gerry said. The men walked to the front of the C-123 and stared out at the Mekong River. "Look," Gerry said and pointed, "You can see the town."

"How do we get off this island?" Watson asked. "Can't swim to the bank. It's too far."

"We wait for a fisherman to come by and hope he isn't a VC," Gerry said.

"Let's look around to be sure we're alone here. Tripp, take the interior, Gerry the right side and I'll do the left. And for Christ's sake let's not shoot each other," Watson ordered.

The three men turned the safety on their AR15s off and started walking. When they reached the end of the island, they turned around and walked back. So far no hostiles. Gerry moved to the waterline and started walking back to the aircraft. When he was halfway there, bullets hit the water next to him. Gerry dove back into the brush and turned his AR15 towards where he thought the shots had come from. He shot four times.

Watson ran up to Gerry and said, "Stop. You're wasting ammo. Wait until you see something. Where'd the gunfire come from?"

Gerry pointed towards a clump of trees on the bank of the river. "How many?" Watson asked.

"No idea," Gerry answered.

Tripp ran up and flopped next to Gerry but didn't say anything. He just pointed his rifle at the bank of the river.

"You know how to use that thing, Tripp," Watson asked.

"Oh yeah. I've been shooting my whole life."

"Shit, now I wish I had paid more attention when they checked us out on these babies," Gerry said patting the AR15. The Air Force wasn't big on combat training for support and air crews. Gerry had only shot an M1 Carbine twice during training. The third Carbine training session was called off because of rain. Since he had been in Nam he had only fired the AR15 once.

"Gerry, you better put something on that wound before it gets infected," Al said and pointed to Gerry's chest.

"Nah it's just a scratch from a tiger's tooth."

"You sure? It's bleeding a lot," Watson said.

"Gerry opened his shirt and saw a five-inch bleeding gash a few inches below the tiger tooth's wound and said, "Shit, I didn't even feel that."

"You will. Get some dressing on it," Al said.

Gerry quickly poured antiseptic on the wounds, placed a bandage on it and taped it tightly to help stop the bleeding. The wound was not too deep so he wasn't worried.

"Tripp, Gerry stay here. I'm going to patrol the island to be sure we're not getting visitors from the other bank. Don't shoot unless you actually see something. We don't have a lot of ammo," Watson ordered and started for the other side of the small island.

A few minutes later Tripp whispered to Gerry, "You see that?"

"No, what?"

"I saw something move over near those red fruit-looking things," Tripp said and pointed.

"Dragon fruit."

"What?" Tripp said.

"Those red things are dragon fruit. Good to eat," Gerry said.

"Tripp pulled his trigger once. There was a short scream and a black clad VC rolled down the bank of the river. Then all hell broke loose when ten other VC starting firing.

"Oh shit," Gerry said and hugged the ground as the bullets whizzed over his head.

Tripp fired again and another VC rolled down the bank, then another when Tripp fired for the third time. The shooting stopped as the remaining VC moved back behind the trees.

Watson ran up and lay down next to Gerry. Gerry said, "Tripp got three."

"What?" Watson asked.

"He killed three VC," Gerry said.

"Good job. How many you think there are?" Watson asked.

Tripp said, "Ten, eleven. Something like that."

"If they figure out how to get across the river or radio their buddies we're fucked," Watson said.

A bullet hit the dirt in front of Gerry and a split second later, they heard the rifle report. He jumped back and lay flat behind a fallen tree.

"Sniper. Must be up in a tree," Tripp said. "If I can see where he is I can get him."

Watson took off his shirt, found a tree limb with two branches extending from it and put his shirt on it. Then he took his hat off and placed it on top of the branch. "How's this?"

"Looks just like you, but better looking," Gerry said.

"I saw this is some war movie," Watson said ignoring Gerry. "You ready, Tripp."

"Yep."

Watson slowly pushed the branch man up and in sight of the enemy. Nothing happened. He started to wiggle the branch. A few seconds later two shots hit his hat on the branch. Then Tripp fired twice at the slight muzzle flash he had seen. A VC fell out of a clump of trees and rolled into the water.

"Fucking A," Gerry said.

It started to rain. Rain in Vietnam was unlike anything Gerry had ever experienced. It was as if some deity just started pouring water from the sky. It came down so hard sometimes it hurt. It lasted an hour and the only positive of the rain was it kept the VC from attacking them. The rain stopped as fast as it had started.

A few minutes after the rain ceased, Gerry heard a loud popping sound and a second later, the water in front of them exploded.

"Fall back to the plane," Watson yelled. The three men crawled back behind the tree line and then stood up and ran towards the destroyed C-123. Another explosion erupted, this time closer to where they had just been. The VC were getting the range. By the time they reached the plane, they had heard three more explosions.

"What're they using?" Gerry gasped out of breath from running.

"How the hell do I know? I've never been in a battle on the ground," Watson said. "Maybe a mortar or rifle-launched grenades."

Tripp moved towards the front of the plane then to the west side of the island. He carefully looked across to the riverbank. They were about 1,000 feet from where the first explosion happened. What he saw sent a chill through his body. The VCs were entering the water holding what looked like floats or inner tubes. There were at least fourteen of them. Somehow, they had gotten reinforcements. Meanwhile the VC continued to shell the area where they had been when Watson's crew had first encountered them.

Tripp ran back to Gerry and Watson and told them what was happening. Watson sat on the ground and said, "Well, gents, it's been nice knowing you."

Gerry looked at him and said, "We're not dead yet so get your ass up and let's take some of them with us."

"You think we got some fuel left in the tanks," Tripp asked.

"Some, maybe. I don't know. Try the left tank," Watson answered. "Why?"

"I was thinking we could put up a fire barrier across the island. It's not that wide. It'll slow them down," Tripp said.

"We have the C4 and grenades," Gerry said.

Tripp and Gerry ran to the plane and Tripp found an old bucket inside and started to fill it with fuel. Gerry grabbed the grenades and C4 and returned to Watson. They set up behind a large fallen tree, while Tripp laid down a line of fuel from one side of the 200 foot wide island to the other.

"We'll use the C4 explosion to light the fuel," Gerry said as he placed the detonators into each brick.

Tripp finished and took his place behind the tree and said, "When we light that fuel it should burn for a little while, but I don't think the vegetation will. So, we won't have much time."

"Enough to kill some of those bastards," Gerry said.

It wasn't long before they heard movement in the jungle in front of them. Gerry picked up a brick of C4 and set the timer for 30 seconds. Then he threw it as close to the fuel as he could. The three men ducked behind the tree and hugged the ground. The C4 exploded in flames and ignited the fuel creating an eight-foot firewall. Then they heard the screams.

Gerry, Tripp and Watson each picked up a hand grenade, pulled the pin and threw it as hard as they could. Seconds later, there were three separate explosions and more screaming. Small weapons fire peppered the tree they were hiding behind as the VC widely shot through the fire.

The fuel burned off quickly revealing 10 advancing VC. Gerry, Watson and Tripp each shot a single round, saving the ammunition. Two VC fell to the ground, one obviously dead from a head wound and the other screaming in pain with a stomach shot. The remaining VC hit the dirt and began firing back.

Tripp yelled out, "Fuck you, Charlie." then he crawled to the edge of the tree, leaned out and shot once at the low profile of one of the VC. He had time to see the blood spray from the VC's head before the enemy started shooting again.

Something hit the trunk of the fallen tree and fell to the ground. The explosion pushed the huge tree a few inches towards the three men.

Gerry yelled, "Grenades, fall back." Then he held up his hand with a hand grenade in it. The other men pulled out their own, and the last of the grenades. Each pulled the pin in unison and tossed them as far as they could. The three explosions were almost simultaneous.

Crouching low Gerry, Al and Tripp starting running towards the front of the airplane. Still crouched they stepped into the water behind the aircraft just as the VC opened fire again. They had little ammo and no other weapons, save their handguns, left.

Gerry pulled out his necklace with a silver cross from under his shirt, made the sign of the cross, bowed his head and said to himself, *O, my God, I am heartily sorry for having offended You. I detest all my sins because of Your just punishment, but most of all because they offend You, my God, who are all-good and deserving of all my love. I firmly resolve, with the help of Your grace, to sin no more and to avoid the near occasion of sin. Amen.*

Tripp closed his eyes and prayed to God to protect the three men. Watson watched them, then staying low, leaned out from behind the front of the plane and shot once. An advancing VC fell backwards, a bullet in his heart.

The VC were now laying down a barrage of cover fire as they advanced on both sides of the aircraft. Just as the first VC reached the midpoint of the aircraft, a storm of .50 caliber hot lead ripped into each side of the fuselage and the VC. Hearing the new gunfire, the three men dove into the water thinking it was coming from Viet Cong who had somehow got behind them.

The barrage of lead lasted a full minute. When it stopped the plane's chassis looked like Swiss cheese, and all of the VC lay dead or dying on the jungle floor.

Two U.S. PBRs, officially known as Patrol Boat River, hit the bank on both sides of Gerry, Watson and Tripp. A young lieutenant leaned over the side of the boat, saluted Watson, and said, "Good evening, sir. You fellas need a ride?" He stuck his hand out and pulled Watson aboard. The other PBR crew members helped Gerry and Tripp onto the boat.

Once Watson was aboard, he shook the lieutenant's hand and said, "Al Watson. Call me Al."

The lieutenant said, "John. The crew calls me Crazy John."

"I'm not going to ask why, but to me you will always be John the savior," Watson said.

Tripp jumped off the boat and ran to the plane.

"Where's he going?" Crazy John asked.

Gerry jumped off the boat and followed Tripp.

"And they call me crazy," Crazy John said.

A couple minutes later Tripp and Gerry returned carrying Jim's lifeless body. The crew helped pull the body aboard. Tripp and Gerry jumped on the boat.

"Now if you don't mind leaving this paradise, how about we get the three of you home?" Crazy John said as he pulled his .45, pointed in the air and emptied the clip.

# Chapter Nine

Three weeks after his rescue, and two weeks after Rose's funeral, Gerry was a civilian and home in Philadelphia. He spent several days at Travis Air Base in San Francisco finalizing his discharge and then took a flight to Philadelphia. After he greeted the family, the first thing he did was to order a Philly cheese steak from Mary's hoagie and steak shop at Westmoreland and Hope Streets. After eating his steak sandwich he walked over to the A&P store at Front and Westmorland Streets and bought 10 large Philly soft pretzels from Joe the pretzel man, who had been there since Gerry was a kid. He ate five of them and brought five to his mother, Mercy. Gerry gained five pounds his first week at home, eating his favorite foods.

He visited Rose's gravesite at Holy Sepulchre Cemetery and paid his respects to her and George Graham. He then traveled south on the Schuylkill Expressway to City Line Avenue and then on to Holy Cross Cemetery in Yeadon to visit his father's grave. Gerry knew that his father wasn't buried in the grave. His body wasn't recovered after the German's sunk his ship in WW2. Still he always felt closer to the father he had never met when his visited his grave.

Gerry placed a Philly steak sandwich on his father's grave stone. Mercy had told him it was his Father's favorite food. He knew it was a little odd for a Catholic boy to do this, but it was something he saw the Vietnamese do for their departed family members and he liked the idea. His friend Hung had said it was a sign of respect and a message that the departed were still remembered. They truly believed that their spirits would eat the food in heaven. Being a practical people, the living Vietnamese ate the offerings after their departed family members had enough.

For 10 days, Gerry visited old friends, traveled around Philly to his old haunts and in general just enjoyed his time off. He flew to Saint Petersburg,

Florida, where his Grandfather Anthony Amato and Grandmother Carmella moved when Anthony retired as Don of the South Philly Mob. No one actually retired from the mob. He was still influential and a key advisor to his successor, Mario Costanzo.

When he returned from Florida, he and Jerome Washington checked out the two surplus C-123 aircraft Jerome had purchased. A day later Byrne Air Freight Inc. was born. Two days after that Jerome and Gerry flew one of the C-123s to LaGrange, GA, and then on to Tamaulipas, Mexico where they arranged to carry various food products such as rice, beans and coffee to an importer in the Philadelphia market. The importer was a secret Byrne corporation. They also solidified a deal with a local marijuana grower Jerome had worked on for the last three months. Byrne Air Freight would carry 5,000 kilos of weed, placed in hidden compartments on the aircraft and special crates, each trip. To start they would make three trips per month and increase them if the grower could keep up. Street value would be about three million dollars per trip. The grower was charging more than his Cambodian connections, but it was much cheaper to ship, so profits were almost the same. The trip to Mexico was a success and Gerry planned to start bringing in marijuana within the next three weeks.

It was customary for Jake, Charlie, Jimmy, and Mike Kelly to get together on Friday nights to play cards, drink beer and discuss everything from politics to religion. When Gerry was a teenager, he often joined the group of older men. Jake told Mercy it was better that Gerry learn to drink responsibly with them, than to sneak around the neighborhood with the other kids and get in trouble.

The first couple of weeks that he was home, Gerry was too busy to join them. Now that he had firmed up his business, he looked forward to getting together with the guys. As expected, he had to endure a period of good-natured ribbing, but eventually the men got down to playing cards.

"I hear you got yourself a Purple Heart over there, Gerry. What happened?" Mike asked.

"Nothing much. We had to ditch our plane in the Mekong River. The plane flipped over." Gerry said.

"You get hurt?" Mike asked.

"Yeah a little," Gerry said avoiding the exact details.

"Yeah. Let's see it. It's not on your ass, is it? If it is your ass, I don't want to see it," Jake said laughing.

"It's not a hundred percent healed yet," Gerry said as he unbuttoned his shirt and showed his scar.

"What? That's nothing," Jimmy said, "I got one too." Jimmy took off his shirt to reveal a scar on his back and another on his side."German asshole got me when I was in Africa."

"That had to hurt," Gerry said.

"Wasn't pleasant," Jimmy replied. "How about you, Charlie? Show us your boo boos."

"Don't want to show you up, Jimmy. Oh right, yes I do," Charlie said and took off his shirt. On his back were five distinct scars. He pulled his pants down a little and there were several more scars on his posterior. "Jap grenade."

"How about you, Uncle Mike? You got a scar?" Gerry asked.

"A few," Mike answered.

"Well, show us," Gerry said.

Mike unbuttoned his shirt. On his shoulder was a round scar. "Got this on a job in New York."

"How about you, Uncle Jake? You get a Purple Heart in Korea?" Gerry asked.

"No medal, but I did get a scar," Jake answered.

"Well, what're you waiting for? Show us," Jimmy said.

Jake stood up, unbuckled his pants and dropped them to the floor. He lifted his shorts to reveal a twelve-inch scar running from his knee up to his thigh.

"Oh shit," Gerry said.

Jimmy cringed and said, "That's way too close to the family jewels."

Charlie and Mike just stared in disbelief.

"You should have gotten a Purple Heart for that. What happened?" Gerry asked.

"Well, you get a Purple Heart for being hurt in action. This didn't happen that way," Jake said and paused.

"We're waiting," Charlie said.

"I don't like to talk about it," Jake said.

"Come on Jake, we're family. You can trust us," Charlie said.

"Ok, but if you laugh I'm going to bust you one," Jake said then hesitated and continued. "I was seeing these two Korean bar girls. One found out and decided to relieve me of my schlong. I was able to stop her, but got this instead," Jake said.

Everyone laughed. Jake jokingly went after Charlie. "I told you not to laugh," Jake yelled as he grabbed Charlie and put him in a headlock.

Mercy walked into the room and saw Jake with his pants to his ankles and Charlie with his shirt off, wrestling on the floor. "What the hell are you two doing?" Mercy said.

Jake tried to pull up his pants, but his belt buckle was stuck on Charlie's shoe. He fumbled to cover himself. Everyone laughed even harder, including Mercy.

"Forget it. I'm not even going to ask again?" Mercy said still chuckling. "Can I get you anything, more beer, some sandwiches, some clothes maybe?" Everyone broke out laughing again.

"Okay then. If you need anything I'll be in the living room watching Dark Shadows," Mercy said.

"You still watching that vampire crap," Jake said.

"I do. It's a good show," Mercy replied.

"It won't last another year. Nobody cares about vampires," Jake said.

"We'll see. I like it," Mercy said and left.

After the men put their clothes back on, they resumed their card game.

"Hey Gerry, we got a little job to do tomorrow. Want to tag along?" Jake asked.

"He don't need to be involved in that shit," Jimmy said.

"No. I would like to go, Uncle Jake. Getting a little bored, you know," Gerry said. "What're we doing?"

"Nothing much, just going to see a couple of guys. One won't listen to reason and the other has sticky fingers," Mike said.

# Chapter Ten

Early the next morning Gerry met Mike and Jake for breakfast at the Olympia Restaurant. The Olympia was a neighborhood restaurant owned by a Greek immigrant and it was conveniently located at Howard Street and Alleghany Avenue, just around the corner from Mercy Row.

"My best bud Phil, his brother Bob and I use to skip Sunday mass and come here for burgers and fries. They have the best greasy burger in North Philly," Gerry said.

"I'm sure they'll make you one if you want it," Mike said.

"Nah, too early for that. I'll stick with the eggs and bacon," Gerry said.

"Get some Scrapple," Jake suggested.

"Don't think so! You know what they put in that?" Gerry said. The three men laughed.

"Eat up. We need to leave in ten minutes. Gerry, you sure you're up for this? Could get dicey," Jake asked.

"I'm good. I've seen dicey before." Gerry replied.

"One thing. We don't kill these guys. I made a promise," Jake said.

"But we can break them up a little. We didn't promise not to do that," Mike said and laughed.

Fifteen minutes later Mike parked his 1967 Cadillac DeVille two doors down from the address Father George had given him. Tom Gentry lived in a simple two-story row home built by Gerry's grandfather, Charles Byrne in the 1920s, as were most of the homes in North Philly. They could hear a man yelling and a woman yelling back. Suddenly the front door of the house opened and a man pushed the storm door so hard it broke the glass. He stopped and yelled back into the house. "When I get home from work, we'll fucking finish this, bitch."

"That's Gentry. Gerry, get out and ask him for a light," Mike said and handed Gerry a cigarette.

Gerry quickly opened the door and came around the car as Gentry was passing by. Gerry stood in front of him and asked, "Gotta light buddy."

Gentry stopped, looked at Gerry, then pushed him with two hands and said, "Get the fuck out of my way."

Gerry stumbled back a few steps then quickly came forward and threw a right-handed punch at Gentry. Gentry blocked the punch with his left arm and hit Gerry in the chest with his right fist. Gerry fell back a couple of feet then rushed forward and brought his knee up and into the Gentry's groin. Gentry bent over and groaned. Gerry hit him with an uppercut to the jaw. Gentry fell over unconscious.

Jake jumped out of the car, opened the Caddy's trunk door and said, "Throw him in."

Gerry picked Gentry up by his shoulders and dragged him over to the car. "I could use a little help, Uncle Jake."

Jake smiled, grabbed Gentry's legs and they threw him in the trunk. He took some duct tape and wrapped it around his mouth, tied his hands and legs with rope and closed the trunk lid. When everyone was in the car and Mike drove off, Gerry asked, "What're we going do with him?"

"Don't know yet. We'll come up with something. By the way, good job, kid," Jake said.

"You don't know? Did you two think this out beforehand?" Gerry asked.

"No, not really." Mike said.

"Maybe, don't you think, you should have?" Gerry asked.

"Nah, it's a simple job and we always come up with something. We're better when we… what's that word?" Mike said, scratching his head.

"Ad lib?" Jake answered.

"No."

"Improvise?" Gerry said.

"Yeah! That's it. Improvise," Mike said.

Gerry shook his head and asked, "Where to now?"

"Fishtown. Norris and Almond Streets." Jake said.

"What's there?" Gerry asked.

"One of your Mother's men. He's sticky fingered and needs a lesson," Mike said.

On the corner of Norris and Almond Street there was a small candy and sandwich shop run by Joe Morris. The shop was a front for Morris' fencing operation. He took in stolen merchandise from the K&A Gang crews, resold it and turned over fifty percent of the profit to the Mercy Row Foundation. It was a lucrative operation and one of ten throughout North and Northeast Philly. The money was entered in the foundation ledger as donations from neighborhood collections. To Mercy's way of thinking, this was just a small redistribution of wealth from those who had a lot to those who had nothing.

Morris had been a good earner until about six months ago. He claimed his suppliers were not providing enough goods, because several of them had been arrested. The real problem was Morris became greedy and began skimming the money for himself. Mercy devised a sting where she had some men bring goods to Morris. The rule was everything was to be logged in when it arrived and again when it was sold. These items did not get on the list, so Mercy asked Jake and Mike to handle the problem.

"Gerry, go to the side entrance. If I signal you, kick it in and stop whoever tries to get out," Mike said.

"Got it," Gerry replied.

When Gerry was in place, Mike opened the store door and Jake walked in. Mike stayed by the door as a lookout. The door chimed, telling the proprietor someone had entered.

"Be right with you," Morris said from his office behind the store.

As he walked through the door, he saw Jake and panicked. He turned and ran, trying to get to the back door before Jake could get around the counter.

Jake yelled, "Joe where you going. We just want to talk."

Mike signaled Gerry and Gerry kicked the door twice before it broke. He pushed the door open with force and it hit something and bounced back. He pushed again and ran into the office. Joe Morris's ample body was lying on the floor and he was holding his nose as the blood ran through his fingers. Mike ran in just behind Jake.

"Mike, Gerry pick him up and put him in that chair," Jake said.

"You pick him up. I got a bad back," Mike said.

Jake motioned to Gerry and each took an arm and pulled Morris to a standing position. They plopped him in the office chair. "What the fuck is this all about," Morris asked in a muffled voice as he was still trying to stop the blood with his hands.

Jake took a clean hanky from his back pocket and threw it at Morris. "Here, put your head back and hold this to you nose," Jake said and then grabbed Morris's little finger on his right hand and snapped it. Morris screamed and blood from his nose splattered onto Jake.

"God damn it, Gerry. Did you have to break his nose? Now he ruined this suit," Jake said over Morris's screams.

It took a few minutes for Morris to stop yelling and crying. When he did, Mike said calmly, "Joe, you know why we're here. Just tell me where the money is and Jake won't have to break the rest of your fingers."

"I don't… I don't know what you are talking about," Morris yelled.

Jake took Morris's left little finger and snapped it. Morris screamed again. "God damn it, Joe, you took money from Mercy. She uses that money to feed hungry families and get kids medical treatment. What the fuck's wrong with you?" Jake yelled.

Morris was crying again. "Where is the money?" Mike asked.

"By the cash register on the floor. Loose floor board," Morris said shuddering from pain.

Mike looked at Gerry. Gerry walked into the store, pried open the loose board and whistled. "Holy shit," he said aloud. He grabbed a paper bag and filled it with the cash from Joe's hiding place.

"I got it," Gerry said as he walked over to Mike.

Mike looked into the bag, pulled some stacks of cash out and said, "Gotta be a hundred k in here." Then he punched Morris in his already broken nose. Morris fell off the chair, balled himself up on the floor. "Son of a bitch," Mike said and kicked Morris in the ass.

"Take it easy, Mike," Jake said.

"I'm cool," Mike said as he pulled his .45 and pointed at Morris's head.

Gerry slowly pushed Mike's arm so the gun pointed to the ceiling and said, "You made a promise to my Mom."

Mike looked at Gerry for a full minute and then holstered his gun.

"Gerry, go get the tape and rope," Jake said. When Gerry returned he tied Morris's hands and was about to tie his feet when Mike said," Leave his feet. I'll be damned if I'm carrying him to the car. He can walk."

"Gerry, make a sign for the front door and lock it. We'll take him to the car," Jake ordered.

Gerry found a marker and a piece of paper and wrote *New Owner. Will Open Again Soon.* He found some tape and fastened it to the front door. Before he left he opened the cash drawer, took the cash and put it in the bag that Mike had left on Morris's desk and took it with him.

When Gerry reached the car, Mike and Jake where standing by the trunk looking at Joe Morris.

"What are you guys doing?" Gerry asked.

"I think Morris is having a heart attack," Mike said.

Morris's chest was heaving, he was groaning and his complexion was pale. Gerry walked over to the trunk and pulled the tape from Morris's mouth. Morris took several quick deep breaths.

"Christ, Uncle Jake. You broke his nose and you taped his mouth. How's he supposed to breathe?"

Jake looked at Mike and Mike shrugged, pulled his gun, placed it on Morris's forehead and said, "Joe, you son of a bitch, if you make one sound I swear I'll blow your head off."

Morris cringed. Mike closed the trunk and they got in the car.

"What're we going to do with the two of them?" Gerry asked.

"Don't know. We'll come up with something," Jake said.

Gerry rolled his eyes. Mike saw him in the rear view mirror and said, "You, got a better idea kid?"

"Maybe?"

"Well, spit it out," Mike said.

"On Wednesday Jerome and I are flying to Mexico for a pickup. How about we box these guys up and I take them with us. I'll get our supplier to hang onto them. They can work in the fields or something. In a few, years, if they're still kicking, we can let them go and make sure they don't come back to Philly," Gerry said.

"Why don't we just drop them in the ocean on the way?" Mike said and looked at Jake.

"No, we made a promise to Mercy and George. Gerry, you got somewhere to stash these two until you leave?" Jake said.

"Yeah, the hangar. I got a couple big wooden crates. I'll throw some blankets in one, punch some air holes and nail down the top. Give me a couple of your guys to guard them until we leave," Gerry said.

When they arrived at the Byrne Air Freight hangar, Gerry prepared the crate. Jake forced the two captives to write letters to their families explaining that they decided to leave. When Gerry and Jerome stopped to refuel, they would mail the letters. Joe Morris had no family so Jake had him send the letter to a friend.

Mercy agreed to offer Mrs. Gentry a position with the Mercy Row Foundation. The day before Gerry flew to Mexico with his human cargo, he dropped an envelope with $5,000 and a note in Mrs. Gentry's mailbox. The note was typed and said, *I'm sorry.* It was signed simply *Tom.*

# Chapter Eleven

Three days later Gerry had Morris and Gentry cleaned up, then put them ina new crate and loaded it on the airplane. They flew to Florida instead of LaGrange, Georgia for their first fuel stop, mailed the letters and took off for Mexico. When they were safely in the air, Gerry turned the controls over to Jerome, and pried the lid off the crate to let Gentry and Morris out.

"If you two give me any trouble, I swear I'll dump you out over the ocean. Understand?" Gerry warned. The two men nodded yes.

Gerry ripped the tape from Gentry's mouth, and then he helped both men out of the crate and onto the floor. Their legs and hands were still bound so they offered no resistance.

"Who the fuck are you and why am I here?" Gentry yelled.

"Who I am is none of your business. The reason you're here is because your wife and kids have a guardian angel. That angel didn't like the way you treated them," Gerry said.

"You have no right to…" Gentry began to say when Gerry interrupted.

"We have every right, you piece of shit. You had no right beating up your wife, cheating on her and fucking every clap-ridded whore in Philly. So shut the fuck up or I'll toss you out the door," Gerry yelled.

Gentry leaned back and said nothing.

"Here's what's going to happen. You're going to Mexico to work for a friend. Consider it a work release program. If you do well you'll be released in a few years. If you don't, I can assure you my Mexican friends have no tolerance for assholes. When and if you're released, you will never come back to Philadelphia. If you do, you won't last a night. Do you know who the K&A Gang is, Gentry?" Gerry asked.

"Yeah," Gentry answered.

"Then you know this is no idle threat. Comeback and you're dead. Got it?"

Both men nodded yes, but said nothing.

Gerry grabbed a machete from a tool chest. He then pulled Morris to the bulkhead.

"What're you doing, I thought..." Morris was interrupted by Gerry.

"Take it easy," Gerry said and cut the ropes from his hands. He placed handcuffs on his left wrist and fixed it to the bulkhead. Then he did the same to Gentry. Gerry opened a cooler, pulled out two beers and handed one each to Morris and Gentry. He took out his church key, and opened the bottles. Then he took out two bags from the cooler and gave one to each man.

"Hoagies. Now eat and I don't want any trouble from you," Gerry said as he took two more beers and two hoagies from the cooler and walked back to the cockpit. He handed Jerome a beer and a sandwich and said, "I got it."

"It's yours," Jerome replied. "How are our guests?"

"I don't think they'll be any trouble. I told them I'd throw them out the door if they were," Gerry said and smiled.

Jerome laughed and said, "I bet you would."

"You mind if I drop her down?" Gerry asked.

"What's with you wanting to fly so low over the ocean anyway?" Jerome asked.

"I don't know. Just makes me happy," Gerry said.

"Then go ahead. God forbid if you're not happy," Jerome said and laughed. Then he tightened his seat belt. "And what's with you and that raggedy ass hat. Can't you afford a new one?"

"This," Gerry said touching the brim of his sweat-stained, grubby old fatigue cap." It's my lucky hat. Had it since I first went to Vietnam. It got me home alive," Gerry said.

"How about you wash it. It's getting a bit ripe," Jerome suggested.

"Are you fucking kidding? I can't clean this. It'll wash out all the luck," Gerry said, paused and continued, "Put the eight track in, will you."

As the music blared Gerry put the plane into a step drive and when they were just 300 feet above the ocean, he pulled back on the yoke. The plane leveled out at approximately 100 feet above the water. It was a calm sunny day on the Gulf and the waves gently rolled as the aircraft's shadow passed over them.

"Look at that. 2 o'clock," Gerry said pointing.

"Humpback, right?" Jerome asked.

"Yep and a calf. Don't see that often," Gerry said.

"Looks like we're not the only ones watching," Jerome said.

Several hundred yards from the whale and her calf, was a white classic 60 foot yacht. Three women in bikinis were waving at the plane. Gerry pulled up and banked the plane until it was in line with the yacht. Then he dropped it to about 50 feet as they flew past the women. He pulled up to about 300 feet banked again and came around. As he flew over the yacht, he tipped his wings first left then right, and continued on to Mexico.

"Holy crap! Did you see those girls. They didn't have no tops on," Jerome said.

"Take it easy, Jerome, they're just tits. They come in all colors, shapes and sizes," Gerry said as he gained altitude and continued on to Mexico. Several hours later, he landed the plane on a small landing strip on a farm in the state of Tamaulipas, Mexico. The closest town was Tampico about twenty miles to the east.

Gerry pulled the C-123 to the end of the runway and turned off the engines. Within minutes, two trucks and a fuel tanker pulled up beside them.

"Jerome, stay here with these two while I fill in Alberto," Gerry said pointing at Gentry and Morris. Then he lowered the cargo door and walked out.

Alberto Rivera was waiting for Gerry at the bottom of the ramp. He hugged Gerry, patted his back and said, "My friend. It is so good to see you."

Alberto Rivera was tall for a Mexican. At age fifty, he had kept the looks of his youth. The only hint of his age was the graying of his jet-black hair above his temple. He always dressed in suits he had tailored in London and a straw fedora hat, no matter how warm and humid it was.

Rivera reminded Gerry of his Grandfather Tony Amato, with one exception. Rivera was even more powerful than his grandfather, which was impressive since Amato controlled all of South Philadelphia. Rivera headed one of the largest crime organizations in Mexico and not trusting local politicians, he had himself appointed Governor of the state of Tamaulipas. Rivera was educated at Harvard University and held a Master's in Business Administration.

Gerry explained to Rivera the situation with Morris and Gentry and Rivera agreed to keep the men until Gerry decided it was time to release them.

"Don't worry, my friend, I will keep these two safe until you tell me otherwise. Nothing is as important as a man's word, and I would not like to see a promise you made broken," Rivera said.

"Thank you, Mr. Rivera, I appreciate your help," Gerry said.

"Gerry, my son, we are friends and we will make millions together. Please call me Alberto," Rivera said and put his arm around Gerry's shoulder. "Now let's get that rascal Jerome and tonight you stay with me, we have dinner and after we have some tequila and talk about American football. Okay?"

With Jerome in hand, Rivera held up his hand and within minutes a white 1967 Lincoln Continental convertible pulled up in front of them. The driver opened the back door and all three men got in. Jerome made a mental note that he would buy one of these cars.

While Gerry and Jerome spent a comfortable evening drinking Jose Cuervo tequila, Rivera's men took Morris and Gentry to a small building at the rear of Rivera's hacienda. They were given rice, beans, and a bottle of beer each. In a couple of days, they would be transported to the marijuana growing fields where they would help to cultivate and harvest the plant.

After a breakfast of Mexican-style sausage, scrambled eggs and corn tortillas, Gerry and Jerome were driven back to their plane. Rivera's men had carefully packed the marijuana in the secret compartments and loaded the plane with crates of roasted coffee, which helped to mask the smell of the drug. Each crate had a false bottom full of the newly processed plants.

The trip back to the States was smooth and when they landed in LaGrange, Georgia, Gerry passed an envelope to the customs agent. He cleared them without looking in the plane. The weather was clear and sunny when they left, but as they approached Philadelphia, they started to experience rain and high winds. This made landing at the North Philadelphia Airport difficult.

"Jerome, help me with the yoke. I'm having trouble keeping her lined up," Gerry ordered.

Jerome took his yoke and they were able to get the plane lined up to land.

"This could be a hard landing," Jerome said.

"Buckle up. Here we go," Gerry said.

When they were twenty-five feet above the runway a downwind pushed the plane to the tarmac. It thudded into the concrete, bounced once and then came back to the ground. Gerry pulled the plane to the hangar and let out his breath.

"That was no fun," Gerry said.

Gerry sent Jerome home and stayed to check out the landing gear. It seemed fine to him but he made a mental note to have a mechanic look at it in the morning. There was a small stack of mail on his desk and on top was a telegram. He opened the telegram and read it.

*To: G Amato*
*From: G Barra*
*URGENT!*
*Arrive 11/22/67 10 AM Eastern Air Lines 223.*
*Paris not happy. Take precautions.*

# Chapter Twelve

Gerry picked up the phone and dialed Jake's home number. It was 6:00 pm and he was hoping Jake would be home having dinner. It was a good bet he would be because Maria, Jake's wife, insisted that the family eat together. It was a custom from her Italian heritage and her mother Carmella Amato's family rule.

"Hello?"

"Aunt Maria, it's Gerry."

"Gerry, where have you been? I haven't seen you for a while. You need to come for dinner Sunday," Maria said.

"I will. I promise. Right now, I need to talk to Uncle Jake. It's urgent," Gerry said.

"Okay, okay. I'll get him," Maria said.

A minute later Jake answered the phone. "Gerry, you alright? Any trouble with the delivery?"

"No. That went fine. I need you to send a few men to Grandpop's and Uncle Franklin's houses. Send a couple more to my mom's house. Be sure they come heavy," Gerry said impatiently.

"Why? What's happening," Jake asked.

"Can you come to the hangar? I don't want to talk on the phone. I'll explain when you get here."

"Okay, I'll be there just as soon as I can," Jake said.

"Jake, better have Maria and the kids go to Mercy's or Grandpop's house," Gerry said and hung up the phone.

Gerry pulled the tarp off a large wooden box he had secured in the hangar's storeroom.  He opened the lid and pulled out an old leather flight jacket Jerome had given him before he left for his tour in Vietnam. It had been one Jerome used when he flew fighter aircraft in Europe during

WW2. Gerry laid it aside then pulled out his leather double shoulder holster with two older Colt 1911 .45s that had belonged to George Graham. He strapped the holsters on then put the flight jacket on to conceal the weapons. Before he closed the lid to the box, he pulled out two AR15s he had been able to liberate from the Air Force before he left Vietnam, and several clips for both weapons.

The main door to the hangar was located on the parking lot side of the building. There was a small door on the runway side as well. Gerry locked the runway side door and using a forklift placed two heavy crates in front of it. The large hangar door was made of steel and he was confident no one could get into the building from the runway. He then locked the parking lot door, turned the lights out, pulled a chair to where he could see out of a window, and waited for Jake.

Fifteen minutes later he heard a car pull up in the parking lot. It was difficult to see as there were no overhead outdoor lights in that area and there was no moon out. Gerry squinted to see better and hoped it was Jake. What he saw sent a shiver down his spine. Four shadowy figures exited the vehicle. As they walked towards the hangar, they spread out and Gerry could see two of them were carrying rifles. He grabbed his AR15, put a clip in and took aim at one of the men.

He hesitated, thinking that they might be Jake and some of the crew. As the men came closer a single light above the hangar allowed Gerry to see their faces. These men were Asians. Gerry shot hitting one of the men in the leg. The man screamed, dropped his rifle and fell to the ground. The other three men started backing up while shooting at the hangar. The man Gerry shot started crawling back to the car, leaving his rifle on the ground.

Gerry ducked behind a crate hoping the metal walls and the thick wood of the crate would stop any bullets. He was partly correct. The crate wood and coffee in the crate stopped the bullets, but the thin metal walls began to look like Swiss cheese. In Gerry's mind this was a repeat of the time he and Watson crashed in the Mekong River near Tan Chau. The only difference was this time there would be no Navy patrol boat or a

Crazy John to save him. His only hope was his Uncle Jake and he would be walking into a shit storm.

After Gerry called, Jake sent men to Mercy, Jacob and Franklin's homes. He called Mercy and Jacob and explained, then met with Mike to go to the hangar.

When they turned into the airport parking lot, Jake and Mike heard gunfire. Jake quickly turned off the lights and pulled over. Jake grabbed an old Thompson he kept in the trunk and handed it to Mike. He took a pump action shotgun and filled his pockets with shells.

Jake and Mike slipped behind the hedges that separated the parking lot from a wide-open expanse of dirt fields. They slowly made their way towards Gerry's hangar. Stepping from behind the hedge onto the asphalt in front of the building, Jake tripped over something. He heard a moan and looked down to see the man Gerry had shot. The man looked at Jake and started to open his mouth, but before he could Jake smashed the butt of his shotgun into the man's head. The man slumped back unconscious.

Jake and Mike positioned themselves behind one of the assailants cars. The three other assailants were still firing blindly into the hangar. Mike stepped out from one side and Jake from the other. They both fired. Jake hit the man on the right. He flew forward with the force of the blast and hit the ground, half of his head pulverized into mist. At the same time, Mike opened up with the Thompson hitting both of the other men. One of the men immediately crumbled to the ground. The third man turned his automatic rifle still firing. Jake fired and hit the man in the chest. The man flew backwards a couple of feet and hit the ground dead.

"Mike, go back and see if you can wake that guy up. Bring him inside. I'll check on Gerry," Jake said.

Mike nodded and left.

"Gerry," Jake yelled. "It's okay, we got them."

Gerry looked out of the window, what was left of it, and waved.

Jake smiled and said, "Open up."

Gerry opened the door and Jake hugged him. "I thought…."

"Nah, I have my lucky hat on," Gerry said as he put his hand on the peak of the hat.

"Hey, give an old man a hand, will ya," Mike yelled.

Jake and Gerry looked into the parking lot. Mike was dragging the man Gerry shot across the lot by the collar with one hand, and in the other was the Thompson.

"I wish I had a camera," Gerry said.

"Looks like you got everything in hand, Mike," Jake said.

Mike dropped the man in front of Jake and said, "You can take him the rest of the way."

Jake laughed, motioned to Gerry to help. They took the man by the arms and pulled him into the hangar. "Put him on that crate," Gerry said.

Jake slapped the man's face to try to wake him up, but it didn't work. He filled a bucket with water and poured it over the man's head. The man started to come around. Gerry searched him and found a passport and wallet. The passport was Cambodian.

"You speak English? Gerry said.

"The man looked at him and said, "Little."

"Who sent you? Who do you work for?" Gerry asked.

The man shook his head no. Mike ripped the pants off the leg where the bullet wound was. He then put his finger in the wound and twisted it. The man screamed. Mike continued. The man passed out.

Jake took a new pail of water and poured it over the man's head. When the man was awake again Jerry asked, "Who do you work for?"

The man hesitated and Mike started toward his leg again. The man screamed "Beaumont, Beaumont."

Jake looked at Gerry and then pulled his .45 and shot the man in the head.

# Chapter Thirteen

While Gerry and Jake wrapped the four bodies in plastic, Mike hosed down the blood in the driveway. By midnight, they had the bodies in a wooden crate with a couple hundred pounds of scrap metal attached to each of them. Gerry used the forklift to place the crate in the second aircraft, which was parked outside the hangar. He called Jerome and told him what had happened and to get the plane ready for a flight at 2 PM that afternoon.

After a few hours sleep, Gerry borrowed his mother's Mustang and drove to the Philadelphia International Airport with four guards following him in two cars. He met Gabriel Barra at the Eastern Airlines gate and told him he was to stay at his Grandfather Jacob's house in Lower Moreland. On the way to Jacob's house, Gerry filled Barra in about the events of the previous night.

"I am truly sorry I was not able to warn you before this. My people in Marseille sent me a telegram telling me about the Paris gang's intentions. I sent you a telegram and I booked the very next flight I could get," Barra said.

"Mr. Barra, you have done much more than I would have expected. Don't trouble yourself with this, please," Gerry said. "I was out of town anyway and just saw your telegram last night.

Barra lifted his hands indicating he understood, and then patted Gerry on the shoulder.

"What is this road? It is very large," Barra asked.

"It's called the Schuylkill Expressway. We like to call it the Surekill Expressway."

"Why is that?" Barra asked

"Good question. I don't really know. I guess because it's such a busy highway they have a lot of accidents," Gerry replied.

"Ahhh," Barra said laughing. "Then, perhaps we should take another road."

Gerry laughed and said, "We will. I am taking you the scenic route, past my airport. We're taking one of the planes for a flight later today. You could come along if you like."

"I would love to. What are you flying?" Barra asked

"C-123, just like I flew in Nam."

As they drove north on the Roosevelt Boulevard, Gerry pointed out some of the various landmarks. There was the Sears Tower on Adams Road. Built in the 1920s it was one of the largest buildings in Northeast Philly. The Big Boys drive-in restaurant was a favorite hangout for the teen-age Gerry and his pals. They would drive through the parking lot in their cars with the mufflers disabled so their cars made a loud noise. The idea was the louder the car the more girls you could attract. The Roosevelt Pools at Tyson Avenue was another place Gerry and his pals went to pick up girls. Gerry pointed out the Northeast Airport at Grant Avenue where his hangar was located and where they would come later in the day.

"What is that wonderful smell?" Barra asked.

"That, my friend, is the Nabisco Bakery. I always get hungry when I pass by," Gerry said.

"I would like to try some of their goods," Barra said. "I am, you know, a connoisseur of baked goods."

"Well, we can do better. I'll treat you to some Tastykakes before you leave," Gerry said.

"What is a tasty cake?"

"It's a Philadelphia gourmet food. I have traveled, as you know, and have never found anything so good. My favorites are the lemon pie and the chocolate peanut butter cakes," Gerry said licking his lips.

"I cannot wait to try them," Barra said.

"This is our turnoff," Gerry explained as they came up to Byberry Road.

A half mile down the road Gerry suddenly pulled into a new Wawa store and told Barra to wait. He went into the store and came out ten minutes later with three bags. He gave each of the drivers in the guard cars a bag and handed the third one to Barra. Barra opened the bag and pulled out a lemon pie. He opened it and gave Gerry half and ate the other half himself.

"Nourriture des dieux," Barra said. "How you say? Food of the Gods."

Gerry smiled and said, "Don't eat too much. My Grandmother Molly has a big lunch planned."

When they arrived at Jacob and Molly's home, Gerry's guards joined the men already guarding the home and he and Barra, using the back entrance, went into the house. Molly and Jacob were waiting. Gerry introduced Barra to his grandparents and Molly ushered them into the dining room.

"Mr. Barra, please sit here next to Jacob," Molly said.

"Please, call me Gabe. May I call you Molly?" Barra asked.

"Of course, Gabe," Molly answered. "Do you like roast beef?"

"But of course. Sadly, I do not get much in Cambodia. They favor pork and chicken. It will be a great treat," Barra said.

"Oh good, it is an old family recipe. I'll be right back," Molly said as she left for the kitchen.

"Gabe, where's your coat?" Jacob asked.

"I do not have one. No need for them in Cambodia. I thought I would buy one here," Barra replied.

"Give me a minute," Jacob said and left the room. Five minutes later, he returned and handed Barra two coats. "This one is for dress and this one for casual. And this scarf will keep you warm. You'll need a hat as well," Jacob said handing Barra a Newsboy cap. "We're about the same size. I am sure they will fit."

"You are too generous, Jacob. Thank you."

Molly came in the room holding a large tray of thinly sliced roast beef and placed it on the table. The meat was still steaming, filling the room with a wonderful spicy aroma. Barra stared at the plate wide eyed. Molly left and returned with a platter of Kaiser rolls and a large bowl of potato salad.

"Gabe, would you like a nice glass of wine? Sorry, all we have is California wine. I didn't have time to buy some of that wonderful French wine your country makes," Molly asked.

"I would. Thank you, Molly," Barra said.

Molly took her seat and looked at Jacob. Jacob made the sign of the cross saying, "In the name of the Father, Son and Holy Ghost." Barra, Molly and Gerry did the same. Jacob continued," Bless us, O Lord, and these your gifts, which we are about to receive from your bounty. And, please care of the soul of our beloved Rose, who brought so much love to our family. Through Christ our Lord. Amen."

"Thank you, Jacob. Now let's eat," Molly said.

"Mr. Barra. Let me show you how I make my roast beef sandwich," Gerry said. Barra nodded. "First I take a Kaiser roll. I take some gravy and pour some on each half of the roll. Then I take a large spoon full of horseradish, then…"

Barra interrupted Gerry and asked, "What is this horseradish?"

Gerry held the spoon close to Barra's nose and Barra took a sniff and exclaimed, "Oh! We call this raifort. It is very good."

Gerry continued, "Then I put the beef on the bread. A lot of beef."

Barra made his sandwich as Gerry had shown him.

"Take some potato salad. It was my Grandma Rose's favorite dish," Gerry said as he piled the potato salad on Barra's plate.

Barra slid his fork in the potato salad and lifted it to his mouth. He savored the taste, swallowed, rolled his eyes and said, "Magnifique."

After lunch, Gerry and Barra drove to the Northeast Airport. Jerome was there and had the plane checked out and the engines warming up.

After the introductions, Gerry pulled the plane onto the runway and waited for clearance.

"Where we really going, Gerry?" Jerome asked.

"You filed the flight plan right? Straight to the Atlantic Ocean, couple hundred miles out and then back," Gerry said.

"Yeah, yeah, but what are we really doing," Jerome said.

"Go get Mr. Barra from the back. I'll fill you both in," Gerry said.

When Jerome returned with Barra, Gerry said," You both know what happened last night. I was lucky and if it hadn't been for Uncle Jake and Mike I wouldn't be here now. We have the four men that attacked us in that big wooden crate back in the cargo area. So we're going to fly out over the Atlantic ocean about 160 miles. Then we're going to drop those boys in the Gulf Stream. Chances are, with weights on them, they'll sink to the bottom. But, if for some reason they don't the current of the stream will push them north and eventually over to Europe. Unless, that is, something eats them first. Either way they'll never be seen again."

Barra nodded his head in approval, held out the paper bag Gerry had given him and said, "Tastykake, anyone."

Two and a half hours later Gerry turned over the controls to Jerome and asked Barra to come to the cargo area with him.

"Mr. Barra. Do you mind helping?" Gerry asked.

"No, not at all. It's not the first body I have disposed of. Of course, we usually just take them into the jungle and leave them," Barra said.

Gerry broke open the crate and with Barra's help they pulled the four weighted bodies to the tailgate area. He helped Barra put on a harness and attached a safety strap. Then he did the same for himself.

"I'm going to open the tailgate now so hold on," Gerry said as he picked up the microphone and told Jerome the same thing. Then he pulled the lever and the tailgate began to drop. The plane shook and lurched momentarily until Jerome corrected it. Barra and Gerry began pushing the four bodies toward the opening until they were half way on the dropped tailgate. Gerry picked up the microphone and told Jerome to take her up as steep as possible.

"Hold on tight, Mr. Barra."

The plane began to climb and the angle of ascent increased. After a couple of minutes, the bodies started to move towards the end of the tailgate. One by one, they fell out of the plane, landing in the ocean and sinking under the waves. When all the bodies had fallen, Gerry told Jerome to level out and when he did, Gerry pushed the crate to the opening and out. When it hit the water Gerry closed the door.

"That was exciting," Barra said, wiping the sweat off his brow.

Gerry smiled, undid Barra's and his own harness and walked back to the cockpit. He sat Barra in a third seat, took his seat and said, "You ready for a little more excitement, Mr Barra?"

"Yes, sure," Barra said.

"Come on, Gerry not with a passenger on board," Jerome pleaded.

"Gotta do it, Jerome. Gotta do it," Gerry said as his put his lucky hat on and picked up a cartridge."

"What is that Gerry? Barra asked.

"That, Mr. Barra is the latest and greatest in music technology, an eight track cartridge," Gerry said and placed it in the player. "And this is the best song of the year."

As the singer belted out the song, *"Your Love Keeps Lifting Me Higher And Higher,"* Gerry put the aircraft into a steep dive. When he reached 500 feet he started to level out until he was traveling 100 feet off the ocean waves. Gerry took a quick look at Barra, who was holding on to the seat with both hands with beads of sweat on his brow.

"Mr. Barra, please come up here. I want you to see this," Gerry said.

Barra undid his seat belt and leaned forward. The white-capped waves sped past at 180 miles an hour. Barra caught his breath at the beauty of it all.

"Over there, 2 o'clock. See the school of porpoises. Beautiful," Gerry yelled over the song.

The song played four times before Gerry began to pull the plane to a higher, safer altitude. It was getting dark and the lights from the Jersey coast began to twinkle as the C-123 headed for Northeast Philadelphia Airport.

# Chapter Fourteen

Gabriel Barra didn't sleep well. The time difference between Cambodia and Philadelphia was twelve hours, so his night was now his day. And, he was worried about the Paris Mob. He knew they wouldn't stop until Gerry Amato was dead. He got out of bed at 4 AM and read for a while. He loved Ian Fleming's James Bond series and was currently reading You Only Live Twice. At 6:30 AM he dressed and went downstairs to see if anyone else was awake.

"Gabe, good morning. Did you sleep well?" Molly asked.

"Yes. yes. Thank you," Barra lied.

"Do you drink coffee Gabe?" Molly asked.

"Oh yes."

Molly told Barra to sit at the kitchen table and placed a cup in front of him. She filled the cup with fresh brewed coffee and said, "Milk and sugar are on the table if you use them. If you'll excuse me, I just have to take these thermoses of coffee and egg sandwiches to our guards. Be back in a jiffy."

"Of course," Barra said wondering what a jiffy was.

Barra poured milk in his coffee and two spoons of sugar. He tasted the brew and frowned. It was very weak. He was used to the strong blends of France and Cambodia.

When Molly returned she asked, "How's the coffee?"

"Wonderful, thank you," Barra lied again.

"Can I make you some breakfast?" Molly asked.

"If it's not too much trouble, thank you."

"Not at all. Eggs and bacon okay? Maybe some Scrapple?"

"What is Scrapple?" Barra asked.

"Oh, it's a Philadelphia treat. Ground pork mixed with cornflower. Very tasty," Molly said.

"Sounds wonderful. Yes, I would love to try Scrapple," Barra said.

As Molly went about making breakfast, Barra marveled that even rich Americans did their own cooking. His first wife, a French debutant wouldn't be caught dead in a kitchen, and here was Molly Byrne, obviously wealthy, cooking him breakfast. *Americans,* he thought, *were a strangely wonderful people.*

Molly placed a plate of scrambled eggs, bacon and three slices of Scrapple in front of Barra and then sat down across the table from him and said, "Try the Scrapple."

Barra cut the Scrapple with his knife and ate a piece. He looked at Molly and his eyes widened. "This is very good."

Molly smiled and took a sip of her coffee.

"Molly, is there a bank near, where I can exchange money?"

"Yes, not too far away, but banks are closed today. It's Thanksgiving," Molly said.

"Oh, I have heard about Thanksgiving," Barra said.

"It's a big holiday for us. It's a time when we give thanks to God for all we have and it starts the Christmas season. I'm so happy you'll be able to experience it. We'll be having a big dinner for the whole family and closest friends," Molly said.

"Ahhh. The Canadians have this as well. They call it the Action de grâce," Barra said.

"Well, I'm happy you're here and will get a chance to meet our family. We'll also be celebrating Gerry's birthday," Molly said.

"It's Gerry's birthday?" Barra asked, "I must buy him a gift today."

"Actually, tomorrow is his birthday but since we're all together we'll celebrate it today. I'm sorry, all the stores are closed. You being here is present enough," Molly said.

A half hour later Jacob walked into the kitchen. Molly was dressing two 22 lb turkeys and Barra was watching her in amazement. Jacob put his hand on Barra's shoulder and said, "Good morning Gabe.

Barra rose from his chair, shook Jacob's hand and said "Bonjour, Jacob, bonjour. I was just watching your wife prepare these, how you say it, tur-key. Fascinating."

"Have you eaten turkey before," Jacob asked.

"Yes, a few times in Canada. It is very good," Barra said.

"It's our tradition to eat turkey on Thanksgiving and Christmas. Speaking about traditions, we have a couple more I think you'll like. We watch the Thanksgiving Day parade on television and then football. Come with me," Jacob said as he led Barra to the living room.

Jacob turned on the television, dialed to channel 6 and sat next to Barra on the sofa. "Gabe, the parade won't start for a while, but I wanted to talk to you. I hope you don't mind," Jacob said.

"Of course," Barra answered.

"It's been twenty-four years since we have had the kind of problems this Beaumont is bringing us. What can you tell me about this guy?" Jacob asked.

"The Beaumont gang controls a large area of Paris. They run drugs, gambling and prostitution. They also terrorize local businesses so they pay them protection. After I began supplying my crop from Indochina, they decided to become growers as well. We had no problem with that. They were in Paris and we were in Marseille. But, they are greedy and wanted Gerry to use them and not me. That's when all the trouble started," Barra said.

"Tell me about the leaders," Jacob asked.

"The boss is Henri Beaumont. His father started the business in the early 1900s and had a reputation for being brutal. He had two sons and a daughter. Henri is the oldest and took over the family business ten years ago when his father died. John Beaumont was his younger brother. He's the one who died in Cambodia. The father sent John to be educated in the U.S. When he returned to Paris John worked as an enforcer. Six years ago, John was sent to run the Cambodia business. They are all sadistic bastards, and do not care if innocents are killed as long as they succeed. They are hated by many in Paris, even in their own gang," Barra explained.

"What about the daughter," Jacob asked.

"She is not in the business that I know," Barra said.

"How do we stop them? Can we negotiate?" Jacob asked.

"Doubtful. Henri will not stop until Gerry is dead and he will not care who else dies in the process," Barra answered.

"Nevertheless I would like to try. Can you have your people contact them to see if we can talk."

"Yes, yes. We can try, but I would not hold too much hope for a peaceful resolution," Barra said.

Jacob nodded and said, "Thank you, Gabe. Can I get you some more coffee?"

"No thank you, but if I can use your phone I would like to call my cousin and see if he can arrange something with Beaumont," Barra said.

As Thanksgiving Day progressed, the house filled with the pleasant aroma of roasting turkey, pumpkin spices and apples and cinnamon. Mercy and Catherine, Franklin's wife, came early to help Molly and Franklin joined Jacob and Gabe watching the Los Angeles Rams play the Detroit Lions. It was a lackluster game and the Rams trounced the Lions.

By 5 PM the entire family arrived as well as invited friends, except for Mary Byrne, Jimmy Byrne's daughter. She was coming separately as she had to study for a final exam. Dinner was traditionally at 5:30 PM but Molly waited until 6 PM then decided they would start without Mary. Jimmy had called Mary at 5:30 but there was no answer.

"We're going to get started. Mary will be here soon, I'm sure. Gabe you may be wondering why there are two empty seats at our table. One is for Mary, of course, and the other is for our wonderful Rose who has recently left this earth for a better place," Jacob said blinking away a tear. "George, will you say Grace for us."

Father George rose from his chair and made the sign of the cross saying, "In the name of the Father, Son and Holy Ghost." Everyone at the table did the same, except Jerome who was a Baptist.

George continued. "O Gracious God, we give you thanks for your overflowing generosity to us. Thank you for the blessings of the food we eat and especially for this feast today. Thank you for our health, our work and our play. Please send help to those who are hungry, alone, sick and suffering war and violence. Open our hearts to your love.

And this day and every day we give special thanks for our friend Gabe who has traveled far, and Jerome who has been part of our lives for many years. We thank you for our family, Uncle Frank and Aunt Catherine, my mother Molly and father Jacob. And my brother Charlie, his wife Janet and their children Bella, Mark and Jeff. And my brother Jake and Maria and their children Alicia and Joey and my brother Jimmy and his wife Sally and their very late daughter Mary. Lastly, my sister Mercy and her son Gerry. We thank you for bringing Gerry back safe from Vietnam. We ask your blessing through Christ your son and we beseech you to hold close to your bosom our Grandmom Rose. Amen."

"Let's eat," Jacob said.

Several times during the meal, Jimmy excused himself and called his daughter Mary. Each time there was no answer from her apartment phone. After the meal of turkey, stuffing, mashed potatoes, four different vegetables and a sweet potato casserole with miniature marshmallows on top, Molly brewed coffee and offered everyone dessert.

"Molly, Jacob, thank you for allowing me to be part of your family's celebration. You have a wonderful family," Gabe proclaimed.

The phone rang. "I'll get it. It's probably Mary," Jimmy said.

Jimmy picked up the dining room phone and said, "Mary, where the hell have you been?"

The person on the phone answered back, "May I speak to Mr. Gerry Amato?"

"Hold on. Gerry, it's for you," Jimmy said not hiding his disappointment.

Gerry looked surprised that someone would call him at his Grandparents' house. He took the phone from Jimmy and said, "Hello, Gerry here."

"Mr. Amato, I'm an associate of Henri Beaumont," the person on the phone said.

Gerry stiffened, "How nice for you," he answered.

"Listen carefully. We have Mary Byrne and if you want to see her alive again, you'll do exactly what I say," the person on the phone said.

Gerry's face turned red with anger. "If she's hurt in any way I swear to you that I won't rest until everyone in the Beaumont gang is dead," Gerry said slowly and deliberately.

"That's up to you. I'll call again tomorrow morning at 10. If you don't answer, she dies. If you call the cops, she dies. Understand?" the person on the phone said.

Gerry said, "Yes."

The person on the phone hung up. Gerry put the phone back on the cradle and turned around to see everyone at the table looking at him.

# Chapter Fifteen

The moments after Gerry explained what the caller had said were chaotic. Molly and Sally began to cry and that started the younger children crying. Jake and Jimmy were threatening to kill everyone involved. Jacob realizing they needed a logical well-thought-out plan to get Mary back and keep Gerry safe, had the men and Mercy meet in his office. When everyone was in the office, Jacob asked them to take a seat and said, "I know the first thing you want to do is kill the bastards that have Mary. And we will do that, but the most important job at hand is to get Mary back safe."

"They said they'll call back tomorrow, so we don't have much choice but to wait," Gerry said.

"Frank, can you call Mike and tell him about this. Ask him to connect with the crews and anyone else that might have any information," Jacob asked. Frank walked over to the phone to call Mike.

"Jimmy, you okay," Jacob said.

"No! No, I'm not okay, Pop."

"Uncle Jimmy, it'll be alright. They want me, not her," Gerry said.

Jimmy shook his head and put his hands to his face. Jake put his hand on Jimmy's shoulder and said, "We'll get her back, Jimmy. I promise and then we'll kill Beaumont.

"Jerome, can you do me a favor?" Gerry asked.

"Sure," Jerome answered.

Gerry slid a piece of paper across the table. "What's this," Jerome asked.

"Call my buddy Al Watson. The number's on the paper. Tell him what's going on and ask him if he can come to Philadelphia," Gerry said.

"He's going to ask why," Jerome said.

"He's a pilot. You're going to need someone to fly with you," Gerry said.

Jerome looked at Gerry for a long moment, but said nothing and shook his head yes.

"Gabe, we need your help. Please tell us everything you know about Beaumont and anyone associated with him," Jacob asked. "Give me a minute first. I'll be right back."

Jacob walked into the dining room where things had calmed down a little and said, "Molly, I think it's best that everyone stay here tonight."

"Yes. Yes, that's a good idea. I'll find blankets and places for them to sleep," Molly said.

"Catherine, will you join us in my office?" Jacob asked.

"I'll make some coffee, Dad, "Maria said.

"Thanks, I think we'll need it," Jacob said.

Jacob walked over to Sally and hugged her. He whispered in her ear, "Sally, I promise you we'll get Mary back unharmed." As Jacob walked back to his office with Catherine he thought, *Oh God, I hope I can keep that promise.*

"None of us are leaving this room until we have a plan to get Mary back and a way to end this Beaumont problem once and for all," Jacob said.

"Sorry Gabe, to get you in the middle of this. Now tell us what you know," Jacob said.

By 8 AM the next morning, everyone agreed they had as good a plan as possible considering they didn't know where Mary was being held.

"Gerry, call Mario Costanzo and tell him we may need his help. Jake, call Mickey Callahan and ask him to come to Philly. Tell him to pack for a long visit and to bring his best man with him," Jacob said.

Franklin looked at Jacob, half smiled and said, "I guess we're at war again." Jacob just slowly nodded his head up and down.

"Jake, you have the combo for the safe in the basement. Take Charlie and go check the weapons. It's been a while since we needed them." Jake tapped Charlie on the shoulder and indicated that he should come with him.

"We have about an hour and fifteen minutes before the call. Go get some breakfast. Take a shower if you like and meet us back in my office at 9:45," Jacob said loudly so he could be heard over the din of people talking.

Mercy was the first one to return. She found her father at his desk doodling on a pad of paper and said, "What're you doing Papa?"

"Just thinking," Jacob said.

"Having second thoughts?" Mercy asked.

"No, just thinking about Mary. You know she reminds me a lot of you."

"Really," Mercy said.

"When Mary was a kid she always worried about the welfare of other people. If she saw a homeless person, she wanted to do something to help. I guess that's why she's becoming a doctor. You were the same way. Do you remember when you first suggested we use the old homes on Wishart Street to help the homeless families during the Depression?" Jacob said

"I do," Mercy said subconsciously rubbing her arm where a Chicago Mob hit man had shot her.

"I remember like it was yesterday. You were just ten years old. Ten years old, with the heart as big as the sun. You were still in the hospital when I told you we were going to do as you asked and convert the houses for the use of the homeless. You were so happy. Here you were shot up, in the hospital and still thinking of others. There wouldn't be a Mercy Row Foundation without you and the thousands of people you've helped would have been out of luck," Jacob said.

"Papa, we all did that. It's not just me. It's the family," Mercy said.

Jacob looked down at the table so Mercy couldn't see the tears in his eyes and said, "You know when you were a baby, I would come into your room and watch you sleeping. Sometimes I was there for hours. I was so scared that something would happen to you overnight. When you started to walk, I put pads on the corners of the tables so you wouldn't hit your head. When you got your driver's license, I swear I went crazy anytime you drove the car. I couldn't do anything until you got home safe. I felt the same way about Mary and now those bastards have her. I wasn't able to protect her."

"Papa," Mercy said as she hugged Jacob. "You have always been there for me, for Mary, for all of your children and grandkids. You're going to get Mary back."

The others started coming into the room. Jacob patted Mercy's hand and said, "Thanks kiddo."

At 10 AM the phone rang.

"Okay, quiet," Gerry said and then picked up the phone. "Hello."

"This is what we want, Amato. We'll give you Mary back in exchange for you. Otherwise first we'll have our way with her, and then we'll kill her," the man on the phone said calmly.

"No. I'll make the exchange. Don't hurt her. How do you want to do it?" Gerry said.

"At 2 PM you come alone to the Japanese Pavilion in Fairmount Park. We let Mary go and you come with us," the man on the phone said.

"No, I want a more public place. No people will be around there this time of the year," Gerry said as they had planned.

"You don't trust us, Amato?" the man said.

"What do you think, bozo?" Gerry said.

"Watch it, Amato. We're dealing the cards in this game," the man said.

"You want me. Beaumont wants me. We pick a public place," Gerry said.

The man hesitated for a moment and then said," Okay, okay a public place it is."

"There's a restaurant on Roosevelt Boulevard called Hammond's. We'll make the exchange there," Gerry said.

"I don't think so, Amato. Not in North Philly. I'll call you at 1:00 and let you know where," the man said and hung up.

Gerry hung up the phone, looked at the family sitting at the table, and said, "I think they took the bait. They'll call back at 1:00 and tell me where."

It was a tense three hours while they waited for the call. Jimmy paced back and forth in the room, leaving periodically to check on Sally. Jake sat at the table, checking and rechecking the weapons they had retrieved from the safe in Jacob's basement. Gerry sat behind his Grandfather's desk outwardly cool and collected, but inwardly terrified something would happen to Mary. The rest had scattered throughout the house to check on their families.

"Hey Gerry, what's with that raggedy ass hat you're always wearing," Jake asked.

"It's my lucky hat," Gerry answered.

"How so?"

"Al Watson gave me these wings when we first started flying together in Vietnam," Gerry said taking his hat off and fingering the wings he had pinned on the cap. "I've worn them on my hat whenever I flew and his hat got me out of a lot of tight spots."

"You scared kid?" Jake asked.

"Yeah. Who the fuck wouldn't be?" Gerry answered.

"We got your back. Those sons of bitches won't know what hit them. You do your part and we'll do ours and both you and Mary will be alright," Jake said.

By 12:30 everyone was back in the room waiting for the call from Beaumont's man. Each person knew their part and was ready.

"Dad, I heard from Mike. No one knows anything about these Beaumont guys. We don't know how many there are or where they're at," Jake said.

"Okay, it was worth a try. Is Mike ready?" Jacob asked.

"He's good. Just waiting for our call."

"Jerome, did you get hold of Al Watson?" Gerry asked.

"Yep. He wasn't too happy. Said he was just about to go to the beach," Jerome answered.

"I don't blame him. He just got home from Vietnam. Is he coming?"

"Yeah, he's coming. Said give him a couple days," Jerome said.

"Jake, you talk to Mickey?" Jacob asked.

"Yeah, he'll be here next week," Jake said.

"Gerry, please tell me you talked to Costanzo," Jacob asked.

"He's on board. Just waiting for our call," Gerry answered.

"I'm hoping they took our cue and pick a restaurant. If so, it will probably be in West or South Philly. If they don't pick a restaurant and do something on the street, it will be a lot harder to deal with. I'm hoping the cold weather will make them want to be inside," Jacob said.

The phone rang precisely at 1 PM. Gerry picked the phone up and said, "Yeah."

"2 PM, Lucky Dragon at 10th and Arch. Be alone," the man on the phone said.

"My Grandfather will be coming with me to take Mary home," Gerry said.

"I said be alone," the man said again.

"He's an old man, what the fuck's he going to do. I need a ride and someone's got to take Mary home," Gerry said.

There was a long pause and finally the man said, "Okay, but he stays outside. Don't be late." The phone clicked off.

"It's the Lucky Dragon at 10th and Arch," Gerry said feeling deflated.

"Shit. I didn't see that coming. The one place we have no influence. Gerry, call Costanzo and tell him. Jake, call Mike and get him and his men in position. Tell them to keep a very low profile," Jacob said.

"Jimmy, you and Jake join Mike as soon as you can. Frank, you and Charlie take what weapons you need," Jacob said as he picked out two .45 Colts and slid them in his back waistband. "Gerry, we need to leave in 15 minutes."

Ten minutes later Gerry walked up to Jacob and said, "Good news. Costanzo says he has connections in Chinatown."

"I don't like it," Jacob said. "We don't know those people."

"We don't have much choice, Grandpop," Gerry said."Time to go."

# Chapter Sixteen

Jacob pulled his car into a parking spot several doors from the corner of 10th and Arch where the Lucky Dragon restaurant was located. Gerry and Jacob got out of the car. Gerry started walking towards the restaurant, and Jacob stood leaning against the car. Jacob dressed in loose fitting clothing and wore one of his old newspaper boy hats to make him appear old and feeble.

Gerry entered the restaurant and paused, allowing his eyes to adjust to the dark interior. It was a small place with just ten tables. Four tables were occupied with two men each. A fifth table had one man sitting and another standing behind him. Gerry assumed the leader was the man who was sitting. He had jet-black hair, which was obviously a toupee, and was wearing what looked to be a custom-made suit. Gerry guessed he was about 50 years old. The most striking feature of the man was his eyes. One was blue and the other green.

The leader gestured to the man behind him who walked over to Gerry and indicated that he should lift his arms. The man searched Gerry and said, "He's okay," then walked out of the restaurant.

The leader waved his hand beckoning Gerry to come to his table. When Gerry reached him he said, "Please sit down, Mr. Amato."

Gerry took a seat and said, "Where's Mary?"

"My associate has gone for her. Please have some tea," the leader said as he poured the hot liquid into a porcelain cup. "My orders are very specific, Gerry. May I call you Gerry?" Gerry shrugged his shoulders and the man continued, "I'm to keep you alive, take you to Paris where you will meet the brother of the man you killed."

"And who are you?" Gerry asked.

"An associate of Mr. Beaumont. Let's just leave it at that," the man said.

"You're not French. Your accent is more like New England," Gerry said.

"Yes, I'm American. Beaumont and my organization do work together, but that's enough about me," the man said. "Gerry, can you take that piece of shit hat you're wearing off while you're sitting at my table. I swear your fucking generation has no manners," he continued.

Gerry took his hat off and put it on the table. "Happy?"

"Yes, that's better. Ahh, my associate's back with your Mary," the leader said.

Gerry got up from his seat and turned to see Mary at the doorway. The associate was grasping her arm and held a ten-inch hunting knife in his other hand. Two men came from behind a drape that separated the dining area from the food preparation area. They were holding pistols.

"Oh, I forgot to tell you. Mr. Beaumont had one other request," the leader said and paused. "He wants you to experience the sorrow he felt when he lost someone he loved."

The leader nodded and the man holding Mary began to lift the knife to Mary's throat.

"Too bad, she was a good fuck," the leader said.

Gerry not hearing anything yelled, "No. Don't."

The knife was almost at Mary's throat when the front side of the man's head exploded spewing blood and brains on the restaurant floor. Mary screamed as she was pulled backwards out of the doorway. The two Beaumont men standing by the drapery began to raise their pistols and stopped abruptly. One fell to the floor with a hatchet protruding from the back of his skull and the other stood for a few seconds with a large butcher knife sticking out of his throat and then fell. Standing behind them were two Chinese waiters.

After pushing Jacob and Mary out of the way, Mike Kelly and Jake Byrne ran into the restaurant, guns in their hands. The Chinese waiters pulled their own pistols and all four men began shooting at the Beaumont men at the tables.

During the seconds this all took place, Gerry saw the leader reaching for his gun. He grabbed his hat and threw himself at the man. The chair the leader was sitting on toppled backwards taking the man and Gerry with it. Gerry landed on top of the leader and pushed the pointed end of the wings on his hat into the man's green eye. The leader screamed in pain. Gerry grabbed the teapot that had fallen off the table with them and smashed it into his head.

A minute later, it was all over. All but three of Beaumont's men were dead. Two men stood with their hands up and the leader was unconscious on the floor.

Gerry ran to Jake and asked, "Where's Mary? Is she okay?"

"She's fine. Probably with her father. He was outside waiting for her, Jake said.

"You okay, kid?"

"I'm good," Gerry said as he flopped down on a chair and sighed with relief.

"What's that blood on your face?" Jake asked examining Gerry closer.

"Not mine. His," Gerry said pointing at the leader lying on the floor.

A well-dressed Chinese man came from behind the drapery and said, "We take care. You go."

Jake walked over to him, shook his hand and said, "Thank you. We appreciate your help in this matter. If you ever need anything, please contact me."

The man bowed to Jake and said, "Please, you go."

"We'll take these three," Jake said pointing at the three still-alive Beaumont men.

The well-dressed Chinese man nodded.

Gerry walked over to the leader and threw a glass of water on him. The leader came around and Gerry helped him to a chair, picked up a cloth napkin and handed it him. "Here wrap this around your eye."

Once the man did as Gerry suggested, Gerry helped him up and started walking towards the door. As Jake, Mike and Gerry ushered the three Beaumont men through the door, the two Chinese waiters began to drag the dead bodies behind the drapes.

Jacob was waiting for them as they came out of the restaurant. They put the three men in cars and told the drivers to take them to Gerry's hangar. Jacob put his arm around Gerry and said, "You did good." Looking at Jake and Mike, Jacob said, "You too."

"You saved Mary's life, Pop," Jake said.

"What do you think they'll do with those bodies? I can tell you one thing. I am never eating Chinese food again," Mike said.

The four men laughed as they got into the car and began driving to the hangar.

# Chapter Seventeen

An hour later Jacob, Gerry, Jake and Mike arrived at the Byrne Air Freight hangar. The three Beaumont men were sitting in chairs with their arms and legs bound. Blood was seeping from the cloth napkin the leader had put over his eye. Jake walked up to him and put his thumb in the man's wound. The leader screamed.

"What's your name," Jake asked. The leader said nothing. "What's your fucking name," Jake yelled and pressed his thumb in the man's eye socket again.

The man screamed then croaked," Okay, okay." He paused to let the pain subside a bit and then said, "Henry Mason."

"Henry, who do you work for?" Jake said putting his hand on Mason's head ready to apply his thumb to Mason's wound again.

"No don't," Mason whimpered. "Gang out of Hartford."

"Who runs it?" Jake asked.

Mason looked at the other two men and said, "Jim Brennan."

"Are you fucking kidding me? An Irishman working for the frogs, against other Irishmen. Un-fucking believable," Jake said.

"If you let us go there won't be any trouble. I'll talk to Brennan and tell him we was wrong to do this," Mason said.

Jake leaned in close to Mason's face and said, "Oh yeah. You think I give a flying fuck about Jim the Jerk Off?"

Jacob put his hand on Jake's shoulder, pulled him back, looked at Mason for a full minute and said, "Why'd you look at these two jamokes when you mentioned Jim Brennan's name?"

Mason looked at his men again and said, "He's Jim's kid."

"Which one?" Jacob asked.

"The one with blond hair," Mason said.

Jacob walked over to the young Brennan and asked, "What's your name?"

"Jim, they call me Junior," Brennan answered.

Mike Kelly laughed and said, "Now we have two Jim the Jerk Offs."

"Hey Jerk Off Jr. How many more of your guys are in Philly?" Jake asked.

The younger Brennan didn't answer.

Jake pulled his .45 and put it on Brennan's forehead and said," I hope you don't answer me. I would love to blow the top of your head off."

"None. We don't have nobody else here," Brennan blurted out.

"Is that right, Mason?" Jacob asked.

Mason lifted his head and said, 'That's right. Nobody else."

"I'm letting you three go back to Hartford. Irishmen don't need to fight Irishmen. You tell your boss to stay out of Philly and that'll be the end of it. If not I'll kill him and wipe out your gang," Jacob said. "You unders...." A banging on the hangar door interrupted Jacob.

"I'll see who it is," Gerry said.

"Mike, go with him," Jacob said.

A couple minutes later Gerry and Mike returned with Jimmy Byrne. Jimmy immediately ran over to Mason and smashed him in the face, knocking him backwards. By the time he hit the floor, Jimmy was next to him and kicked Mason in the head. Jacob grabbed Jimmy, pulling him backwards and away from Mason.

"Take it easy, Jimmy," Jacob said.

"This piece of shit, this fucking piece of shit raped my baby," Jimmy said and kicked out to try to hit Mason again.

Jacob and the others stood in shocked silence for a moment. Junior's eyes opened wide and he yelled, "Mason, you fucking bastard. You just killed us all."

Jacob pulled the stiletto Gerardo Amato gave to him many years ago, after he cut Franky Capaci's throat and took over the South Philly Mob. Jacob handed the knife to Jimmy, who was still shaking with fury.

"Jake, Gerry, pull Mason back up," Jacob said.

Jake, Mike, Gerry and Jacob watched as Jimmy walked over to Mason. He hesitated for a moment and then, without saying a word, he drove the eight inch stiletto blade through Mason's blue eye and into his brain killing him instantly.

A large urine stain appeared on Junior's pants and he began to sob as the hot liquid flowed to the floor under his chair. Jimmy handed the knife back to Jacob, who took a hanky from his back pocket and wiped it off.

"Pop, give me the hanky and the knife for a minute, will you. Let's send Jim the Jerk Off a message he'll understand," Jake said.

Jacob handed the knife and hanky to Jake and asked, "What're you going to do?"

Jake said nothing, walked over to Mason's body, undid Mason's, belt and pulled his pants down. Using the hanky, he pulled Mason's penis out, cut it off, wrapped it in the hanky, and asked Gerry to find a small box. When Gerry gave him the box, he placed the hanky and Mason's penis in it.

Jake said, "Cut these two loose, Mike." When Mike had released Junior and the other man, Jake handed the box to Brennan and said, "Give this to your father and give him the message my father told you."

"Mike, take a couple of our guys and get these two started back to Hartford," Jacob said.

When Mike had ushered Junior and his associate out of the hangar Jacob said, "Jimmy, you okay?"

"I'm okay," Jimmy lied. Inside he was shaking. He had killed men before when he served in Africa during the war. He even had killed men who invaded the family home in an attempt to take over the K&A Gang back in 1943. He knew Mason deserved to die, and he was happy he could provide retribution for his daughter Mary. But, this was close up and very personal. He was shaken but he also knew he would get over it.

"How's Mary," Jacob said.

"As good as can be expected. She's happy to be home and alive," Jimmy said.

"Me too, Jimmy. Me too," Jacob said.

"Jake, what about him?" Jacob said pointing at Mason's body.

"I'll take care of that, Grandpop," Gerry said. "Jerome and I will take him swimming tomorrow."

Jacob nodded and said, "Okay, then let's go home. I need a bit of the old Irish."

After Gerry and Jake wrapped Mason in plastic and loaded him on Gerry's airplane, they all left for Jacob's house. When they arrived, Jacob checked on Mary then he asked the men, Mercy and Catherine to meet in his office.

Gabriel Barra had spent the day trying to get his cousin Pierre Barra, the head of the Marseille Mob on the phone. He was desperate to find out if his cousin was able to broker the peace between the Paris Mob and the K&A Gang. An hour before Jacob returned he got his answer.

Jacob poured everyone a glass of Irish whiskey and said, "To Mary and her safe return to us." When everyone drank their whiskey Jacob continued, "Gabe, do we have any news from your cousin?"

"Yes, Pierre sent a man to Paris to talk to Beaumont yesterday. Today at noon, my cousin received a package specially delivered by a courier. In that package was a severed human hand. The fingers had been arranged so as just the middle finger was sticking out. By the ring on the hand, my cousin saw that it was from the man he had sent to Paris. Beaumont has always had a flare for the dramatic," Barra answered shaking his head.

Jake looked at Gerry and smiled.

"Well, we tried. So now, we have to do it the hard way, as we planned. Gabe, you mentioned that some of Beaumont's men were not happy with their situation. Can your cousin reach out to them and try to get their support?" Jacob said.

"Yes, I already suggested it to Pierre. He is, as you can imagine, very angry and wants Beaumont gone. It may take some time and he must be careful. If Beaumont finds out we are talking to his men, he will kill them and come after Pierre," Gabe said.

"Understood and we appreciate his help," Jacob said. "Frank, are you sure you're okay with you and Catherine going to Paris?"

Franklin took Catherine's hand and said, "Yes, of course. Who wouldn't want to spend Christmas and the New Year in Paris with a beautiful woman? Besides, Catherine's an old hand at espionage. She's a regular Mata Hari."

"It's important we know Beaumont's habits and where he hangs out. Pierre will assign a couple of his men to you to help. Catherine being able to speak French will be a great help," Jacob said.

"I wish I could go to help you," Barra said.

"We understand, Gabe. After all we don't want you spending the rest of your life in a French hoosegow," Frank said.

"Hoosegow? What is a hoosegow?" Gabe asked.

"The pokey, clink, the slammer," Gerry said and laughed.

"It means prison, Gabe," Mercy said.

"Ahhh, yes, I wouldn't want to end up in the, how did you say it, whose cow. Gab," said.

"Close enough Gabe," Mercy said.

"Frank, we'll meet you and Catherine in Paris on January 4th," Jacob said.

"Pierre has rented you a large house on the left bank. There are five bedrooms. There will be two servants and a driver at your disposal. They will, of course, be his people and they are there for your safety and to help you with tracking Beaumont. To anyone looking you will just be two rich Americans enjoying the holidays in Paris," Gabe said.

"It's important that you do all the things tourists would do. Go see the Eiffel Tower, enjoy the best restaurants and take long walks along the Seine River. Just get us the information we need," Jacob said.

"It's a tough job, but someone's got to do it," Franklin said and laughed.

"We have two goals. One is to get Beaumont. The other is to keep the family safe while we are doing it. Jake, Mickey, Mickey's man, Gerry and me will handle Beaumont. Mike's in charge of security for the family while we're in Paris. Jake, move your family into our house until this is over.

Charlie, Jimmy you'll be in Frank and Catherine's house. Both homes have safe rooms if we need them. Mercy, your house has a safe room so you can stay there and Gerry's friend Al Watson will stay in Rose's old room," Jacob said

"Papa, we already know this. It'll be okay," Mercy said.

"I know. It's just that.... well, you know me. It's always better to be safe than sorry," Jacob said.

"Yeah Pop, we'll be safe and Beaumont will be sorry," Jake said.

# Chapter Eighteen

Two days after Mary's rescue, Al Watson arrived at the Byrne Air Freight hangar and office. He looked at the sign for a few seconds, shook his head and smiled. He couldn't help feel a sense of pride. Gerry had started out a green kid co-pilot and Al had helped him become a great pilot. Now he was a businessman as well. In return, Gerry had made Al Watson a wealthy man. They broke a few laws and made a boatload of money. Now Gerry needed his help. There was no way Al Watson was not going to give it.

As Al approached the door two men, who had been sitting in a car, stopped him.

"What's your business here?" One of the men asked Al.

"I'm the Fuller Brush man, what's it to you?" Al replied.

The second man grabbed Al's arms from behind while the first man patted him down.

"What the fuck?" Al said.

When the man was finished, he banged on the steel door. A minute later Gerry opened the door, saw Al and said. "Al, you son of a bitch. How the hell are you?"

"I'd be better if this goon would let me go," Al said.

"It's okay, Pete, he's a friend," Gerry said.

Pete let Al go and Gerry shook Al's hand, hugged him and said, "Come in, Al. I want you to meet my partner, Jerome."

Jerome Washington was standing just inside the door holding a .45 automatic. When he saw it was safe he placed it back in his shoulder holster and waited for Gerry to introduce him.

"Al Watson, meet Jerome Washington."

The two men shook hands.

"Pleased to meet you, Jerome," Al said.

"Same here. Gerry told me about you. Says you flew in Korea," Jerome said.

"Yep, how about you?" Al asked.

"WW2. Flew a P40," Jerome said.

"Really! Let me shake your hand again," Al said. "That was tough duty."

"I hear you two had some excitement too," Jerome said.

"A little," Al replied.

The three men walked over to a small lounge area Gerry had made in the back of the hangar. Gerry poured each man a large glass of whiskey and said, "To our brothers we lost in our wars." Gerry poured a small amount of whiskey on the floor and Jerome did likewise. They both looked at Al, who was in turn looking at Jerome with a quizzical frown.

Jerome laughed and said, "It's an Irish thing."

"Oh," Al said and poured some whiskey on the ground as well.

All three men finished their drinks and sat down. Gerry explained the situation in detail then gave Al a tour of their two aircraft.

"When do I start," Al asked.

"Tomorrow. The three of us will take one of the planes up and let you check it out," Gerry said.

"Good," Al replied.

"Okay then, let's get you something to eat then you can get some rest," Gerry said.

"Sounds good. Is there a hotel nearby?" Al asked

"You'll be staying with me and my mother," Gerry said.

"You sure. I don't want to be a bother," Al said.

"You kidding? You're family, Al," Gerry said as he put his arm around Al's shoulder and started to walk him to the door. "Jerome, tomorrow at 9 okay with you?"

"Sounds good. Al, good to meet you. Looking forward to flying together," Jerome said as he shook Al's hand.

"Me too," Al said.

A half hour later, Gerry pulled up in front of the Wishart Street house. Al pulled up behind him. Mercy was standing on the step with a coffee pot in one hand and a tray with cakes from the German Bakery at Clearfield and Front Streets. Two of the K&A Gang guards assigned to protect Mercy were standing on the pavement in front of the step, each with a cup of coffee and a half eaten Danish in their hands.

Gerry and Al got out of their cars as Gerry's guards pulled up behind him. Mercy seeing them walked down the steps, kissed Gerry on the cheek and handed him the pot of coffee and tray of cakes. She then walked over to Al and said, "You must be the famous Al Watson Gerry is always going on about."

"More like infamous, depending who you talk to, but yes, I'm Al."

Mercy kissed him on the cheek and said, "I want to thank you for taking such good care of Gerry when you two were in Vietnam."

"Actually, Mrs. Amato, he took care of me," Al said.

"Call me Mercy please, Al. Are you two hungry?"

"Yes ma'am," Al said

"Well, come in. I have a roast in the oven with your name on it," Mercy said as she took Al's arm and guided him into the house and then to the dining room. "Sit here, Al. I'll be right back. Gerry, get Al something to drink."

Gerry looked at Al and widened his eyes and Al said, "Beer."

Gerry went to the kitchen, took a quart of Ortlieb's from the refrigerator, picked up two beer glasses and placed one in front of Al. "Looks like my mom, how do you say it in the south, has taken a fancy to you," Gerry said.

Surprised, Al said, "Why do you say that?"

"She gave you my seat at the front of the table," Gerry said as he sat next to Al on the side of the table.

"Well, maybe she just knows a real man when she sees one," Al said and laughed.

"Or maybe she just feels sorry for you because you look like a decrepit old fart," Gerry said as he poured beer into Al's glass and gave a half smile.

Al silently lipped the words *Fuck You.* Gerry laughed.

Gerry held up his glass and said, "To our long and profitable friendship."

"Here, here," Al replied.

Mercy brought the roast beef and placed it on the table. "Can I help you, Mercy?" Al asked.

"No, but thank you. I'll be right back," Mercy said and left the room.

"Ass kisser," Gerry said. Al smiled.

Mercy returned with bowls of mashed potatoes, corn and string beans. She took her seat and said "Al, would you say grace. please?"

Al hesitated trying to remember any prayers he knew. Then said, "My mother use to say this prayer at every meal.

We Give Our Thanks

For food that stays our hunger,

For rest that brings us ease,

For homes where memories linger,

We give our thanks for these."

When Al finished Mercy and Gerry made the sign of the cross and said, "Amen."

"Thank you, Al. That was a wonderful prayer. Is your mother still with us?"

"No, she passed a few years back," Al said and his eyes watered.

Mercy saw this and said, "I'm sorry, Al, but she's with the Lord now and no doubt looking down on you with pride."

"I like to think so," Al said, but he didn't believe it. He had been raised a Baptist and his mother and father were devoted to the church. They read a passage from the bible every night before dinner and often quizzed their children to be sure they were listening. And Al did listen and believed until he fought in Korea where he witnessed so much cruelty and death. His time in Vietnam did nothing but support his disbelief in God. The God he was taught to love was kind. If he existed, he would not allow such violence against his women and children.

"Al, on Sunday we go to mass. Come with us? We'll go early and light a candle for your mother," Mercy said.

"Thank you, Mercy, I am not sure they would want a half-baked Baptist like me in your church," Al said.

"Nonsense, we welcome everyone, Al," Mercy said.

Gerry tilted his head and gave Al a hard look to remind him of his promise to God if they got out of Vietnam alive. Al got the message and said, "Well in that case I would be happy to go." Then he kicked Gerry in the shin under the table. Gerry smiled.

That evening Gerry, Mercy and Al watched television, but did more talking than watching. Mercy told the family story leaving out the more nefarious parts. She explained how the Mercy Row Foundation worked and even how they got most of their money.

"That's kind of like Robin Hood. I like it," Al said.

"I guess you could say that," Mercy said.

Al told Mercy and Gerry what it was like growing up in Georgia and how his mother and father were very strict Baptists until his father ran off with a younger woman, taking the contents of their bank account with him. After that, it was very difficult. They lost their house in Decatur and rented a small place on Pine Street in Atlanta.

"It was a row house, kind of like this. I think they might have been the only row houses in the city. At the turn of the century, the homes were upscale, but by the time we got there they were run down. I heard that someone opened a hippy bar in the basement of one of the homes. Glad I'm out of there," Al said.

"Well, I need to get some sleep. Long day today," Gerry said. He kissed his mother and walked up the steps.

"Al, do you like Gun Smoke? It's on in fifteen minutes," Mercy said.

"I do," Al answered.

"Give me a minute. I want to make some coffee for the guards. Will you drink some?"

"Sure, thank you," Al said

"Be right back," Mercy said and left for the kitchen. She made the coffee and gave the guards a thermos full and some sandwiches she had made earlier. Then she brought a tray with two cups of coffee and some cakes from the bakery and set them on the table in front of Al.

"Did I miss much," Mercy asked.

"No, it just started," Al said.

They sat on the sofa drinking the coffee, eating the cakes and talking about everything from religion to family to politics. Al was amazed at how much Mercy knew about the space program, a subject he was very interested in. They laughed at each other's jokes and showed dismay over how things were changing. Sometime after midnight, Mercy showed Al his room and as she walked up the stairs to her room, she was smiling. Al flopped on the bed, put his hands behind his head and grinned.

# Chapter Nineteen

Catherine and Franklin Garrett sat at a small table outside of a cafe across the street from the Notre-Dame Cathedral in Paris. That morning they had visited the Musée du Louvre and walked the banks of the Seine River from the Eiffel Tower to Notre-Dame. It was a very pleasant day, sunny, blue sky and unusually warm for December.

The waiter placed a baguette sandwich and a cup of aromatic French coffee in front of Catherine and then another in front of Franklin.

Catherine said, "Merci beaucoup." The waiter nodded and walked away.

Franklin picked up his coffee, held it out to their bodyguard Jules, who was sitting at a table near them. Jules did the same, then Franklin clicked Catherine's cup and took a sip. He picked up the baguette sandwich and took a bite.

"It's no hoagie but this," he held up the sandwich, "is pretty damn good. You know, I could get used to living in Paris," Franklin said.

"Frank, I get the shivers when I realize how old things are here. Did you know that Norte-Dame was first opened in 1345? It took them almost 200 years to build it. Imagine that? The U.S. isn't even 200 years old yet," Catherine said.

"Boggles the mind," Frank said and took another bite of the baguette.

"Paris dates back to the third century before Christ. That's over twenty two hundred years ago. Catherine paused and then said, "I bet you don't know how the city got its name."

"No idea," Franklin answered, his voice muffled by a full mouthful of baguette."

"Well, it comes from the Celtic tribe called the Parisii who settled the area in 250 BC. In 52 BC Jules Caesar conquered the city and named it

Lutetia Parisiorum. They ruled until the fall of Rome in fifth century AD." Catherine said.

"You're quite the tour guide, Catherine," Franklin said and then ate the last part of his baguette. He motioned to the waiter to come to the table, picked up the plate, and put one finger up. The waiter took the plate and went off to get Franklin another sandwich. "I wonder how long they've been eating these sandwiches," Franklin continued.

Catherine shook her head and said, "We're going to have do some serious running tomorrow to work off all this food."

The waiter brought Franklin's second baguette sandwich just as a black Citroen Limousine pulled up to a building directly across from the cafe. Jules came to their table and said, "That's him."

Henri Beaumont's guard exited the Citroen, perused the area, and then opened the car's back door. Henri Beaumont stepped out of the car and quickly, shielded by his bodyguard, entered the building.

"That's the third day in a row Beaumont visited that building," Franklin said, then motioned the bodyguard to sit with them. "What time is it?"

"4 o'clock. Catherine, answered then asked, "Jules, what's that building?"

"A hotel with some apartments and some offices," Jules said his accent strong but clear.

At 5 PM Henri Beaumont left the building, surrounded by three bodyguards. All four men walked to the Notre-Dame Cathedral. Beaumont stayed there for thirty minutes, returned to his car, and drove off.

"I would say that's a habit. Every day he visits this building for an hour, then the Cathedral for thirty minutes and then off to his home," Franklin said. "I think this is the place we do it."

Two days later Pierre Barra, head of the Marseille Mob, visited the home he had arranged for Catherine and Franklin to stay at while they were visiting Paris. Pierre was a slightly older version of Gabriel Barra. The family resemblance was obvious. The biggest difference between the two men was that Pierre's hair was white, while the younger Gabriel's hair was still black with gray temples.

"Catherine, are you happy with your accommodations," Pierre asked in French

"Oh yes, Mr. Barra. Overwhelmed with joy would be a better way to describe it," Catherine answered, also in French.

"No, no, please call me Pierre." Then Pierre, speaking English asked, "Franklin, and you? How do you like Paris?"

"I was telling Catherine the other day, how I could get used to living in your fine country," Franklin said.

"Well, maybe someday. We hope anyway," Pierre said. "Jules has told me you have a plan for Beaumont."

Franklin explained his plan to Pierre, who listened intently occasionally asking Catherine for a translation of a word he didn't understand. When Franklin finished Pierre bobbed his head back and forth, thinking, and finally said, "Dangerous. But it can be done."

"Yes," Franklin said.

"When?" Pierre asked.

"First week of the New Year."

Pierre nodded his consent and said, "My source in Beaumont's organization says he is not finished with Gerry Amato. He is sending several men and his second in command, Albert Montfort, to Philadelphia," Pierre said.

"When?" Franklin asked.

"Now. He said they plan to be back by Noel." Pierre paused, thought for a second then said, "Christmas. But they will stay until they get the job done."

"I'll pass that information along," Franklin said.

"Beaumont is a relentless man. He will not stop. He has no problem killing anyone who gets in his way," Pierre said.

"We'll stop him," Franklin said with more bravado then he felt. "What happens after?"

"My contact says there are two factions in his organization. One backs Beaumont. The other backs my contact. If we take out Beaumont, there will be a civil war. It has happened before, in the late 40s. The Beaumonts won that war," Pierre said.

"We'll make sure Beaumont won't be around to win this war," Franklin said.

Pierre shook his head up and down slowly, not fully confident that all would work as Franklin said. He put his hands on the table and said, "Well, now that you have your plan you can take some time to enjoy France. What are your plans today?"

"Franklin has promised me that we will go shopping today. Would you like to come with us?" Catherine asked.

"Oh no. I am sorry, but I must get back to Marseille. I do not want to be seen in Paris. Please enjoy your shopping," Pierre said. "Now I must go."

"It's been a pleasure to meet you, Pierre," Franklin said holding out his hand.

"The pleasure has been mine," Pierre said ignoring Franklin's hand and instead kissed him on each cheek. Then he turned to Catherine and took her hand and said, "Au revoir, Belle Dame."

Catherine kissed Pierre on each cheek and said, "Que ce soit bientôt."

"When this is over, maybe you can visit me in Marseille. It is a wonderful city and the Mediterranean beaches are wonderful," Pierre said.

"We would love that," Catherine said.

When Pierre had gone, Catherine walked up to Franklin, held him tightly and gave him a long kiss on his lips. "Tell me everything's going to be okay."

Franklin kissed her back and said, "I promise."

"That kiss was very French of you," Catherine purred.

"Let's put off shopping for an hour or so," Franklin said as he guided Catherine to their bedroom. "But first, I have to call Jacob and tell him what Pierre told us."

As Franklin started to dial the phone Catherine unbuttoned her blouse and took it off. Then she dropped her skirt. She stood in her red bikini panties and matching bra, her long legs accentuating her shapely body. The phone began to ring and Catherine turned her back to Franklin and bent slowly to pick up her skirt. Franklin felt a warm tingly sensation in his groin. He kicked off his shoes and said, "I'll make it a fast call."

# Chapter Twenty

Mickey Callahan arrived in Philly from Los Angeles, with his man Sean Mulligan, the week Franklin and Catherine left for Paris. Both men had worked for Mike Kelly and Jake Byrne as enforcers before Callahan took over the Los Angeles chapter of the gang.

Mulligan's mother lived on Wishart Street just three doors from Mercy's house, so Mike assigned them to protect Mercy until they left for Paris with Jacob. They would stay with Mulligan's mother. It didn't take long before Al Watson and Gerry became friends with Callahan and Mulligan. They had a lot in common. All had seen action in one or more of America's wars and they liked to play pool.

Gerry introduced them to the Circle Billiards Room located at Lee Street and Alleghany Avenue. It was a short walk from Wishart Street and a great diversion when the men were off duty. They took every opportunity to visit the poolroom. Mickey Callahan was a very good player and usually won when they played.

On his third visit, Gerry suggested Mickey challenge the owner of the poolroom to a game. He did and they agreed to bet $1.00 per ball. Whoever sunk 100 balls first would win all. Mickey won the break and put ten balls in the pockets before he missed. The owner, whose name was Harry, only put four balls in the pockets before his miscued. Callahan feeling he could easily beat Harry upped the bet to two dollars for each ball. Callahan lined up the cue ball and easily sunk the last ball of the first rack. Harry set up another rack. Callahan broke the balls but didn't sink any. That was the last shot Callahan had in that game. Harry went on to sink 96 balls in a row and won the game and the $200.

What Gerry had failed to tell Mickey was that Harry had won the Philadelphia Billiards Championship during the 1950s and was a well-known pool shark. "And that, my friend Mickey is the lesson of the day," Gerry had said. "Never try to hustle a hustler."

Harry was of medium height with a powerful build. Not fat and not thin. He was in his late 50s and had played pool with some of history's great players. He avoided the limelight stating that if too many people knew who he was and what skills he had, he would never get a game for money. Harry even refused to be on a local television show featuring players from around the country. Instead, a mediocre player who started using a name made famous in a movie about hustlers became host of the show.

Over the next three weeks Gerry, Callahan and Mulligan visited the poolroom regularly. They often played cards in a back room that Harry told them was the Pinochle room. In reality, there were two tables in the room for men to play poker. One table was for high stakes and the other was for the more moderate players.

After a week or so, Al Watson started to put off trips to the Circle Billiards Room, and made excuses to stay home with Mercy. Gerry realized that his mother and Al were becoming close and he was okay with that. It had been 24 years since his father had passed and he could think of no one better for her than Al.

Hoping to increase his skill level, Callahan asked Harry to give him some tips and Harry agreed to give the men a fifteen-minute lesson each time they visited. Over the weeks he had shown them how to hold the cue stick for better control, how to use the diamond system for bank shots and even taught them how to replace a cue tip.

"What's Harry teaching today?" Gerry asked Callahan.

"Says he's going to show us how to use English," Callahan said.

"What's that?" Mulligan asked.

"It's a way to hit the cue ball and make it spin. It's supposed to give you more control," Callahan explained.

"Well, I don't like it," Mulligan said.

"You don't even know what the fuck it is. So why don't you like it?" Gerry asked.

"I don't like the name English." Mulligan said being serious.

"Why do you hate the English so much?" Gerry asked.

"I don't really know. My Pa was from Northern Ireland and hated them. So I guess it's a family tradition," Mulligan said.

Gerry rubbed his hand over his face, then trying to change the subject said, "Hey listen, you're both welcome to come to Christmas dinner at my Pop and Mom's house."

"Nah, thanks Gerry, but Mulligan's Ma invited me, so if it's okay with you, I'll be with them," Callahan said.

"Sure, sure. No problem. If anything changes, dinner's at 5.

"The real key to winning is in positioning your cue ball to have another shot after you sink a ball," Harry said. " If you hit the cue ball straight on but a little to the right, the ball will spin counter clockwise and when it hits an object, such as a rail it will make the ball go more right and if you hit it to left, it will spin clockwise and when it hits an object it goes left. Hit the ball low and it will draw back to you and hit it high it will follow the ball it hits. Learn English and you'll dominate the game," Harry said and then demonstrated.

"That's a load of bullshit," a man who was playing on the next table said slurring his words, and obviously drunk.

"Watch your mouth, asshole," Mickey yelled.

"It's okay, Mickey I got this," Harry said calmly. Then he said to the man, "This is your first time here so I'm going to give you a pass for the insult. If you believe its bullshit, put your money where your mouth is."

The man walked over to Harry and said, "Fuck you, old man," and slapped a twenty-dollar bill on the table.

"Put another twenty down and I'll prove it isn't bullshit," Harry said

The man took a twenty from his pocket and threw it on the table. Harry pulled a wad of bills out of his pocket, peeled off two twenties and said, "Here's what I'll do. Shooting from the end of the table here, I'll hit all four cushions, and then the ball will go into the left side pocket."

"How the hell can he do that?" Callahan whispered to Gerry. "After it hits the rail in front of him, the ball would have to bounce back and twist to the left to go in the pocket. It's impossible."

"Wait and see," Gerry whispered back.

The man pulled another twenty from his pocket, threw it on the table and said, "Can't fucking be done. I'll be happy to take your money."

Harry placed a twenty on top of the pile and said, "Gerry, you hold the money."

Gerry picked the money up.

Harry picked up the chalk, twisted against the tip of his custom-made cue stick and then said, "Ready?"

The man replied, "Go at it, old timer," and laughed.

Harry hit the ball; the ball hit the right rail, then the back rail, then the left rail. Then it hit the rail in front of Harry, flipped up and off the table. At the same time, Harry held his left coat pocket open and the ball landed in it.

"Callahan, laughed and said, "Holy shit. How the hell did he do that?"

The man wasn't laughing and said, "I win. It didn't go in the pocket. Give me my money."

Harry picked the ball out of his left coat pocket and said, "Here it is. It went into my left pocket. Sorry, you lose."

The man turned red and took a swing at Harry. Harry sidestepped, hit the man in the stomach with his right hand and then a left uppercut to the jaw with the ball still in his hand. The man fell like a sack of potatoes. His friend seeing this, rushed at Harry. Harry quickly threw the ball hitting the friend on the forehead. He fell on top of the other man.

Callahan looked at Mulligan and slowly shook his head in amazement.

Harry grabbed one man by the collar then said, "Help me out here, will you?"

Gerry and Callahan picked the second man up as Harry dragged the first man to the door. He opened the door and tossed the man to the pavement. Gerry and Callahan threw the second man out the door. They waited a few minutes until the men started to come around. Then Harry said, "Don't come back. And never call me old timer again."

The two battered men slowly got up and started to walk east on Allegheny Avenue. As the two men staggered down the street, Gerry heard several gunshots coming from the west. He yelled, "Come on," and started running west to Wishart Street and Mercy's house. Callahan and Mulligan followed. As they ran they drew their guns.

"Sean, take the alley," Gerry said as he and Callahan continued another 100 feet to Wishart Street. They slowed down and looked around the corner. There were two cars stopped in the middle of the street in front of Mercy's house. Three men were crouched behind the cars and firing into the house. One of four guards Gerry had left at the house was lying by the step.

Gunfire was coming from the front windows on the first and second levels of the house. It was dinnertime and the street was full of parked cars. Gerry said, "Mickey, make your way up the street. I'll go around to Lippincott Street and make my way around. We'll flank them."

Callahan ducked behind the cars, crouched and started up the street. Gerry ran one block south to Lippincott, then west to Howard Street and north to the corner of Howard and Wishart. He stopped and began to look around at the shooters just as a man came running out of the Wishart Street alley. The man turned and started running south on Howard Street towards Gerry. When the man saw him, he pointed his gun at Gerry. Gerry fell to the ground and fired four times, hitting the man twice in the chest. The man fell and landed in the middle of Wishart Street.

The men who were attacking Mercy's home heard the gunfire and turned their weapons to where their associate had fallen. At the same time, Mickey Callahan opened fire. The men had their doors open and Mickey's bullets made a metallic ping as they hit the metal. Sean Mulligan, who had been chasing the now-dead assailant exited the alley and ran to the north side of Howard and Wishart Streets. He and Gerry started to fire at the would-be assassins. Seeing they were taking fire from the front, left and right, the men decided to retreat. They crawled into one of the cars and staying low they sped east on Wishart.

Gerry and Mulligan fearing they would hit Callahan didn't fire at them, but Callahan empty his clip at the cars as they passed him. The assailants bounced off several parked cars as the made their way up the street and then turned left onto Front Street.

Mulligan checked the assailant who was lying in the street and said, "He's a goner," They ran to Mercy's house. As they came to the stairs, the guard who had been shot sat up. He was holding his shoulder and blood ran down his fingers and dripped on his lap. Mulligan and Callahan helped the man to the steps while Gerry checked on Mercy and Al.

Al was just coming down the stairs holding an AR15 as Gerry entered the house. "Where's my Mom? Is she okay?" Gerry asked frantically.

"She's okay. In the safe room," Al said.

"Thank God," Gerry said, then he turned to the two guards who had been firing from the front window. "Call an ambulance. Matt's been shot."

Al opened the door to the safe room and Mercy climbed up the steps. They hugged each other and then Mercy hugged Gerry and said, "Thank God you're okay." Still hugging Gerry, Mercy took Al's hand and said, "Al saved my life."

In the distance, they could hear sirens.

# Chapter Twenty-One

Jacob decided it would be easier to defend just his and Franklin's house, which were side by side, so, Mercy, Gerry and Al moved to Jacob's house the next morning. It was crowded in both homes, but the kids doubled up and Gerry found a comfortable sofa in his father's den.

Molly was in her glory. She had a full house of children and grand-children as well as two other guests to fuss over. Mercy, Jimmy's wife Sally, Jake's wife Maria and Janet, Charlie's wife helped to prepare meals. Jacob had arranged that the children start their Christmas break early. This made for some very energetic days and evenings. Fortunately, Franklin had a large game room in his finished basement complete with two pinball machines, a pool table, a television and one of those large shuffle board games you find in bars.

The children pretty much hung out in the Franklin's recreation room, except for times when they argued over what to watch on TV. One particular cause of disagreement happened on Friday nights. The boys wanted to watch Star Trek and the girls wanted to watch Hondo, a western series with a very handsome star. After some fun arguing, the girls would leave and go to Jacob's TV room where there was a new 25 inch RCA large screen color TV.

Gabriel Barra was delighted with all of the Byrne's children. He had no offspring of his own and this was an opportunity for him to act like a grandpop. Like most grandfathers, he spoiled the children rotten, or at least that's what Mary Byrne told him. He taught the boys how to play poker using dry beans as chips. The girls loved his stories about the women of Cambodia, Vietnam and France, so Barra spent many hours in the recreation room as well.

Jake had twenty men surrounding the houses. Some stayed in cars and relieved those who were outside and vice versa. There were four additional guards, all close friends with Mike and Jake, in the homes. They accompanied anyone who had to leave the house to shop or work. Mary went to classes, Janet and Maria did the shopping and Al and Gerry went to work at Byrne Air Freight. Jake, Jimmy and Charlie conducted business as usual but with additional men guarding them. There had been two additional half-hearted attempts by the Paris mobsters to get to Gerry, but both were thwarted with no casualties on either side.

During the time prior to Christmas, Gerry, Al and Jerome traveled to Mexico to bring back a shipment of pot and introduced Al Watson to the Alberto Rivera organization. Rivera was delighted to see that Gerry was expanding his operation and promised to increase his production of marijuana to accommodate Gerry's plans for growth. Al knew a good pilot and after the holidays and the threat from the Beaumont's gang was taken care of they would start flying both planes to Rivera's farm thus doubling their revenues.

Christmas came and went without incident. The children trimmed the tree on Christmas Eve, opened their presents and stockings the next morning. The two households had a typically traditional Christmas dinner. The only difference this year was they had to forego the yearly ritual of the whole family going to Christmas Eve mass. Jacob thought there were just too many people at the Christmas mass to be safe. Instead, he had arranged that the entire family attend a private mass conducted by Father George Byrne at Saint Hugh's Church near Mercy's house. He chose the day of Wednesday the 27th at 2 pm for the gathering. After church, they would return home and have a special dinner. On the appointed day the entire family, their guests and guards drove in a caravan to Saint Hugh's Church. The guards who were Catholic were also invited to the mass and those who were not guarded the doors.

Before he began the mass Father George said a prayer for Rose Reilly Graham and beseeched God to care for her as she had cared for the Byrne family. Mercy began to cry and this started the other women and the children in the family to weep. In the tradition of Irish male machismo the men held it in, but they felt the same way. This was the first Christmas without Rose.

After the mass, the family gathered at the back of the church to thank Father George. The family members were escorted to their cars ringed by the guards. Gerry held back to talk to Father George.

"Uncle George, do you have a minute?" Gerry asked.

"Of course."

"I just wanted you to know that Tom Gentry is doing well in Mexico. They have him supervising the farm workers. Don't worry, he won't get away until we decide to let him. I just wanted to let you know he is healthy and hopefully regretting what he did," Gerry said.

"Thank you Gerry," Father George said as he motioned for Gerry to kneel.

Gerry did as Father George blessed him and ended with, "In the name of the Father, Son and Holy Ghost."

Gerry stood up and Father George took his arm and walked him to the door of the church. Only one door was open. They stood in the doorway and Father George took Gerry's hand and shook it. George heard the faint sound of glass breaking and quickly pushed Gerry to the side. A split second later, a bullet ripped into George's side. He fell back into the church.

The guards pulled their weapons and shot at the third story window of the William Cramp Elementary School where they thought the shot came from.

Jacob yelled, "Get the women out of here. Jimmy, go with them. Jake, stay with me. Charlie, get an ambulance."

Jake took five of the guards and ran to the school. One of the cars followed down Howard Street to cut off anyone trying to exit. Another Byrne car sped down Waterloo Street to do the same thing. Waterloo Street was very small and had parking on only one side. It was a tight fit for a car traveling fast and the driver sideswiped several cars before his tires screeched as he turned left onto Ontario Street.

As Jake and his men ran out of the schoolyard, the second Byrne car sped down Howard Street. When the Byrne car was about 100 feet down the street, a vehicle a couple of hundred feet further down turned out from a parking spot, tires screeching. The car fishtailed and hit a parked car, then sped down Howard Street towards Ontario. Just as it reached the intersection, the Byrne car that had driven down Waterloo blocked them.

The Byrne car driving down Howard quickly pulled up behind the assailant's car. A minute later Jake and his men circled the vehicle pointing their guns at the men in the car.

Jake yelled at his men, "Don't Shoot." Then to the men in the car he said,"Throw your guns out the window and get out with your hands up."

There was no answer for 30 second and then the front seat passenger tossed his pistol out of the window. The driver followed and then the two back seat passengers dropped their guns on the street.

Jake said, "Get them out. Search them."

The guards did as Jake asked and then made the four men lay face down in the street.

"Gerry, take the three cars and these pieces of shit to your hangar. I'm going to check on George. I'll be there as soon as I can," Jake ordered.

Gerry did as Jake asked and when he had left, Jake asked Charlie to find out who owned the cars they had hit and be sure they get money to fix them. Jake ran back to the church. When he reached the church's doorway he saw his father Jacob kneeling over George. He was holding his hand over a wound on the lower left side of George's abdomen.

"Pop, how is he?" Jake asked.

George answered, "God is with me." And then he passed out.

# Chapter Twenty-Two

When the ambulance arrived George was still unconscious, but breathing. After a quick assessment of George's condition, he was placed in the ambulance and rushed to the Episcopal Hospital on Lehigh Avenue. It was a short ride and Jacob rode with George. Before they left Jacob asked Jake to follow in George's car. During the ride, Jacob held George's hand and repeatedly said, "It'll be alright, Georgie. It'll be alright."

The ambulance pulled up to the emergency room entrance and they rushed George into an examining room. After the doctor evaluated him, the head doctor informed Jacob that George needed an operation. Jacob consented and reluctantly took a seat in the waiting room after the nurses insisted he leave the examining room.

For Jacob, the wait was excruciating. He was used to being in charge, being the one that got things done. Now he had to wait while strangers held his youngest child's life in their hands. He detested waiting for anything and the awful realization that one of his children was in eminent danger ate at his soul. Every fiber of his being was on fire. His emotions cycled through rage and hate for those who did this to George, to fear of the outcome of the operation, to utter helplessness.

"Pop, what's the plan?" Jacob asked.

Jacob, still in a fog, took a minute to answer.

"Pop, you alright?" Jake persisted.

Jacob looked at Jake and saw his concern. It was as if someone threw a cold glass of water on Jacob's face. All of the sudden he snapped out of his melancholy and it was replaced with a calculated rage for those who did this to George.

"I'm okay," Jacob said and paused to think. "Jake, go to the hangar. Find out who the, bastard was that shot George. When you do, I don't want anyone to ever see him again."

"What about the others?" Jake asked.

"Franklin said Beaumont's second in command is with them. His name is Albert Montfort. Find out which one he is and send him with the shooter. Put the other two on ice. After we take care of Beaumont, we may need them to show goodwill to whoever takes over," Franklin said.

"Okay, Pop," Jake said and left for the hangar.

Ten minutes later Molly and Mercy arrived. Jacob kissed Mercy and tightly hugged Molly. Molly began to cry and said, "How is he?"

"I don't know yet. They're operating on him now," Jacob said.

Molly began to sob and Mercy put her arm around her and said, "It'll be okay, Mama. I just know it will."

The three sat in silence for a few minutes then Jacob asked, "Where's everyone?"

"At your house, Papa. I told them to stay there. I'll go call them and let them know about George," Mercy said.

"Let me do it," Molly said.

"Okay, Mama."

Molly walked off to find a pay phone and Mercy said, "Do you remember the last time we were here, Papa?" Mercy asked.

"How can I forget? Thanksgiving Day 1943."

"Gerry's birthday. Remember how, when I was in labor you told me that everything would work out and that you would keep the family safe from the Johnson Family?"

"Yes," Jacob said.

"And you were right. You did work it out. Papa, you and Uncle Frank have always kept us safe. You saved Mary. You saved me. George will be okay. I know it in my heart," Mercy said.

Jacob hugged Mercy and kissed her on the forehead. Mercy said, "Let's say a prayer for George."

Both Jacob and Mercy made the sign of the cross and silently prayed that George would recover quickly.

Jake Byrne arrived at the Byrne Air Freight hangar 30 minutes after he left the hospital. He briefed Gerry, Al and Gabriel Barra on George's condition. Barra made the sign of the cross.

"Who's with the family," Jake asked.

"Mike, Mickey, and Mickey's man, Sean Mulligan. They have ten men with them," Gerry said.

"Good. Where's the phone?" Jake asked.

"There's one on the wall," Gerry answered and pointed to the wall in front of the office.

Jake called his father's house and had Mike send Mickey and three men to the hospital to guard Jake, Molly and Mercy.

"Okay, where are these sons of bitches," Jake said.

"Tied up in my office," Gerry answered.

"Mr. Barra, Al you should leave now. No reason you need to be part of this," Jake said.

"Jake, my boy," Barra began to say and paused for a moment. "What do you Americans say? I think it is, this is not my first radeo."

Jake smiled and said, "It's Rodeo. It's not my first rodeo."

Barra said, "Oh! Well, anyway you may need someone who speaks French."

Jake looked at Al. Al shook his head back and forth and said," I'm not going anywhere."

Gerry opened the office door and the four men were sitting in folding chairs with their hands bound behind them. Their feet were also tied to the chair and each man had duct tape over their mouths. The four men looked up when Jake walked into the room. When Barra entered the room, two of the men looked surprised to see him.

Jake ripped the tape off each man's mouth and stood in front of them. He pulled his gun from his shoulder holster, held it at his side, and said, "I have three questions I need answered. If you tell me the truth, then you might live. If not..." Jake shrugged his shoulders.

"Who pulled the trigger today?" Jake asked.

The men said nothing so Barra, speaking in French said, "Look you miserable pieces of shit. This man's a maniac. He's killed more men then you even know, so when he asks a question, you better fucking answer. He asked who pulled the trigger today." Then in a loud angry voice Barra said, "Who was the shooter?"

Two of the men turned their heads and looked at the man in the third chair.

"Gerry, could you please untie this man," Barra said pointing at the man in the third chair. "Just his hands."

Gerry untied the man and then Barra grabbed the man's right hand and smelled it.

"Gun powder," Barra said.

Jake walked over to the man, pointed his gun at the man's heart and pulled the trigger. The man fell backwards taking the chair with him. Jake shot him twice more.

"Question two. Who's Albert Montfort?"

No translation was needed this time. One man looked surprised and the other two men looked at him. Jake pointed his gun at Montfort and said, "Last question. Montfort, are there any more Beaumont men in Philadelphia?" Jake paused then said, "Strike that. Anywhere in the USA?"

Jake cocked his .45 and pointed it at Montfort's head. Barra translated. Montfort leaned back in fear and said, "No."

"Will your boss send more men?" Jake asked.

Barra translated and open hand slapped Montfort in the face.

Montfort paused for a minute and said, "Yes."

"When?" Jake asked pressing the gun into Montfort's head.

Montfort laughed and said in English, "Beaumont will send men here until he," Montfort pointed at Gerry and continued, "is rotting in his grave."

Jake bashed the gun into the side of Montfort's head and said, "So you understand English. So understand this. If you don't answer me I'll blow your fucking brains all over Gerry's office. Gerry probably won't like that because he'll have to clean up the pieces of gray matter and blood. As for me, I would very much enjoy it. Now when will he send more men?"

"Not until after the holidays," Montfort reluctantly said.

The next morning Gerry and Al loaded the three men and the dead man's body in their C-123 aircraft. When they were in the middle of the Gulf of Mexico, they pushed the dead man's body out of the plane's side door. The body seemed to float mid air for a second and then quickly fell to the water below.

Alberto Rivera was waiting when Gerry landed the plane and he took possession of the three men who would now be field hands until Gerry said to release them. After a long lunch with Rivera their aircraft was loaded with product and Gerry and Al headed home. Before they left Gerry informed Rivera that it would make his family happy if Albert Montfort had a fatal accident while working in the fields.

Jacob, Molly and Mercy stayed with George in his hospital room through the night. Several hours after George went to the operating room, the doctors told the family that the operation was successful and that George should have a complete recovery. No organs had been hit and there was no permanent damage. Barring any infection, they promised he would be home by New Year's Day. George woke up at 4:00 am and said he was hungry. After he ate he slept again until 9:00 am.

Jacob was relieved and happy about George's condition, but he was very concerned about the information Jake had given him the night before. Montfort had said Beaumont men wouldn't come until after the Holidays. *But, how soon after, he thought? Can I believe Montfort?*

"Molly, I've decided we have to deal with Beaumont sooner rather than later. I know I said I would be home for New Year's Eve, but we have to go to Paris as soon as possible," Jacob said.

"I know. I have been thinking the same thing. That man won't stop and I'm afraid for the children. I don't want you to go, but I understand why you have to," Molly said and began to cry.

Jacob took her into his arms and said, "It'll work out. By the time I get home, I promise this will be over and we can start looking for a house in Florida."

"I'll pray every day that God looks over you all," Molly said.

Jacob said, "I know you will," and then kissed Molly on the head. "Can you wake up Mercy? I'd like her to arrange our tickets to Paris."

# Chapter Twenty-Three

On December 29th Jacob, Jake, Gerry, Mickey Callahan and Sean Mulligan drove to New York City's John F. Kennedy Airport where they boarded a Pan American Boeing 707 Jetliner. When they arrived in Paris Franklin was waiting with a large Mercedes van, to take them to his rented home.

"Wow, this is some house," Gerry said in amazement.

"Take a look out of the living room window. You can see the Eiffel Tower," Franklin said.

"That's about all we're going to see. Remember what I told you about laying low till we get the job finished," Jacob said.

"It's a damn shame. Come all the way to Paris and can't see anything," Sean Mulligan said. Mickey looked at him and squinted his eyes. Sean quickly said, "Don't get me wrong, I understand why. But it's a shame."

"Tell you what, Sean. When we get our work done and make peace with the Paris Mob, I'll pay for a one-week trip back here for you and your girlfriend. That goes for everyone," Franklin said.

"I just might take you up on that," Sean said.

"Me too. That's when I find a girlfriend," Gerry said and smiled. "You know Paris looks a lot like Saigon. Or, vice versa, I guess. Vietnam was a French colony for almost 100 years, before the Vietnamese kicked their asses out in 1954."

"Thanks for the history lesson, kiddo, but if you don't mind I would like to get a shower and eat something. I'm starving," Jake said.

"Oh crap. That reminds me," Gerry said as he opened a large paper bag he had brought with him. "My mom sent you these." Gerry held up two Philadelphia hoagies. "There's a couple more in the bag and some soft pretzels. She thought you and Uncle Frank might enjoy a little taste of Philly."

"She's such a considerate person," Catherine said. "I'll eat one later. First, let's get you all situated in your rooms and you can take that shower, Jake. Then we'll have lunch."

Catherine arranged for a typical French cuisine for the group's first meal in France. To start they were served soupe à l'oignon, an onion soup with a crusty bread topping. The soup was followed by the entre, Hachis Parmentier, a sophisticated version of Shepherd's Pie. The cheese dish included several local favorites and this was followed by an assortment of French pastries and strong coffee. There was, of course, plenty of baguettes. Franklin and Catherine ate their hoagies.

When everyone had finished the meal, the discussion turned to the planning of the hit on Henri Beaumont. Franklin explained that one thing Beaumont did on a regular basis was to visit someone in a building across from the Notre-Dame Cathedral every weekday. After an hour, sometimes two, he would walk to the cathedral, guarded by three men, where he sat in a left side pew close to the main altar. His guards always sat 10 pews behind him and wouldn't allow anyone to sit in the first 10 pews on either side until Beaumont left the church. Franklin and Catherine had followed him into the church on a couple of occasions and saw that Beaumont spent about 30 minutes with his head bowed then he left the way he came in.

Jacob decided that Notre Dame would be their best chance to take Beaumont. Gabriel Barra had advised Jacob that it would be better to have Beaumont disappear than to leave his body to be found. That way it would create some doubt in Beaumont's followers's minds as to whether he had been killed or he just took off to avoid the K&A Gang's retribution. So, they planned to take Beaumont alive.

Notre Dame always had people visiting and often nuns and priests from around the world would come on pilgrimages. It was decided that Gerry, Mickey and Sean, being the shortest, would dress as nuns and sit as close as possible to the guards. When the time came to take Beaumont, they would dispatch the guards with knives so as not to make a disturbance. Then they would grab Beaumont and take him out the front entrance where Jacob and Jake would be waiting. Franklin would be in a stolen ambulance. They would all pile in the vehicle, then take Beaumont somewhere and dispose of him.

"Nuns. Really?" Gerry asked. "Can't we be priests?"

"No," Jake said smiling. "No one will suspect a nun. Anyway I always thought you would make a good-looking girl."

Gerry put his left hand up to hide his right hand, so Catherine wouldn't see him give Jake the finger.

The planning continued until every detail was clear to everyone. By December 31st, despite the luxurious surrounding, Gerry and Sean Mulligan were exhibiting cabin fever symptoms and they asked Jacob if the could spend a couple hours enjoying the New Year's Eve fun on the Champs-Elysées.

At first, Jacob refused to let them out of the house, fearing someone would somehow recognize them and inform Beaumont. Jules, one of Franklin's bodyguards assigned by Pierre Barra, convinced him that it should be safe. The Champs-Elysées would be very crowded and as far as any of them knew, no one in Paris would recognize Gerry anyway.

Jacob reluctantly agreed, but ordered Jules to go with them and to be back before midnight so they could celebrate the beginning of 1968 together. By 9 pm Gerry, Sean and Jules were walking along the Champs-Elysées enjoying the Parisian revelers and sipping Cognac from silver flasks Jules had supplied.

It was a dazzling affair with the Champs-Elysées lit up like a Christmas tree. The City of Lights was celebrating the New Year like no other place on earth and Gerry relished every moment. He made a promise to himself that he would return someday with his wife. He didn't know who the wife would be or when he would marry, but he was sure he was coming back to Paris.

By 11:00 o'clock, the trio had made their way from the Avenue de Franklin Delano Roosevelt to the Arc de Triomphe.

"What's this Arc all about, Jules?" Sean asked.

Jules looked at the Arc de Triomphe for a long minute and then said, "I have no idea. Something about Napoleon, I think?"

"What the hell, Jules. You're French. You should know," Gerry said.

Jules shrugged his shoulders and said, "I had to quit school when the Germans invaded France. By the time they were gone it was too late to go back. So I am fucking sorry if I don't know anything."

"I didn't mean anything by it. I'm sorry, Jules," Gerry said trying to make amends.

"I watched the German army march under that Arc. The German soldiers had come to all the houses near the Arc and forced the people to stand and cheer the shit face Nazis as they marched under our Arc. It was the saddest day in my life," Jules explained.

"I'm sorry, Jules I really am," Gerry said.

Jules was a large man at 6'5" tall and 250 lbs of muscle. He quickly put his arm around Gerry's neck, drew him close, and bent him down. As he rubbed Gerry's head he said, "In 1944 I watched American troops as they marched under the Arc. It was the happiest day of my young life. That's why I love Americans." Jules laughed, kissed Gerry on the top of the head and let him go.

A second later, someone from the crowd bumped into Jules. Jules turned to see who it was. The man made his excuses, then stopped for a moment and looked at Jules. Then he said, "Jules? Is that you?"

Jules saw fear in the man's eyes and immediately put his arm around the man's shoulder holding him tight. He then asked, "Who are you with?"

The man eyes darted back and forth and he looked at a man standing about 10 feet away. Jules looked at Gerry and said, "Get that guy."

Gerry taken by surprise looked at where Jules was pointing and hesitated for a few seconds. The man also saw Jules pointing and he started to run. As the man ran under the Arc Gerry followed, but he was a good 30 feet behind and was impeded by the crowd. But so was the man. Now the man was frantically pushing people out of the way and the crowd became angry. He pushed one woman and she fell to the ground. Her husband, who was 10 feet behind her, put out his foot and tripped the man as he ran by. He flew a few feet and smashed into another man. The man he crashed into pushed the man Gerry was chasing to the ground and a few seconds later Gerry pounced on him.

Gerry and the man wrestled on the ground, each trying to throw punches, but none hitting their mark. Gerry rolled on top of him. The man pushed Gerry up and then with lightening fast reflexes, he reached into his coat pocket and pulled a knife. In a split second, the man plunged the knife at Gerry's chest. The impact of being stabbed made Gerry fall backwards. The man, still holding the knife struggled to get up intending to finish Gerry. Before he could the husband of the woman the man had pushed, kicked him in the face. The man fell backwards, unconscious.

Gerry was now sitting on the pavement under the Arc and put his hand on his chest to feel for blood. He felt no pain, but he was sure he was stabbed. He pulled his hand back and looked at it. There was no blood. Then he reached into his inside jacket pocket and pulled out the silver flask Jules had given him and saw it was dented. He shook his head in amazement, opened the flask, and took a swig. He got up from the pavement and walked to the man who had kicked the man Gerry was chasing and handed him the flask. The man took a swig and started to hand it back.

"You keep it. Merci," Gerry said as he pushed the man's hand back. The man said something in French that Gerry didn't understand, so he just nodded. Then he took the knife from the man on the ground and slapped his face to wake him. He wouldn't wake up. A woman, who was carrying a bottle of Champagne, saw Gerry trying to revive the man and poured some of the bubbly on the man's face.

The man Gerry had given the flask to said, in broken English, "She must be German. No French woman would waste good Champagne." Then he walked on.

Gerry helped up the man he had chased, held the knife to his back and marched him to where Jules was waiting. Jules had the man he had caught flung over his shoulder. The man was unconscious. None of the revelers thought anything of it. After all, it was New Year's Eve. One was expected to over celebrate.

Jules had prearrange to meet their driver on Avenue Victor Hugo, a city block down from the Place de l'Étoile. Jules dropped the man he was carrying into the trunk of the Citron limousine and then told the man Gerry had caught to get in the trunk. Sean closed the trunk lid and they drove back to Franklin's rented home.

"This is exactly what the fuck I was afraid would happen. Damn it! How did they know who you were?" Jacob said.

"One of the men was at a meeting Mr. Barra had with Beaumont a couple years ago. We were posted outside the building and shared some laughs and Cognac," Jules said.

"We got them before they could tell anyone. Beaumont still has no idea we are here," Gerry said.

"Gerry, you almost got killed. Holy Christ what would I have told your mother if I brought you back in a body bag?"

Gerry said, "I'm sorry."

"Okay, okay." Jacob said shaking his head. "Nobody goes out again until we take care of Beaumont," Jacob said.

"What about these two?" Sean asked.

"Tie them up and put them in kitchen. Stay with them," Jacob ordered. "Don't hurt them. When this is over we'll need to make peace with their new boss."

"Jules, go with them and see what information you can get," Franklin said.

# Chapter Twenty-Four

Mercy Amato carefully measured out five scoopes of coffee grounds and placed them in the round basket of the metal coffee pot. Her hands were shaking and she spilled some of the grounds in the sink. In frustration, she threw the whole basket in the sink, put her hands to face and sobbed.

Al Watson, who along with Mercy and the entire family was staying in Jacob and Molly's house, saw her and asked, "What's wrong?"

Mercy patted her eyes with her hanky and replied, "I just talked to my father in Paris. Gerry went out last night to celebrate and almost got himself killed. What's wrong with that boy? Haven't I given enough?" Mercy began to cry again.

Al turned her to him, put his arms around Mercy and held tight. "Is he hurt?"

Mercy sniffed and said, "No, he's okay."

Al kissed her on the forehead and said, "Gerry's a tough guy and he has skills. He'll be okay. I promise."

Mercy looked up at Al and nodded. Al pulled her tighter and kissed her on the lips. It was a long passionate kiss. When he was finished Mercy opened her eyes, looked up and returned his kiss.

From the doorway they heard,

*"Mercy and Al sitting in the tree*
*K-i-s-s-i-n-g!*
*First comes love.*
*Then comes marriage.*
*Then comes baby in the baby carriage,*
*Sucking his thumb,*
*Wetting his pants,*
*Doing the hula, hula dance!"*

Mercy and Al quickly turned to see Bella, Charlie's fifteen-year-old daughter, in the doorway. She was smiling.

Mercy put her arm up, beckoning Bella to come to her. Bella ran over and hugged

Mercy and Al.

"I haven't heard that since I was a little girl," Mercy said.

Bella who was as tall as Mercy, leaned over and whispered, "I like him. I'm happy you two are hooking up."

"What do you mean hooking up?" Mercy asked.

"You know. Like when you're girlfriend and boyfriend," Bella explained.

Mercy turned to look at Al, but said nothing. Al looked at Mercy, then Bella, then back to Mercy, and said, "Yep, if it means that, yes we're hooking up."

Mercy kissed Al lightly on the lips.

"Well then, Uncle Al, I have to warn you. Aunt Mercy has four mean brothers and if you don't treat her right, they won't be happy," Bella said.

"Somehow, I think you may be tougher than all of them," Al said and smiled.

"Right on," Bella replied, gave the peace sign and left the room.

Al turned to Mercy and said, "Umm, four tough brothers. I better be careful."

"You better," Mercy said then kissed Al again. This time it was a longer and more passionate kiss.

When they finished Al said, "Here let me make the coffee," and picked up the coffee basket, rinsed it out and began to fill it.

Mercy stood close to him as Al put five scoopes in the basket and one more to give the coffee more body.

"Oh, so brave. I like that in a man," Mercy said.

Al gave Mercy a bewildered look and said, "What do you mean?"

"Mom likes to use five scoopes. You don't want to be on her bad side before she has her morning coffee," Mercy answered and smiled.

Al took one scoope out of the basket, put the basket in the pot and paceded the pot on the stove.

"No, I don't," Al said.

A few minutes later, Charlie walked into the kitchen and said, "If you two love birds are finished, we'll be picking up George from the hospital in fifteen minutes."

Mercy looked at Jake and said, "Bella."

"Yeah, she's telling everyone you're boyfriend and girlfriend," Charlie said and smiled.

An hour later Molly, Mercy, and Charlie arrived at the Episcopal Hospital. Charlie tried to talk Molly out of coming to pick George up, telling her it wasn't safe, but Molly stubbornly insisted. Mercy also insisted on coming and before they left, she placed a stub-nosed .38 revolver in her pocketbook, just in case.

Two cars with three guards each accompanied the family. Traffic was light because it was New Year's Day. When they arrived at the hospital three guards stayed at the main door and the other three followed the family to George's room. When they entered the room George was dressed and sitting in a chair. He had been awake since 5 am in anticipation of leaving at 9 am. He hated hospitals and couldn't wait to get out and get home. George had asked a nurse to help him get dressed and by 6:30 am he was fully dressed in his immaculate priestly garb. He was very particular about the way he dressed and was obsessed about his auburn shock of hair. He couldn't stand it if even a few hairs were out of place.

Charlie was well aware of this obsession when he approached his brother, clapped him on the shoulder and said, "Happy New Year, brother. Georgie, you're looking fit as a fiddle." Then he put his hand on George's head and mussed his hair.

George pulled away and said, "Surely, you'll go to hell for that." Then he took out his comb and started to repair the damage Charlie had done.

Molly kissed him, took the comb, and began to straighten out the mess Charlie had made. Mercy kissed George on the cheek and laughed.

"What's so funny?" George asked.

Mercy took out a hanky and wiped the two red lipstick marks from George's face. "It wouldn't do for a priest to be seen in public with lipstick on his face."

The nurse pushed George's wheelchair through the hospital doors and to the car. Charlie and Mercy helped George into the back seat.

"I'll ride with the lead car so George will have more room to stretch out," Charlie said. To the driver of Molly's car he said, "Stay close to us."

The three vehicles drove out of the hospital parking area and onto Lehigh Avenue, then north on Kensington Avenue. Charlie had decided it would be safer to take a different route home. It was a little longer but it would put off any would-be attackers. They would follow the elevated train route on Kensington Avenue.

Kensington Avenue turned into Frankford Avenue. When they reached Bustleton Avenue they would turn left and follow that to U.S. Route 1, the Roosevelt Boulevard, where they would travel north. This road passed the Northeast Airport where Gerry's business was located. A short distance later, they would turn left onto Byberry Road and then north on Buck Road and on to Jacob's house.

As they pasded under the elevated train, or as most Philadelphians called it the El, Molly couldn't help but recall the days when this part of the city was the go to place where the people from the surrounding neighborhoods went to shop. She lamented over how this wonderful shopping thoroughfare had deteriorated so much. Where once quality furniture and clothing stores plied their business, there were empty shops. The street, once so clean was now littered with old newspapers, empty cigarette packs and other debris.

"I used to come over here every Saturday to go to the movies at the Iris Theater," George said.

"The Midway Theater too," Mercy added. "I would buy you and your brothers soft pretzels at Kensington and Allegheny Avenue and we would pay fifteen cents each to see a double feature, cartoons and a serial," Mercy said.

"Yeah, my favorite was The Green Hornet," George said.

As George and Mercy discussed their favorite serial movies, a brown 1967 Chevy Impala pulled out from behind the rear guard car and sped past them on the wrong side of the road. When they were parallel to the car in which Mercy, Molly and George where passengers they turned sharply hitting its left front bumper. The driver of Molly's car lost control and careened into a parked vehicle. The men in the Chevy started shooting at the rear guard car. As they did, one of the men leaped out of the backseat. He was holding a shotgun. He pointed it in the air and fired.

Molly's driver was unconscious and Molly and George had been knocked to the back seat floor. Mercy was sitting in the front passenger seat. Realizing what was happening she grabbed her handbag and pulled out the small .38 special.

The assailant came to the window and yelled, "Get the fuck out now."

Mercy pointed the revolver at the man's head and pulled the trigger. A look of bewilderment flashed on the man's face just before a .38 slug entered his forehead. He dropped like a stone.

As this happened the driver of the car Charlie was in put his car in reverse and smashed into the front end of the Chevy. Charlie and the three guards jumped out of their car and started firing at the assailants. Meanwhile the men in the rear guard car started to return fire at the men in the Chevy. Seeing they were out gunned the two remaining assailants slipped out of the car and behind some parked cars on the west side of Kensington Avenue. They ran into a store and out the back door into an alleyway.

Charlie stopped his men from following because he feared they might have more assailants waiting for their ranks to be thinned out. Charlie's men ringed Molly's car and waited. When it was obvious that no other attack was happening Charlie stuck his head in the driver's side window of Molly's car and asked," Everybody ok?"

The driver was regaining consciousness and groggily said, "I'm okay."

"George's bleeding again. I think his stitches came out," Molly said.

Charlie motioned to his men to get George and said, "Put him in the other car and take him back to the hospital. Mom, Mercy, go with him. I'll wait here for the police."

After Charlie's men removed George and Molly left the car, Mercy climbed to the back seat and exited the damaged vehicle. She was still holding the .38 pistol.

"Give me that," Charlie Said. "I'll take care of it."

Mercy handed Charlie the .38. Then she left with George to go back to the Episcopal Hospital.

# Chapter Twenty-Five

Jacob slowly put the phone in the cradle. He shut his eyes and took a long breath trying to get hold of his emotions. His heart was pounding and neck was stiff. Jacob opened his eyes and said slowly, "We go tomorrow." He paused and then yelled, "And every day we have to until we kill that fucking bastard." Jacob picked up a bottle of whiskey he had been sipping from and threw it at the living room wall.

The others in the room drew back, surprised at the actions of a man who always had his emotions under control.

Franklin walked over to Jacob, grabbed his arm and asked, "What is it? What happened?"

Jacob told everyone what Charlie had conveyed to him. He was careful to start out with the fact that everyone was okay, except that George was back in the hospital. The more Jacob explained the angrier Jake became. He started pacing around the room, his fists clenched and his mood dark and ominous.

"Jake, come over here, please," Jacob said. Jake walked over to his father and Jacob pointed to the chair next to him. When Jake sat down Jacob said, "Save it for tomorrow. Right now, we need to concentrate on the plan. That goes for all of you."

"I think the wall you threw the bottle at disagrees," Franklin said.

Jacob smiled and said, "Well, forgive an old man for losing control for a moment. I'm good now." He continued, "Jules, do we have the nun outfits?"

"We have them," Jules answered.

"Do they fit?"

"Ahhh umm," Jules mumbled and then said, "I don't know."

"Well, we better find out. Go get them," Jacob ordered.

Jules came back with three large boxes and placed them on the table.

"You know how to put them on, right, Jules?" Gerry asked.

"No, I don't know that."

"What the hell. I certainly don't know," Gerry said.

"Calm down, I know how to do it," Catherine said. "Before you ask, I used to help around the convent when I was a child."

"Gerry, you're up," Jacob said and smiled.

"Strip down to your trousers and tee shirt," Catherine said. "Now roll up your pant legs and put on the black shoes."

Gerry did as she asked. Jake made a cat call.

"Funny, Uncle Jake. Funny," Gerry said.

Catherine helped Gerry put on the tunic, then the belt with the rosaries. She was careful to have the rosary beads on the left side and the belt buckle in the rear. Then she lifted the scapular over Gerry's head and straightened the long cloth in the front and back.

"This is important. All three of you listen. When you sit down you must not sit on the scapular. It's a blessed item and no real nun would do that. Just pull it to the side. Understand?" Catherine said.

The three men nodded that they understood.

"Mickey, Sean, put on your shoes and tunic," Catherine said.

The men did as she asked.

"Okay, now the wimple. Watch what I do for Gerry and do the same."

Catherine picked up the wimple and placed it over Gerry's head then tied it in the back. She then placed the collar around his neck and finally she placed the veil and pinned it in the back.

"Now I know why nuns aren't allowed to have sex," Sean said.

Catherine giggled and said, "Okay, now walk across the room."

The three men did as Catherine asked.

"Oh boy," Jacob said.

"Guys, you have to walk like nuns, like women. Take small steps, bow your head and walk slowly. Try keeping your feet closer together," Catherine instructed.

Gerry, Mickey and Sean did as Catherine instructed. "That's better. Pull your veil out more to help cover your face. When you're in the church do your rosaries and keep your heads down like you're praying," Catherine instructed.

"How do we carry our guns?" Mickey asked.

"Put them in the waistband of your pants and there are slits on the side of the tunic where you can get access."

"Can we take these off now?" Gerry asked.

"Okay, I'll help you," Catherine said.

"I can help," Franklin said. "I've taken off a couple of habits in my life."

Catherine looked sideways at Franklin and said, "We'll talk later about that."

Sean, Gerry and Mickey practiced walking for another hour while Jake, Jacob and Franklin sipped on wine and watched. Catherine and Jules were in the kitchen preparing a late night repast. When it was ready, Catherine called everyone to the dining room.

"Gerry, you're the youngest. Can you say grace?"

"Sure," Gerry answered and then made the sign of the cross as he recited, "In the name of the Father, Son and Holy Ghost. Bread is Bread, Meat is Meat, For God's Sake Let's Eat. Amen."

"Really, Gerry. Really," Catherine said rolling her eyes.

"What's wrong with it. Georgie taught me that," Gerry said. "If a priest can say it so can I."

"Quiet," Jake said. "Did you hear that?" He paused to listen. "There it is again. Sounds like someone's trying to open the garden door."

"Catherine, go to the bathroom and get in the tub. Jules stand outside the door and guard her," Franklin ordered. Each of the men pulled their weapons and slowly walked towards the living room. The noise continued and became more frantic.

"Mickey, come with me. The rest stay here and cover us," Jake whispered. Then he motioned to Mike and they both walked into the living room and stood 10 feet from the garden door. The noise continued.

Jake motioned to Gerry and Sean to go outside and around to the garden door. Then he whispered to Mickey, "I don't see anything."

"Me neither," Mickey whispered back.

Jake crouched down and moved closer. Mickey pointed his gun at the door ready to blast anyone trying to get in. The noise increased and they heard a whimpering sound.

From outside he heard Gerry say, "For Christ's sake, it's a dog." Then Jake heard Sean and Gerry laughing. Jake went to the door and opened it. When the door was partially opened a straggly black haired dog burst through the door, stopped a few feet into the room, and wagged its tail.

Jake walked over to the dog and put his hand out palm down. The dog licked his hand. Then he petted the dog's head. He looked her over and said, "Hey girl, where have you been? You don't look so good."

The dog's fur was matted and she was filthy. Her ribs were showing and it was obvious that she was starving. "Sean, grab some food from the table and bring it here, will you?"

Sean returned with a bowl of green beans and handed them to Jake. Jake put the bowl on the floor and said, "I'm guessing you never had a dog. Right?"

"Right, never did," Sean said.

"Well, they like meat. Can you go get some meat?"

"Looks like she's digging the beans," Sean said.

Jake looked down and the dog had finished the whole bowl of green beans and was looking back up at Jake as if to say, "Can I have more, please?"

"You were very hungry, girl. Weren't you?" Jake said in a high-pitched voice as he rubbed her head. Then to Sean he said, "Get some meat, will you?"

Catherine came into the room just after Sean placed a plate of beef in front of the dog.

"Oh my God. That poor thing. She's a mess," Catherine said.

The dog looked up at Catherine, tilted her head and stared.

Catherine rubbed her head and said, "You eat up and then we're going to give you a good bath."

After dinner, Catherine and Jake had to bathe the dog three times to get her clean. When they were done, Catherine dried the dog with her hair drier and then put a green bow on her head. The dog walked into the living room, ran directly to Jake and jumped on his lap. He rubbed her head, sniffed and said, "You smell wonderful." The dog licked Jake's cheek.

"What're you going to do with her Jake? I guess they have pounds here in France," Sean said.

"Not a chance. She's going home with us," Jake said.

"They're not going to let a dog on the plane," Mickey said.

"Pop chartered the plane, remember. It's all ours and if I want a dog on the plane, I'll have her on the plane," Jake said.

"Then what?" Mickey asked.

"I'll sneak her through customs and take her to my shelter in Buck's County or maybe I'll keep her myself," Jake said.

"You have your own pound?" Sean asked surprised.

"Not a pound, a shelter," Gerry said. "He started it in 1958. It's called Bonnie's Retreat. He named it after our family dog."

"Well, I'll be damned," Sean said.

"Okay guys. we have a big day tomorrow. Let's get some rest," Jacob said.

"What are you going to call her, Jake?" Catherine asked.

Jake thought for a second and said, "Beanie." Then he walked off to his room. Beanie followed.

# Chapter Twenty-Six

The next day, January 2, 1968, Jacob Byrne and his crew traveled to the Notre-Dame Cathedral and waited for Henri Beaumont to arrive. Gerry, Mike and Sean, dressed as nuns, remained hidden in the stolen ambulance and waited. Franklin and Catherine sat at a table in the café across the street and Jake and Jacob took their position near the entrance to the church, but out of sight. Jules had arranged for two women to sit near Franklin and when Beaumont arrived, one would walk to the van and the other to the entrance, where Jacob and Jake were, to warn them. They figured they would have about an hour before Beaumont left the hotel and arrived at the church.

After waiting for four hours, Jacob called off the attack. It was obvious that Beaumont would not show up that day. They all agreed they would return the next day at the same time.

On January 3rd at 4 pm Beaumont arrived at the hotel. Once Beaumont entered the hotel, Franklin told the women to deliver their messages.

> Gerry, Mickey and Sean walked slowly to the church, being careful to keep their heads bowed. When they entered, each crossed themselves with holy water and sat in the eleventh row of pews on the left side. If all went well the guards would take their normal seats in the tenth row, right in front of them. Jacob and Jake were already in position.

True to form, Beaumont exited the hotel with three guards and started to walk to the church. After he had crossed the street, Franklin escorted Catherine to a waiting car and opened the door for her.

"Be careful," Catherine said,

"Always am. See you back at the house as soon as I can," Franklin said and kissed Catherine.

When the car drove off Franklin walked to where Jules had parked the ambulance and sat in the passenger side. "We're on," Franklin said.

Jules made the sign of the cross. Franklin changed his shirt for a regulation ambulance driver version and put on a hat.

Once Beaumont entered the church, Jake and Jacob took position just inside the entrance. Beaumont crossed himself with holy water and walked down the long center aisle to the first pew. He genuflected and then took a seat in the middle of the left pew. The three guards stopped at the tenth set of pews, stood there until Beaumont was seated and then two of them took seats, while the third man turned, looked at the nuns, nodded and then walked over to the right side of pews and took a seat.

Gerry looked at Mickey, who shrugged as if to say *sometimes things don't always go exactly how you want*. Mickey tapped Sean on the leg and when he had his attention, he looked at the man on the right side of the church and made an L shape with his thumb and finger. Then he closed his finger. Sean nodded his approval, slipped his hand in his tunic and grasped the handle of his .45. They hadn't brought silencers, because of the bulk under the tunic and hoping to be silent only using knives, so the three men were going to make a lot of noise in the quiet church. Sean silently asked God's forgiveness and nodded in the affirmative to Mickey.

Jacob had arranged that Gerry, Mickey and Sean would take out the guards at exactly fifteen minutes after Beaumont took his seat. Keeping his hand low behind the pew Gerry lifted the tunic sleeve and looked at his watch. Five minutes to go. He tapped Mickey on his arm and held out his hand with all five fingers extended. Mickey nodded and did the same for Sean.

Gerry felt as if the minutes were passing very slowly. He looked at his watch again and only thirty seconds had gone by. Time was in slow motion for him. For the first time since he entered the church he looked up at the altar and then scanned the room and finally the ceiling. He was amazed at the workmanship of the timeless sculptures and beautiful and intricate stained glass windows. It was incredible to him that people living 800 years ago could build something like Notre-Dame. He looked at his watch again then held out three fingers for Mickey to see.

A sudden sadness washed over Gerry like a wave in the ocean. He caught his breath and realized that he was sorry that he had to stain this beautiful building, this tribute to God, with blood. Reality came as quickly as the sadness had. What he was doing was saving his own life and that of his family. No structure or person would ever stop him from protecting his family. He looked at his watch again. He held out one finger to Mickey.

Both Mickey and Gerry put their hands into the slit in their tunics pulled out ten-inch stiletto knives. Gerry's knife was his Grandfather Jacob's who had received it from Gerry's Great Grandfather Gerardo Amato. Sean pulled his .45 and kept it out of sight. Gerry looked at his watch again. It read thirty seconds. The second hand was moving closer to the twelve. Gerry nodded at Mickey.

Both Mickey and Gerry simultaneously thrust their stilettos into the soft area at the base of the skulls and into the brains of the guards sitting in front of them. At the same time, Sean lifted his .45 and fired. At that exact time Mickey's arm hit Sean's back making the shot miss. The guard sitting in the right pew ducked behind the pew and pulled his pistol. The two guards Mickey and Gerry had stabbed were dead and falling forward as Sean fell back towards Mickey seeking some cover. The guard on the right fired and hit the wood on the back of the pew.

Gerry, Mickey and Sean fell to the floor just as Beaumont fired four shots from his automatic. The bullets punctured the wood above their heads and sending small splinters onto them. Sean fired three shots at the guard and the guard returned two shoots. Sean held steady while Gerry and Mickey crawled on their bellies towards the left side of the church. After shooting, Beaumont ran to the left side of the church and passed by the tenth row just as Gerry looked up. Gerry squeezed his trigger, but missed Beaumont. Beaumont continued to run towards the front entrance.

Beaumont's guard saw him and fired several shots at Gerry and Mickey to keep them from going after Beaumont. It was a fatal mistake. Sean seeing the guard break cover shot twice, hitting the man in the chest and throat. Sean yelled," Go."

Gerry and Mickey stood up and ran to the end of the pew and then after Beaumont. Sean followed them. Beaumont was close to the back of the church plowing through some people trying to get out. Other people were screaming and running out the entrance. Jacob and Jake pushed their way through the crowd and into the church. Beaumont saw them and ran into the entrance to the north tower.

By the time Jacob could see what was happening, Gerry, Mickey and Sean were at the entranceway to the north tower. Gerry motioned to Jake to take the south tower stairs. According to the drawings Gerry had seen, there were only two ways out from the towers. You took either the north or south tower stairs. When Jake and Jacob took off for the south tower Gerry started up the north tower stairway.  Sean and Mickey followed

It was a very narrow spiral staircase made from stone. From what he remembered there were several hundred stairs to get to the top. He was sure at Beaumont's age he would be slow to get to the top and when he did he would need a rest. Gerry was wrong. As Gerry started to turn the last spiral to the top of the landing, two shots hit the stone just a couple of feet in front of him. He jumped back bumping into Mickey and almost knocking him down the steps.

Jacob and Jake were making their way up the south tower stairs, which was the exact same design as the north tower stairs. The only difference was that the south tower stairs were general used for tourists to exit. Most had gotten out before Jake and Jacob started up but a few stragglers were still making their way down. This delayed Jake and Jacob, as the stairs were so narrow you had to go sideways to let two people get by each other. A heavyset woman almost knocked Jacob down the stairs as she passed by. Jake grabbed his father's jacket and steadied him.

When they finally reached the top, they started to cross the walkway leading to the north tower. Beaumont was in the walkway close to the north tower. He fired at Jake and Jacob and missed. Gerry, Mickey and Sean were on the other side walking towards Beaumont. Beaumont spun around and fired at Gerry. His gun clicked and he was out of ammunition.

Jacob yelled, "Give it up, Beaumont."

Beaumont threw the gun at Jacob, ran towards the north tower entrance of the walkway and then lifted himself up onto the stone railing. He climbed around the column and crouched behind a horned gargoyle. He realized that if he gave himself up he was a dead man. If he could stay behind the stone gargoyle, at least until the police arrived, he might survive.

As planned a few minutes after Gerry was to take out the guards, Jules turned on the ambulance's siren and started towards Notre Dame. When he arrived, he drove directly up to the main center doorway. People were looking up at the horned gargoyle and the man hanging on to it. They parted to allow the ambulance through.

Beaumont heard the siren of Jules' ambulance and some that seemed further away. He felt a sense of relief, knowing now that Jacob's men would flee so they wouldn't be arrested.

Jacob heard the sirens as well and said, "Go, all of you. Get down to the ambulance and get out of here. I'll deal with Beaumont."

"No way. I'll do it," Gerry said.

"I started this and I will finish it. I know what to do. Just get going. Don't argue with me, Grandpop or we'll all be in a French prison," Gerry said frantically. "Jake, get him out of here, will you?"

Jake hesitated for a few seconds, grabbed his father's arm and pulled him. Jacob reluctantly went with them. When everyone had left, Gerry climbed up the rail and inched his way around closer to the gargoyle and Beaumont. Holding on with one hand he put the other hand into the slit in the tunic and pulled out a gun from his waistband.

From the ground, the spectators gasped. What they saw was a nun climbing out on the ledge to help a man from committing suicide. Jacob, Jake, Sean and Mickey ran out of the main door of the church and stopped at the ambulance. They looked up to see Gerry inching his way to Beaumont. Jake exclaimed, "Oh fuck."

Gerry pointed the gun at Beaumont and said, "Time to come in. Give me your hand, I'll help you."

Beaumont just looked at Gerry and said nothing. Gerry said, "Look if you come in off the ledge maybe the cops will get here in time to save your sorry ass. If not I'll just shoot you now. Give me your hand." Gerry put his gun away.

Beaumont hesitated, but then held out his hand. Gerry took his hand and Beaumont let go of the gargoyle with his other hand. Gerry pushed hard. Beaumont looked surprised and grabbed for gargoyle again, but it was too late. His foot slipped and Beaumont fell silently to the pavement below. Gerry crossed himself and inched back to the walkway.

Franklin and Jules ran to Beaumont's lifeless body and pretended to administer to him. On a whim, Mickey wiped his fingerprints from his stiletto and walked to where the body lay, bent down and asked, "Anything I can do?" While he spoke he slipped the knife in Beaumont's hand.

Jules said something in French and Mickey went back to the ambulance. The first police car arrived as Gerry was running down the steps of the south tower. The two officers ran in the church and started up the steps. Gerry, still dressed as a nun plowed into one of the officers. The officer looked at Gerry for a second and said, "Excusez-moi, Sœur.»

Gerry nodded and ran down the rest of the stairs as the police officers ran up. When he came out of the entrance, he went to the ambulance and jumped in back. The others got in and Jules and Franklin came back to the ambulance, got in, turned the siren on and drove off. Just as they turned onto the main street, three more patrol cars sped past them and with a screech of tires, stopped in front of Notre Dame.

No one spoke until they arrived at the house. There was no celebration, no whopping and hollering. Each person knew it was a serious thing they had done, a thing that had to be done for the safety of the family. It was not something to celebrate.

Jules collected the weapons and placed them in a box. He also asked for the nun's habits from Gerry, Mickey and Sean. They were happy to oblige. Later, after the crew had left for the Unites States, he would dispose of them as well as the stolen ambulance that was currently in the garage.

"We leave first thing in the morning, so be ready at six," Jacob said.

# Chapter Twenty-Seven

The difference between soldiers and mobsters is that soldiers can talk about their exploits with their families and friends and receive medals for their valor. Mobsters avoided discussing their exploits, for good reason. So, when the crew arrived home all that was said was that the family was safe, or would be soon and that no one in the crew was hurt. Wives understood the need for silence as did children, so no one who had stayed home asked questions, with the exception of Mike, Jimmy and Charlie. They also avoided telling George anything about their exploits in Notre-Dame Cathedral.

The day after Jacob and the others returned, Gabe Barra received a telegram from his cousin. He found Jacob in his office looking over the receipts from the Paris trip. Jake was with him.

"Come in, Gabe. Have a seat."

Gabe sat next to Jake, slid the telegram across the desk and said, "Read it."

Jacob picked it up, studied it for a few seconds and said, "It's in French. I don't read French."

"Oh, pardon me. I am sorry. I forgot. Give it and I will translate," Gabe said and took the paper from Jacob.

"It says, Paris Newspaper headline. Henri Beaumont, a reported crime boss goes **berserk**. Kills Three. Commits Suicide."

Jacob and Jake laughed and Jacob said, "And the police believe this?"

"No, of course not. But they are happy he is gone and my cousin Pierre is, how do you Americans say it? A spin doctor."

Jacob smiled and said, "Yep, that's a good term."

"Jake. I hear you abducted a French citizen," Gabe said.

"Yes, a beautiful black lady. Her name is Beanie," Jake said.

"What will you do with her?" Gabe asked.

"Well, Maria says we have too many dogs now, so I'm going to take her to my animal shelter and see if we can get her adopted. How about you? You need a traveling companion?" Jake asked.

"Well, I am sure she is wonderful but I do not think a farm in the jungles of Cambodia would suit her very well. Your mother told me about your shelter. You are to be commended," Gabe said and smiled.

"Thank you, Gabe. You're probably right. We'll treat her like the princess she is until the right family comes along," Jake said.


The next day Jake decided to take Beanie to his shelter in Bucks County. The shelter was an old farm with 20 acres of land. The shelter manager and her family lived in the old farmhouse built in the 1880s. The animals lived in a new facility Jake had Jimmy build. It was a circular shape structure with the center being the veterinarian and administrative offices, the training rooms and storage areas. There were also 10 wedge-shaped rooms accessible from the circular common area. Each room could house 50 dogs or 75 cats. There was a play area, a shallow pool and open space in each room. There were also cages that were used only when necessary to protect the dogs. Most of the dogs roamed throughout the room at will.

Attached to the outside of each room was a very large outdoor fenced-in grassy area. When the weather permitted, the dogs could access the outside from a special easy open and close door. Often, when it wasn't too cold some dogs opted to sleep outside.

Sean and Mickey were leaving to return to Los Angeles in two days so Jake invited them to tour his shelter before they left. Gerry decided to go as well.

"Wait till you see this place," Gerry said."I flew over it once and it was something else. From the plane, all you saw was a very large round building with a red roof that comes to a point. There was a large green circle surrounding it. It looked like some kind of Christmas cake."

"Jake, how did you get into doing this shelter thing?" Sean asked.

"I'm not sure. I've always loved animals, especially dogs. So, I just wanted to do something for those animals that people treat like shit. Unfortunately there is no shortage of them," Jake said.

"Story I heard was that Jake here, when he was a teenager, found a guy mistreating a dog and was going to drown her puppies. Jake broke his arm and told him if he ever saw him with a dog again he would kill him," Mickey said.

"Is that true?" Sean asked.

"Kind of," Jake answered.

"Uncle Jake brought those five puppies and their mother home. He named the mother Bonnie and named the shelter after her. Bonnie's Shelter," Gerry said. "Charlie kept one puppy and named her Ginger. Jake named his puppy Zack, and Uncle Frank and Aunt Catherine even kept one. They named her Bunny. My Mom named her puppy Simone and we were lucky to have her for fourteen years."

"What happened to the fifth puppy?" Sean asked.

"Good question. I don't know," Gerry said.

"I made a deal with old man Schechter to take one. You remember him, Gerry?" Jake asked.

"Yeah, I do. Nice guy. His son's the family lawyer, right?"

"Right, he named his puppy Zara. It's some kind of female name from the bible, I guess," Jake said.

"You have any dogs now?" Mickey asked.

"Jesus Christ, I feel like I'm on that game show *Jeopardy*. Last answer. Yes, I have a mixed breed named Rocco and we have two Chihuahuas named Tomas and Carmen. That's why I'm bringing Beanie here. Maria thinks we have enough dogs at home."

Sean laughed and Jake asked, "What's so fucking funny?"

"Sorry, Jake I was just picturing you carrying around your Chihuahuas in a bag like those Hollywood actresses do," Sean said.

Mike and Gerry laughed. Jake smiled and said, "Well, that ain't gonna happen."

Jake turned into a paved driveway and drove 200 feet to the parking lot. A few minutes after he parked, a black 1968 Cadillac pulled up to the driveway, stopped for a few seconds, then drove on.

# Chapter Twenty-Eight

Gabe Barra hung up the phone and looked at Jacob who was sitting across the table from him. Barra was frowning and to Jacob this signaled that all was not well in Paris. The plan had been once Beaumont was out of the picture, more moderate gang members would take over and a peace could be brokered.

"Okay, Gabe let me have it," Jacob said.

"It is not the best news, but it should be resolved in a couple of days one way or the other. Beaumont's organization has splintered into three groups. One is his supporters led by one of Beaumont's closest men. The second one is the man my cousin is backing and he is aligned with us. A...how do you say it? A dark horse has revealed himself. He will be out of the game by tomorrow. The real battle is between a man named Alain Fontaine and our man, Anton Gaspard," Barra explained.

"What're the odds?" Jacob said.

"Right now 50/50," Barra said and shook his head. "If Fontaine wins I am afraid they will come after your family again. Fontaine's brother-in-law was Beaumont's second in command, Albert Montfort."

Jacob nodded and said, "Well, then Gaspard better win this battle."

"We will pray for that."

"Any word on the two shooters who attacked Molly and Mercy?" Jacob asked.

"No. No one knows where they are. Perhaps they got the word and are back in France."

"Maybe, but I can't take that chance. I have to keep the family bottled up until I know for sure. The kids are going crazy having to be inside so much."

"I will stay until we see who becomes the victor," Barra said.

"I appreciate that. Gabe. We owe you for what you have done for us. Whatever you need, whenever you need it, I will give it if it's in my power," Jacob said.

Father George Byrne finished his prayers, made the sign of the cross and slowly and painfully stood up. It had been only 24 hours since he was released from the hospital for the second time. The doctors told him to rest for a couple of weeks and then he could go back to work. But George had persuaded Charlie to drive him to his church so he could pray. George always felt more comfortable in his church. Seeing the altar, the stained glass windows and the statues of the saints and Jesus gave him peace of mind. *God knows I need It,* George thought.

Charlie assembled five men to come with George and himself to ensure there were no more repeat attacks. The trip to the church had been uneventful.

George swayed a little and Charlie asked, "Are you okay?"

"I'm fine," George said and sat down.

"Look, Mom's already mad at me for bringing you here, so if you're not feeling well I need to get you back," Charlie said.

"I'm okay. Just a little lightheaded. It passed."

Two men entered the church. One was wearing a black suit. He was a big man about 50 years old with a steel hard face. The other man was wearing dungarees and a brown shirt. He was younger and less threatening looking. The two men started to walk up the aisle. Charlie's guards quickly surrounded them with their pistols drawn.

George heard the commotion and turned to look. He whispered to Charlie, "It's okay. That's Deacon Bill. He works here."

Mary Byrne had just arrived at Jacob's house after a day of pre-med classes. She was tired and hungry. She dropped her briefcase on the sofa and walked to the kitchen.

"Good Afternoon, Grandma," Mary said and kissed Molly on the cheek.

"Hello sweetheart. Can I get you something to eat?" Molly asked.

"That would be heaven," Mary said.

"Go sit in the dining room. Frank and Catherine are there having a bite. I'll bring you a sandwich and coffee in a moment," Molly said.

"Want some help?" Mary asked.

"No. I'm not old and decrepit yet," Molly said.

Mary nodded and said, "And you never will be." Then she walked to the dining room.

Franklin and Catherine were sitting at the table. Mary kissed both and said," What are you eating?"

"Avocado and tomato sandwiches," Catherine replied.

"Ugh. No meat?" Mary asked.

"Mary, honey, if you cut down on eating meat now your future self will thank you."

Franklin leaned back and shook his head in the universal gesture of No.

"You may be right, Aunt Catherine but right now my present self is screaming inside for meat," Mary said.

Molly walked into the dining room with a tray. She placed a sandwich in front of Mary then a cup of coffee, and sat down next to Mary.

"Now this is a sandwich, Aunt Catherine," Mary said as she took the top piece of bread off. "Dark mustard, Lebanon baloney, American cheese topped with potato chips."

Catherine shook her head and Franklin, looking mournfully at Mary's sandwich said, "I miss those. I really do."

Boom! A loud gun-like popping sound rang through the room. Mary dove out of her chair and rolled under the table. Molly looked at the dining room doorway and saw Joey, Jake's son, standing there with a broken bag in his hand and smiling. She grabbed her chest and said, "Joey, you almost gave me a heart attack."

Mercy rushed into the room, saw what was happening and grabbed Joey by the ear and said, "Oh my god, you are so much like your father." She marched him to the living room and gave him a lecture.

Franklin helped Mary up from under the table and said, "It's okay. It was just Joey playing a prank. Mary sat back in her chair. She was physically shaking. "Let me get you something to help calm you down."

Franklin walked to the cupboard and pulled out a bottle of Jameson and four glasses. He put one in front of Mary and half filled it and said, "This should help. Anyone else?"

Catherine shook her head no. Molly said, "Oh God, yes."

Franklin poured two more glasses, gave one to Molly and held the other up in the air and said, "May the saddest day of your future be no worse than the happiest day of your past." Then he started to tilt the glass to spill a little on the floor for the spirits.

"If you spill that on my carpet, you'll have a broken toe in your future," Molly said, paused and continued. "Use your plate. The spirits can drink just as well from a plate as they can from the floor."

Mary downed her whiskey in one gulp.

# Chapter Twenty-Nine

"Franny, can you take Beanie to the vet and have her checked out? I'm going to show the boys around. When I'm done I'll take her for a walk outside. After that you can process her and assign a room," Jake said.

"Of course," Franny said and took Beanie's leash and started to walk to the veterinarian's office. Beanie looked back at Jake, tilted her head and barked.

"It's okay, Beanie. Go ahead now," Jake said. Franny gave the leash a little tug and Beanie complied.

Jake showed the men the administration offices, the vet's office and the storage area first.

"Holy shit! I never saw so much dog food," Sean said.

"At any given time we can have over 400 to 500 animals here. Takes a lot of food to feed them," Jake said.

"You buy all this food?" Mickey asked.

"Yeah," Jake said and paused. "Mostly. Some is donated and some fell off the back of a truck," Jake said.

Mickey shook his head in the affirmative and said, "That's what I thought. When I get home, I'm going to send you a couple truckloads."

"I appreciate that, Mickey. Thanks," Jake said.

"Don't thank me. Thank the guys that own the trucks," Mickey said and laughed.

Jake smiled and said, "Still I appreciate it."

"I'm going to write a check for $25 large as a donation," Mickey said.

"Are you kidding? That's generous," Jake said.

"Sean will give you $5 k," Mickey said.

Sean looked at Mickey, hesitated and said, "Sure $5 k"

"Well, let's finish the tour so I can show you how your donations will help," Jake said.

Jake opened the door to one of the outlying rooms and ushered the men in. The noise was deafening as the dogs barked at the strangers and Jake had to shout to be heard. "These are the bigger dogs. We keep them separate so the little ones aren't hurt. I think we have five rooms for the larger dogs at this time."

Gerry looked around the room. Most of the dogs had laid back down, and several were splashing around in the shallow pool. Still others were running around playing with each other. The smell was ripe, but he had expected that with so many animals. He saw one dog running and playing that had a weird contraption strapped to its rear. It was two wheels, like on a shopping cart. "What's her story, Uncle Jake?" Gerry asked.

"That's Cindie. Someone found her on the road. Some bastard hit her and just left her to die. When they got her here, the vet told us she would be paralyzed. We don't put dogs down unless there is no hope and they are suffering. Franny and the Doc came up with that…" Jake hesitated and then said, "wheelchair for dogs, I guess you call it. Gus, that Rottweiler in the pool was owned by a guy who sponsored dog fights. I liberated him and 20 other dogs. Gus was a piece of work at first, but we worked with him and eventually he changed. Nicest dog you ever want to meet now."

"What happened to the dog fighting guy?" Mickey asked.

"Let's just say he'll never be able to fight any other dogs," Jake said.

"Figured," Mickey said and grinned.

Jake showed the trio several other rooms and shared stories of how the dogs came to his shelter. There was the Pomeranian that had been found half beaten to death, the Border Collie that was found outside chained to a fence in the dead of winter. He lost a paw due to frostbite. There was a Boston Terrier that had to have his metal choker surgically removed after his owner refused to replace the dog's collar as it grew. The dog had a permanent scar around his neck.

"I'm impressed, Jake. I had no idea," Mickey said. "I'll make that donation $50k."

Jake finished the tour at the veterinarian's office. The vet said Beanie, aside for needing to gain weight was in pretty good shape. She had some neck abrasions and the doctor suggested Jake use a harness instead of a choke collar. Jake found a harness and placed it on Beanie.

"Guys, I want to take Beanie for a last walk. I'm sure someone will adopt her soon. Come with me and I'll show you the grounds," Jake said.

"I need to hit the latrine first. Meet you outside," Gerry said.

"Me too. We'll catch up," Mickey added.

"Okay, but don't take too long to powder your noses, ladies. I want to get home before five," Jake said and smiled.

Jake, Sean and Beanie walked to the main entrance and out the door. It was a nice day, not very cold for January. Beanie bounced around and pulled on her leash. Jake was happy to see that Beanie liked her surroundings. He was sad to let her go, but Maria was right. They already had three dogs and contrary to what some people think, dogs can be a lot of work. For Jake that didn't matter. He loved having them around.

Sean was impressed with what Jake had been able to do. He never had a dog, not even when he was a kid. Now he was thinking he would go to the local Los Angeles shelter and adopt one. He liked the Rottweiler he saw in one of the rooms and decided he would get that breed when he got back home.

Jake undid Beanie's leash and let her loose. She immediately started running toward the trees and then, abruptly stopped, turned and ran back. When she reached Jake and Sean she ran around them three times and took off to the trees again. She did this twice then ran around the right side of the building and out of sight.

"She might run away," Sean said feeling concern for Beanie.

"Nah, she'll be back," Jake said.

A minute later, they heard Beanie barking. She was still out of sight and seemed very agitated.

"She may have seen a rabbit or squirrel. Come on, I don't want her to get used to hunting small animals," Jake said.

The two men ran to the side of the building the barking was coming from. As they turned the corner, they saw what Beanie was barking at. A man was standing near the trash dumpster trying to shoo Beanie away. When the man saw Jake and Sean, he jumped behind the dumpster, pulled his pistol and loosed two rounds at Jake and Sean. The noise scared Beanie and she backed off 50 feet or so, but kept barking.

Jake hit the ground, rolled over and pulled his .45, rolled back and shot three rounds at the man. All three rounds hit the dumpster. Sean flattened himself against the wall and started towards the dumpster. If the man came out to shoot at him, Jake would be able to take him out.

The assassin leaned out and shot towards Jake again. The bullet hit the dirt a few feet in front of him. Beanie rushed at the man, grabbed his arm and shook. The man stood up, still behind the dumpster, pulled Beanie off his arm and threw her 10 feet back. Then he pointed his pistol at the dog. Sean seeing this rushed the dumpster and pushed as hard as he could. The dumpster moved enough to knock the man's arm. His shot missed Beanie and she ran off towards the woods.

Sean came around the left side of the dumpster his gun in his hand. As he turned to the backside of the dumpster, the assailant heard him and turned. Sean shot once and hit the man in the stomach. The man was knocked back by the shot and was now clear of the dumpster. As he fell backwards he shot once at Sean. Jake seeing his chance shot three times at the man, hitting him once in the arm and once in the head. The man crumpled to the ground. Beanie rushed back and went behind the dumpster.

When Gerry and Mickey heard the first shots, they quickly started towards the door, pulling their weapons as they ran. When they reached the door, they stopped and checked both sides of the area. No one was there.

"Go around," Mike ordered. Gerry started running while Mike followed the same path Jake had taken. As Mike turned the corner, he saw Jake shoot twice at a man near a dumpster. The man fell.

As Gerry ran past the outdoor play areas, the dogs started to bark. It seemed to him that they were barking in all the play areas. Because the building was round, he could only see 10 or so feet of the building as he ran. Suddenly there was a man running in the opposite direction from

Jacob. He tried to miss him but the two men collided. Both men fell backwards stunned. Gerry's gun flew from his hand.

Realizing he had no weapon Gerry started crawling quickly to retrieve his gun. The man had also lost his gun. When he saw Gerry trying to retrieve his weapon, he leaped at Gerry. This knocked Gerry on his back and the man threw three rapid punches at Gerry, connecting with his eye with one of the punches. Gerry rolled back towards the man, grabbed him and threw him back. The man grabbed Gerry and the two rolled several times on the ground. When they stopped rolling Gerry saw the man's gun just a few feet away. The man saw it also and both leaped for it at the same time. Gerry was slower. The man pushed Gerry away and stood up. He pointed the gun at Gerry.

Mickey, seeing Jake had things in hand ran back to help Gerry clear the back of the building. As he passed the third outdoor play area, he saw a man pointing a gun at Gerry. Mickey shot the full clip of the .45 pistol at the man. The man fell where he stood. Mickey ran up to Gerry and asked, "You okay, kid?"

"I am now," Gerry said and stuck his hand out. Mickey grasped it and helped Gerry to his feet.

"I thought I was a goner. Thanks, man. I owe you," Gerry said.

"Let's go see how Jake and Sean are," Mickey said. Both men walked around the building checking for more assailants.

As Gerry and Mickey came to the dumpster, they saw Jake standing next to it, his head pointed downward and his gun in his hand. The assailant lay nearby blood oozing from his three bullet wounds. Mickey checked his pulse and said, "Dead."

Then he saw Beanie was lying next to Sean and whimpering. She took her paw, placed it on Sean's shoulder, and scratched trying to wake him up.

Mickey looked at Jake who shook his head. Mickey made the sign of the cross. Then Jake did the same. Gerry seeing both of them realized what had happened and he made the sign of the cross and said a silent pray for God to accept Sean's soul into Heaven.

Beanie whimpered. Jake looked at her and Beanie cocked her head and opened her eyes wide. Jake said, "Okay girl, you're coming home with me. You can count on eating steak twice a week."

Beanie ran up to Jake and rubbed her head on his pant leg.

# Chapter Thirty

The police decided that the shootings were in self-defense and by eight that evening the men and Beanie were home at Jacob and Molly's house. Sean's body was released after two days, to Mulligan's Funeral Home and he was buried three days later at Resurrection Catholic Cemetery in Cornwell Heights.

The day after Sean was buried Mickey returned to California. He gave Jake a check for $50,000 made out to Bonnie's Shelter. The note in the envelope said *In the Name of Sean Mulligan*. The same day Jake arranged with Mercy to provide Sean's mother with a lifetime endowment from The Mercy Row Foundation.

It took three more weeks for the Paris Mob situation to work out. On January 27th a powerful explosion at the headquarters of Alain Fontaine, the new supposed head of the Paris Mob, settled the dispute. Fontaine was killed along with seven other mobsters and two French citizens who had the misfortune of walking by the building at the wrong time.

On January 28th Anton Gaspar officially took over as boss of the Paris Mob. He formed an alliance with Pierre Barra, the head of the Marseille Mob, and the peace was negotiated with Jacob and Franklin.

"Gabe, there's one thing that still bothers me," Jacob said.

"Oh? You won. What could still concern you?" Gabe Barra said.

"Not really concerned, just curious," Jacob said.

"What is it?" Barra asked.

"Who was Beaumont visiting in that hotel everyday?" Jacob asked.

"Ahhh. Yes. It was his sister," Barra said.

"His sister. Really." Jacob said.

"Yes, we found out after Beaumont died, that she had a stroke a year ago," Barra said.

Jacob said nothing for a minute then asked. "What can I do to help her? Can I send money for her care?" Jacob asked.

"Nothing, my cousin has taken care of that. She will receive a small cut of the Paris profits until she dies."

"Am I interrupting," Molly asked as she entered the living room.

"No, no. We are just reminiscing. Come sit with us. I leave for Cambodia tomorrow and I will miss your company and our conversations," Barra said.

"Me too," Molly said as she took a seat next to Jacob. "I've invited Gerry, Mercy and Al to lunch so they have a chance to say goodbye to you, Gabe. Franklin and Catherine will be here as well. Our boys are working."

"We talked last night and I had a chance to say goodbye to the children, so I am happy about that. I will miss those little devils." Gabe pulled out several $100 bills from his pocket, put it on the coffee table and said, "Would you please share this amongst the children. Maybe they can buy some candy. It is the last of my American money."

"Oh, Gabe that's so kind of you, but, it's too much. You can turn it in at the airport and get Cambodian money."

"I have plenty more at home. Please give this to them," Gabe said and pushed the money towards Molly.

Molly nodded yes.

"What time is lunch?" Jacob asked.

"1:00 o'clock. You two have 15 minutes to freshen up," Molly answered.

Molly prepared all of Gabe's favorite Philly foods. She started with Taylor Pork Roll sandwiches on Kaiser rolls with American cheese and

Gulden's mustard. As a side dish, she served Rose's potato salad as well as pickles, tomatoe's and lettuce. She had a hard time figuring out which dessert to serve. She knew it would be Tastykakes, but Gabe had tried them all and liked every flavor. She decided on a mix of Chocolate Peanut Butter Tandy Kakes, Lemon Pie and French Apple Pie.

A week after Gabe arrived in Philly, Molly learned that he didn't like the coffee, so she purchased an espresso machine at the Italian Market. She hated the taste, but Gabe was ecstatic. In Gabe's honor, she served everyone espresso Coffee.

Jacob took a sip of the coffee, got up and walked over to the liquor cabinet. He picked up a bottle of Jameson and said, "Only one thing can make this French coffee better, a bit of the Irish."

He poured the Jameson into each person's cup and said, "To Gabe. We will miss you. From today forward you are an honorary Irishman." Jacob downed his doctored coffee and the others followed.

Jacob filled their cups again with Jameson.

Gabe stood up, wiped a tear from his left eye and said, "I am proud to be a French Irishman and more proud to have such friends as all of you. When I worked with Gerry in Cambodia I knew he was from a special family, but I didn't know how special. May you all live long and prosper." Gabe drank his whiskey and the others followed.

Gerry started laughing and asked, "Gabe, where did you hear *live long and prosper*?"

"Why? Is it improper?" Gabe said a bit taken back.

"No, no not at all. It is very nice. Just wondered," Gerry said.

"Well, young Joey. I asked what was the proper toast and he said live long and prosper. Then I saw it on television. You know that man with the funny ears says it. Is something wrong?"

"Absolutely not. It's a fine toast and we appreciate it," Jacob said. "How about another drink."

Jacob poured another round. Mercy said, "May I say something," and didn't wait for an answer. "I just want to tell you that Al and I are seeing each other. We talked to Gerry and he's fine with it," Mercy said. Everyone started laughing. "And what's so funny about that?" Mercy said a bit irritated.

Molly got up and kissed Mercy on the head. "Mercy dear, this is common knowledge. Bella has told everyone in the family. I'm surprised it's not on the channel 6 news."

Gerry stood up and said, "To my wonderful sweet mother and to my best friend Al. May you live long and prosper."

"Gerry, you can call me Dad," Al said and laughed.

Gerry scratched his cheek with his middle finger so Al could see it and said, "Sure, Dad." Al laughed again.

The phone rang and Jacob got up and answered it. A minute later, he hung up and asked everyone to come to the TV room. When they were there he turned on the television set and turned to channel 3 and said, "Mary said there's a special bulletin about Vietnam."

The set came to life and showed video of fighting in the streets of Saigon. It was Chinese New Year or as the Vietnamese call it, Tet. They watched and listened in silence as the news anchor explained that the

North Vietnamese and the Viet Cong had broken the Tet Treaty designed to stop all hostilities for the seven days of the holiday. Instead, they had initiated a full scale attack on every major city in South Vietnam.

"I've got to get word to Tripp to check on the orphanage," Gerry said.

"How?" Al asked.

"I don't know," Gerry said.

"I'll call Senator Wise and see if he can find out anything," Jacob said. "Chances are we're not going to learn much for a couple of days. They must be very busy," Jacob said.

"Will he do that," Al said.

"I'm sure he will. He owes me a couple of favors," Jacob answered.

Images of the children and the Sisters at the orphanage being lined up and shot floated through Gerry's head. *No they wouldn't, couldn't do that,* Gerry thought. Then he remembered the mangled bodies of women and kids lying on the street after the bomb blast that killed Hung.

"I gotta go back over there," Gerry said.
"Over where?" Mercy asked

"Saigon. I got to go help them."

"Use your head, Gerry. What're you going to do? It'll be over one way or another before you get there," Al said.

"I can't sit around and do nothing," Gerry said.

"Let's see what the senator says. Give it a day or two," Jacob said.

"I was afraid of this," Gabe said. "I fear that the communists won't stop until they own South Vietnam and maybe Cambodia; all of Indochina."

"They can't win against the United States. We're too powerful," Al said.

"That's what we said in France, but they kicked us out. They had the will to continue to fight and we didn't."

"No offense, Gabe, but we have the finest army in the world. The men and women we have in Vietnam are more than capable and willing," Al said.

"But are your politicians? Are the mothers and fathers of your brave soldiers willing to sacrifice their children to fight a war so far away? That's what people in France asked and the answer was no," Gabe said.

"I'm not willing," Catherine said, "And I don't have children."

"My fear is that the war will go on until my grandchildren are old enough to fight. I couldn't take that. I gave up a husband in one war and a son that was almost killed in a second war. We've given enough," Molly said.

"Right or wrong we're at war. Our country called and these kids answered. Those protesters have no right to call them baby killers and spit on them when they come home," Franklin said.

"Mercy Row Foundation contributes to veterans causes and I've been to the hospitals. I cry every time I go. Men with arms and legs missing, faces distorted with scars, women disfigured for life. It's horrible," Mercy said.

"Look we can argue all day about the war being just or not, but right now a lot of Vietnamese people and our military are in trouble and I feel so helpless," Gerry Said.

Mercy put her arm around Gerry's shoulder, kissed him on the cheek and said, "It'll work out. Gerry. I am sure of that."

Gerry wasn't so sure.

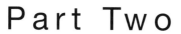

Part Two

# Chapter Thirty-One

*Early April 1975 - Cambodia*

The door to Gabe Barra's villa suddenly blew inward followed by a ball of fire. The noise was deafening and the shock froze Barra to his bed for an instant. It was four in the morning and Barra was still awake. The combination of illness and the news that Vietnam would fall to the communists had given him a wicked case of insomnia.

Barra reached to his nightstand and picked up the new Beretta 92 automatic Tripp Edwards had given him for his birthday. Edwards, who used to fly with Gerry Amato, took Barra up on his offer for employment and joined Barra's organization in 1969, just after he was discharged from the United States Air Force. Over the years, Edwards had proven himself a natural leader, a superb businessman and an excellent gangster. In 1972 he became Barra's second in command of the Cambodian Marijuana growing operation for the Marseille Mob.

Barra's bedroom door burst open and he quickly pointed the gun and readied himself to shoot. He hesitated and saw that it was Tripp Edwards. Tripp was still in his underwear.

"Hold on, Gabe it's me," Tripp Edwards yelled. "Get up we're getting out of here."

Tripp helped Barra out of bed and led him to a door that opened to the rear patio.

"Wait," Barra said and grabbed his robe from the chair.

Barra had been ill for the past week and in his weakened condition, it was difficult for him to walk. Tripp supported him as they went down the steps and then into the jungle behind the house. It was only 100 feet away, but the exertion took its toll on Barra.

"Sit here and I'll go get the Rover. If you see anyone just stay quiet. Don't go anywhere," Tripp said.

"You will not have to worry about that. I can hardly walk," Barra said.

Tripp ran off and Barra pulled himself behind the flora. A couple of minutes later he heard voices. They were definitely speaking Cambodian. Khmer Rouge without a doubt. Barra knew from previous run-ins that the Khmer Rouge soldiers were heartless bastards. They killed men, women and children without any hesitation. Up until now they mostly left him alone because he had a large workforce, all of which Barra had armed. Two days ago, most of his men had deserted him after hearing that Vietnam was going to fall to the Viet Cong. They knew, as did Barra, that Cambodia would also fall under communist rule. It was only a matter of time before a large force came to take Barra's organization out. That time had come faster than Barra had imagined.

Barra could tell by the noise that the Khmer Rouge soldiers were dragging something across the ground. He thought he heard at least three men. They stopped 10 feet in front of him. There was a small clearing between the leaves and Barra could see a man kneeling. It was his Cambodian foreman; one of the few men that did not desert. A Khmer Rouge soldier smacked the foreman on the head and called him a traitor. Then he pointed his rifle at the man and pulled the trigger. The foreman's forehead exploded in a mist of blood. Barra moved slightly backwards.

One of the Khmer Rouge soldiers heard the noise and rushed into the foliage. He was on Barra before he could get his gun from the robe's pocket. The man pulled Barra out of the jungle and pushed him face forward into the dirt. Barra yelled in Cambodian, "I have money. I have a lot of money. I will tell you where it is if you let me go."

The man lifted Barra to his knees and yelled back, "We don't want your money, you imperialist pig shit." Then he lifted his rifle and pointed it at Barra's head.

Barra closed his eyes and said a short prayer and asked God for forgiveness. Then he heard a thunderous noise and he thought maybe that's what you hear when you're shot in the head. He opened his eyes and saw two bright lights coming at him. *Heaven* he thought and that made him happy. An instant later, he realized that it was the Land Rover coming at him. He dropped to his right and rolled.

The three soldiers began firing at the Land Rover. Bullets smashed into the passenger side window shattering it into a thousand pieces. It was a fatal mistake for the soldiers. Barra's Land Rover was purchased in Britain where they drive on the left side of the road and the steering wheel is on the right. Cambodian drivers were on the left side of the car. They had no time to contemplate this because Tripp smashed into the three men knocking one man to the side and rolling over the other two. Just to be sure Tripp backed up over the two men again.

He jumped out of the Land Rover, grabbed Gabe and helped him in the back seat. As he was returning to his seat, the man he had knocked to the side got up and pointed his rifle at Tripp. Three shots rang out and the man fell to the ground. Tripp looked back and saw Gabe holding the Beretta 92 he had given him. Tripp picked up the soldier's rifle and threw it in the vehicle. By the time he was back in the seat, several more soldiers having heard the shots, came from the front of the house. They were about 70 feet in front of the Rover.

Tripp put the vehicle in reverse and floored it. As he did the men opened fire. When he was another 50 feet away, he turned the Rover forward and raced out to the dirt road. The soldiers in front of the house began to fire at the Land Rover. As they raced down the road, Tripp could hear the bullets smashing into the Rover's body. Finally, he was far enough away that the soldiers stopped shooting at him.

"Gabe, you okay?"

"Ok. I am okay. Keep going. Get us to Thailand," Barra said.

"That's about a six hour drive, if we don't run into the Khmer Rouge," Tripp said.

"Do we have enough fuel?"

"Should be. I have a few cans in the back of the Rover," Tripp said.

"Good thing we were leaving today anyway. I was hoping it would have been a little less exciting departure though," Gabe said.

Tripped laughed and said," Rest now. Just lay back and I'll get us to Thailand."

A few minutes later Gabe said, "I smell petro." Tripp drove on and when he thought it was safe, he pulled over and checked the cans of fuel. Two of the three cans were leaking. A bullet had pierced one can midway and the other on the bottom. He put the cans on their side so the leaks stopped. Tripp got in the driver's seat again, shook his head and said, "This is the second time I've been low on fuel in this cesspool of a country."

"Will we make it?" Gabe asked.

"Not sure. We have a full tank and whatever we have left in the cans, which isn't a lot," Tripp answered. "We'll go until we can't go anymore. Gabe, lay back and see if you can sleep a little."

Three hours later, Tripp saw a couple of farmers walking on the road. He had learned conversational Cambodian over the years and asked one of the farmers if he would sell him his pants. They were more like pajama bottoms, but it beat running around in his underwear. He asked the second farmer to sell him his shirt. After some negotiations, Tripp pulled out a wad of Cambodian money, equal to about $400 U.S. dollars and gave it to the men. They quickly took off the clothes and gave them to Tripp, who put the pants on first.

Fortunately, Cambodian farmer clothing was very loose fitting and he was able to get the pants around his waist. The pant legs, however, just covered his knees. The shirt was a different matter. He ripped the back a bit and was able to get his arms in the sleeves but he couldn't button the shirt. The two farmers laughed as they walked away counting their money. Unfortunately for them when the Khmer Rouge took over the country the money probably wouldn't be worth much.

"How are you doing back there, Gabe?" Tripped asked.

"Okay. At least I have a robe that fits," Gabe answered with a small smile.

"Do you want me to stop for a while?"

"No! Keep going. We have to get out of Cambodia," Gabe said.

After four more hours of driving Tripp pulled the Land Rover off the road and into the jungle to hide it. The jostling of the vehicle woke Gabe, who had fallen asleep just after Tripp had left the farmers counting their money.

"What's happening? Is everything alright?" Gabe asked in a sleep groggy voice.

"We got a little problem. The Khmer Rouge have the border crossing guarded. Looks like 10 men," Tripp said.

"Can you bust through?" Gabe asked.

"Nah, not going to happen. We'd be dead before we got a hundred feet. Even if we did make it the Thai guards on the other end would probably take us out." Tripp paused for several seconds and asked,"How you feeling?"

"A little better. Chills have gone away," Gabe said.

"Up for a little stroll in the jungle?" Tripp asked.

"What's your plan?" Gabe asked.

"I'm thinking we make our way a couple hundred yards south of the crossing and the Khmer Rouge. Cross over there and come back on the Thai side and ask the Thai guards for help," Tripp explained.

"I can try."

Tripp helped Gabe from the back seat of the Land Rover, then opened the hood, pulled some wires out and took the distributor cap off and threw it in the foliage.

"No reason to let these assholes have a perfectly good Land Rover," Tripp said.

Tripp and Gabe made their way across the road without being seen, and then moved into the jungle. It was tough going for Gabe. The strength he thought had returned quickly dissipated. Gabe stumbled over a broken tree limb and fell to the ground. Tripp tried to pick him up but Gabe just brushed his hands away and said, "Just leave me."

"Yeah, like that's going to happen," Tripp said and picked Gabe up and threw him over his shoulder. He carried Gabe like that for 200 feet until he came to a dirt road. He carefully laid Gabe on the road and surveyed the area. About 300 feet north of where he was he saw two vehicles and a group of guards. They were wearing Thai Army uniforms.

"We made it, Gabe. This is Thailand," Tripp said. "Can you walk or should I carry you again."

"I can walk," Gabe said, his adrenaline giving him some added strength. There was just no way his would pride allow him to be carried. Tripp took his arm and they walked the 300 feet.

The Thai guards noticed them when they were a couple hundred feet away. They pointed their weapons at Tripp and Gabe, and waited for them to come closer. Once they saw who they were, they grasped the situation and allowed Tripp and Gabe to approach.

"Anyone speak English?" Tripp asked.

The guards looked at each other and shook their heads.

"French?" Tripp asked.

"Yes, I speak a little," one of the guards answered in French.

"We come from Cambodia and seek refuge here. Can you help us?" Gabe asked in French.

The French-speaking guard said, "Yes. We understand. There is a camp a few miles away. We can take you," then he handed Gabe a canteen of water.

"Thank you," Gabe said and took the canteen, drank some water and handed it to Tripp.

The Khmer Rouge guards on the Cambodian side of the boarder had seen the interaction, but didn't seem too interested. That was until a vehicle approached them and four men got out. The guards all came to attention and after a short discussion pointed at the Thai side of the border.

"Looks like they didn't like us offing their men back at the farm. They sent some troops after us," Tripp said.

"Fortunately for us they are a little late," Gabe said.

One of the four men grabbed a rifle from one of the Khmer Rouge guards and began firing at Tripp and Gabe. One of the Thai soldiers fell as the side of his face exploded. The other Khmer Rouge soldiers started to fire as well. The Thai soldiers fell back behind their vehicles and started to fire back. Tripp pushed Gabe to the ground and fell beside him. The Thai soldier who had died had dropped his rifle near Tripp. He grabbed it and started to fire back.

Two Khmer Rouge soldiers dropped as Tripp continued to fire at them. Several more fell to the Thai soldiers efforts. Tripp heard the Thai soldier who had given them water yelling into a radio. He had no idea of what he was saying but Tripp hoped he was calling for help.

Gabe and Tripp were lying behind a small berm, which provided some protection but not much. The Khmer Rouge soldiers stopped firing and took positions behind their own vehicles. Once they felt safe, they began shooting again. Tripp raised his rifle and shot once, hitting one of the enemy in the head. A few seconds later, a bullet ripped through Tripp's upper arm. He fell backwards, rolled over and lay flat on the ground. Meanwhile the Thai soldiers were providing a steady stream of firepower, but it wasn't working. One soldier fell and then another.

Then Tripp heard a familiar sound. It was the sound a rifle makes when it launches a grenade. He covered Gabe with his own body and waited for the blast. The grenade hit the ground and rolled under one of the Thai vehicles. The explosion lifted the vehicle in the air and when it came down it was on its side just five feet from Tripp and Gabe. Tripp grabbed Gabe by the shoulder and said, "Come on. We're getting behind that jeep."

Gabe didn't answer. Tripp shook him again. Still no answer. Then Tripp rolled him over. Gabe stared back at him with lifeless eyes. There was a bullet hole seeping blood in Gabe's chest. Tripp checked Gabe's pulse but he knew Gabe was gone. He kissed the man who had become like a father to him on the forehead, said a short prayer and started shooting at the Khmer Rouge soldiers.

Tripp crawled behind the upturned jeep. Just as he was about to take another shot, he heard the sound of a helicopter. It came in quick and unloaded its Gatling guns on the Khmer Rouge soldiers. After a few seconds, he leaned out from behind the jeep and saw total destruction. The Khmer Rouge vehicles were on fire and he could see limbs and bodies in bloody disarray. Not one of the Khmer Rouge soldiers was left alive. The helicopter turned and headed back to wherever it had come from.

The Thai officer in charge walked over to Gabe and checked his pulse and said to Tripp, "I'm sorry about your friend. One of my men will take you and him to the camp."

"I thought you didn't speak English," Tripp said.

"Well, it's best not to show all your cards to strangers"

"Your English is perfect," Tripp said.

"Berkley graduate. I told everyone and acted like I was one of the oppressed Vietnamese getting a degree so I could return and help my oppressed people. It did wonders for my sex life. Americans like to help oppressed people, I think," the officer said.

"Yeah," Tripp said.

"Come, I'll help you with your friend. It's time to get you back to the camp," the officer said.

"I got him," Tripp said and picked Gabe up with his good arm and hoisted him on his shoulder.

# Chapter Thirty-Two

April 12, 1975

During the seven years after Gabriel Barra, helped the Byrne family fight off attacks from the Paris Mob, Gerry Byrne had visited him in Cambodia three times. Each visit became progressively more dangerous. Communist Cambodians, who called themselves the Khmer Rouge, backed by North Vietnam, were marauding throughout the country killing anyone who resisted them. In 1973 the United States abandoned the War in Vietnam, promising to help with materials and medical aid but most of its military left the country.

When that happened Gerry knew it was the end. America had lost its will to win the war. It was only a matter of time before South Vietnam would fall to the communists. And what happened to Vietnam would happen to Cambodia and Laos. He had spent two years trying to convince Gabe Barra and Tripp Edwards to abandon the farm and leave Cambodia, but Gabe stubbornly refused. Gerry gave up and told Gabe that if he ever needed him he would be there. Gerry also offered Tripp Edwards a position in Byrne Air Freight. He also refused.

Gabe and Tripp were grown man and it was their right to stay, but the children from the orphanage, Hoi Duc Anh, where Gerry volunteered when he was in the Air Force, were innocents. In 1973 he enlisted the help of his now deceased friend Nguyen Van Hung's family to help him to convince the Vietnamese government to allow him to bring these children to the United States. Hung's eldest daughter Mai's position as a translator at the U.S. embassy provided her with the ability to negotiate with both the Vietnamese and U.S. government officials to have the children immigrate to the U.S.

Mai's father, Hung was killed by a Viet Cong terrorist bomb in 1967 while waiting for Gerry outside the orphanage. His daughter, Mai was to be married a few weeks later but she canceled the wedding because of her Father's death. After six months, she married Tran Van Tam, a Captain in the South Vietnamese army. On the one-year anniversary of her father's death, Captain Tam was killed in action in Cu Chi.

Mai worked tirelessly to try to get approval from both governments, but was refused on all levels. The official view of both the U.S. and South Vietnamese was that they would win the war and there was no need to take so desperate of an action. If they allowed the orphans to leave it would send the wrong message.

On April 3rd 1975, when they finally realized that Vietnam was lost, U.S. President Gerald Ford announced Operation Baby Lift. Mai contacted the office controlling Operation Baby Lift but was told that the thirty flights approved for the airlift were already booked and there was no way the children at Hoi Duc Anh would be able to leave on any of these flights. Mai was out of options and informed Gerry that there was no recourse except to ride out the storm should Saigon fall. The prevalent view, by citizens of Saigon was that if the communist took the city there would be a bloodbath. They thought that anyone who had worked with the Americans or South Vietnamese government would be the first to go and that mixed raced children would be burnt alive.

On April 8th Gerry received a telegram from Tripp Edwards informing him of Gabe Barra's death at the hands of the Khmer Rouge. Gerry was devastated. Barra had become a close friend and confidant of Gerry's over the years since Barra had helped save his family from the revenge of Henri Beaumont, the head of the Paris Mob. Barra had made it clear to Tripp that should he die he wanted to be returned to France for burial in the family cemetery with his mother, father and cousin Pierre, who had passed away three years before.

After Barra's body had been sent to France, Tripp called Gerry and told him he was staying in Thailand for a while, so he could settle Gabe Barra's affairs. After that, if the job offer was still open, he would come work for Gerry. Shipments of pot from Barra hadceased in late 1972 when it was clear the U.S. was pulling out of the war in Vietnam. Gerry was able to make up the difference by obtaining increased volume from Alberto Rivera in Mexico and by planting his own fields in New Jersey.

Tripp's opinion was that Vietnam would fall within the month, as would Laos and Cambodia. The situation was dire.

Gerry decided it was time to take action. If the government wouldn't save the orphans at Hoi Duc Anh, he would do it. And while he was there he would save his departed friend Hung's family. He set up a meeting to tell his own family what he was about to do.

"I'm going to Saigon and I'm bringing the kids and nuns from Hoi Duc Anh home to America," Gerry said, as the family and he sat around his Grandfather Jacob's old conference table. When Jacob and Molly Byrne and Franklin and Catherine Garrett retired to Florida, Jacob insisted that Mercy move to his home in Lower Moreland. She reluctantly agreed, sold her Wishart Street houses and she and her husband Al Watson moved to the larger house. Franklin asked Gerry to take his home over and keep it maintained so they would have a place to stay when they visited.

"If the government can't get these kids out, how the hell are you going to do it?" Jake asked.

"Even if you can get them out, how can you get them back here? You need a place for them and you need immigration papers. I don't see how this will work, Gerry," Jimmy said.

"That's why I asked for this meeting. First of all, I have discussed this with my Mom. At first she wasn't very happy, but she understands we are talking about children here, children with no families to protect them. Mom has agreed to try to find a place for them," Gerry explained.

"I have connections in various orphanages we support, so I think I can get them placed. Gerry says there are 73 children. We'll up our support to the orphanages that take the children Gerry brings back," Mercy said.

"What about getting them immigration status? It takes years for people to immigrate here. Do you really think you can bring them in the country with no repercussions?" Jimmy said.

"Yeah I do. We bring in drugs, don't we? If I have to smuggle them in, I will. But, I would rather it be legal. That's why I'm asking you and Jake to grease the way with your politician friends," Gerry said.

"Tall order," Jake said.

"I got plenty of money. Pay them whatever they want. One way or another I'm bringing those kids back here," Gerry said his voice raising in frustration.

"Mercy, are you okay with this?" Charlie asked.

"No. Of course not! Do you think I want my only son to go back to a war-torn country? But, like he said, we're talking about children. It breaks my heart to think what may happen to them."

"Jimmy's going to have to deal with the politicians alone," Jake said.

"Gerry sunk back in his chair feeling deflated and said, "Why, Uncle Jake?"

"Because I'm going with you," Jake said.

Gerry sat up, tilted his head, smiled and said, "I'll need some pilots. Anybody know any good ones?"

"I'm in," Al Watson said.

Gerry had also invited Jerome to the meeting. Everyone now looked at him. Jerome nodded his head up and down and said, "You bet your sweet bippy."

"You been watching reruns of Laugh In?" Gerry asked. Jerome shrugged his shoulders and smiled.

"What's the plan. How do we get them out?" Jake asked.

"I have Tripp buying two C-123 in Thailand. There's a lot of surplus there since we pulled out. He'll make the purchase as Byrne Air Freight. One is a backup. Should anything happen to one of the planes we should be able to fit all the kids and nuns in the other airplane. After we get them back we'll have the planes sent back to Philly and I'll use them at Byrne Air Freight or leave them if we have to." Gerry said.

"So you just fly across Cambodia and into Vietnam. Is that what you're saying?" Al asked.

"That's about it. Things are so screwed up in Cambodia with the government fighting the Khmer Rouge they won't even know we're there. Once we get to Vietnam we'll identify ourselves as Air American planes coming to evacuate VIPs."

"Never heard of that airline," Jerome said.

"And you won't. It's a CIA front. They've been flying in Indochina for years. Most of their aircraft is unmarked so no one will even question us," Gerry answered.

"Okay, so we fly into Ton Son Knut Airport. Then what?" Al asked.

"No, we fly into Bien Hoa. The airbase is smaller and will probably be in chaos since it's a ways out of the city of Saigon. The VC will take that before they can get to Saigon," Gerry answered.

"What if the communists take the airbase before you get there? Can you turn around and come back to Thailand?" Mercy asked.

Al grabbed Mercy's hand and said, "No, by then we would be low on fuel. We would have to land. We would try Ton Son Knut in Saigon and pray."

"In either case we need to be sure we have transportation to go pick up the kids. The airbase is about 20 miles from Saigon. I have Tripp buying two surplus troop transport trucks. We'll fill them with cans of fuel and each aircraft will carry one to Bien Hoa. That way we have fuel for the return trip and transportation to pick up the kids and get them back to Bien Hoa," Gerry explained.

"Then what?" Charlie asked.

"We're going to charter a Boeing 747. Uncle Jimmy, this is important. Our first U.S. port of entry will be Anchorage, Alaska. We need to be sure they clear us so we can fly directly to Philadelphia from Anchorage," Gerry said.

"How much time do we have?"

"We need to leave here in seven days and if it goes well, we should be back in a week," Gerry said.

"I better get on the phone. The wheels of government turn slowly. I have an old army buddy who's a senator in Nevada. I'll start with him, " Jimmy said.

"Gerry, you seem to have this well thought out. How long have you been planning this?" Jake asked.

"About a year. Once I saw how both the Vietnamese and U.S. governments were not going to do anything I thought as Grandpop Jacob always says...," Gerry was interrupted when everyone in the room said in chorus, "Better safe than sorry." They all laughed.

# Chapter Thirty-Three

April 18, 1975

Gerry listened to the right side engine. It sounded good. He then started the left side engine and listened. It also sounded good. Tripp had found two C-123's in very good condition. He had the planes flown to a small airfield at a poppy plant farm near the border with Cambodia. The farm was one of several owned by a friend and supplier of heroin to the Barra Mob.

"Where's Mary?" Gerry asked Tripp after walking down the plane's cargo ramp.

"In the medical tent."

Gerry walked over to a cluster of tents they had erected on the right side of the runway. He opened the flap to the tent and was assailed by the strong odor of medical alcohol. Mary was cleaning a wound on one of the twenty Royal Thailand Army veterans Tripp had hired for security.

"Mary, do you have all the medical supplies you wanted?" Gerry asked.

"Yes, it looks right," Mary Byrne answered

Mary Byrne, Jimmy's daughter, received her Medical Doctorate in 1971 and she interned in pediatrics at the Hospital of the University of Pennsylvania, where she was also a pediatrics resident for two years. Late in 1974 she took a position at a Kensington free clinic that was partially supported by the Mercy Row Foundation. When Mary heard that Gerry was going to Vietnam to rescue children, she insisted that she go along to provide medical aid. Her father forbade her to go, but Mary's bullheadedness and persistence won out. She agreed that she would stay in Thailand and wait for the children there.

"If you need anything else while we're gone, ask Sarawut. He'll get you what you need," Gerry said.

"When are we leaving?" Mary asked.

"Tomorrow morning. What do you mean we?"

Yeah, well you see I'm going with you," Mary said.

"Absolutely not! Uncle Jimmy will kill me if I let you go."

"I'll sing at your funeral then, because I am going," Mary said.

"Mary, no way. This is a dangerous thing we're doing."

"So you think men are the only ones that can face danger? Is that it?" Mary asked.

Gerry stammered and said, "No, but..."

Mary interrupted him. "Look, you have 73 kids to bring back. Do you think some of them won't need my help. If you do then you know nothing about children. I'm going even if I have to sneak one of the planes," Mary said.

Jake Byrne lifted the tent flap, heard the argument, quickly replaced it and started to walk off. Gerry yelled after him, "Uncle Jake. We need you."

Jake stopped, shook his head back and forth and returned to the tent.

"What do you need?" Jake asked.

"Mary won't listen to reason. She's insisting that she come with us to Vietnam. Please talk to her," Gerry pleaded.

Jake patted Gerry on the back and said, "The only woman I have ever met that was more stubborn, more headstrong, and more persistent than your Mother Mercy, is Dr. Mary Byrne. She's already won this augment and you don't even know it."

Mary smiled. Jake winked at her. Gerry walked out of the tent.

Five minutes later Gerry came back to the tent holding a holster and a .45. He placed it on the table next to Mary. "Can you shoot this?"

"Better than you. My dad had me at the range for months after I was kidnapped," Mary said.

"Okay, we leave at 0800, eight o'clock to you. Bring that gun and any medical supplies you need. You'll fly in my plane," Gerry said and walked out of the tent.

"Thanks, Uncle Jake," Mary said.

"Don't get hurt kid," Jake said and left to follow Gerry.

When Jake caught up with Gerry, he said, "I have the guys waiting in your tent. We should go over the details again."

When Gerry entered the tent, it took a minute for his eyes to adjust from the bright sun. When they did he saw, Al, Jerome, and Paul Jefferies, an ex-U.S. Air Force pilot Tripp had found, sitting at a table. Tripp Edwards walked in behind Gerry and Jake and introduced the team to a Thai national who was with him.

"Gentlemen, meet Prem Tag... Ahh Tagula.... Oh fuck it. Just call him Captain Prem. Prem is the leader of our security team," Tripp said. Each man shook Prem's hand and welcomed him to the team.

"Captain Prem has 20 seasoned soldiers, some of who you met already. These are top-notch fighters. Captain Prem is an ex-Royal Army Special Forces officer and he speaks English," Tripp said.

"Captain Prem, 10 of your men will be with Jerome and Paul on their aircraft. The rest of them and yourself will be on my plane. What kind of weapons do you carry?" Gerry asked.

Prem spoke with a slight British accent, "Each man has a M16A1 rifle and a handgun as well. We have two cases of American hand grenades and two M60 machine guns."

"Good, when we get to Bien Hoa, 10 of your men will go with us in the trucks. The other 10 will protect the aircraft. If anything happens to those airplanes, we're all fucked. Understand?"

"Yes, of course," Prem answered.

"Is the 747 ready in Bangkok?" Gerry asked Tripp.

"It arrives tomorrow morning. It'll be waiting when we get there."

"Jerome, when we get to Bien Hoa, we'll identify ourselves as Air America. If they ask you, tell them you're picking up VIPs for evacuation. Hopefully the Vietnamese air controllers will buy it," Gerry said.

"If they don't?"

"We land anyway."

"Okay, that's it. Tripp, have the trucks in the aircraft by 0700. We leave at 0800."

# Chapter Thirty-Four

Gerry leveled off at 11,000 feet and gave control of the C-123 to Al Watson. He turned in his seat and asked, "Mary, you okay?"

"Yep. It's pretty exciting."

"Let's hope this is as exciting as it gets. Keep your seat belt on. We could hit some bumpy air," Gerry said.

"Is that the technical term? Bumpy air," Mary joked.

"No. I just use easy-to-understand language with nitwits like you, cuz," Gerry said, smiled and walked into the cargo area.

"The truck holding?" Gerry asked.

"Yeah, I remember how to tie down cargo," Tripp said.

"Everybody's a smart ass today," Gerry said and patted Tripp on the shoulder. "How you doing, Tripp?"

"Okay, I guess. That old man was like a father to me. I miss him," Tripp said.

"Yeah, me too," Gerry said and paused for a minute. "Tell the men to eat something and get some sleep. We'll be there in about four hours. After that it might be a while until we can rest."

Gerry picked up a large paper bag and a thermos and brought it to the cockpit. He handed both to Mary and said, "Sandwiches. Some coffee too."

Mary opened the bag, took out two sandwiches, and handed one to Al and another to Gerry.

"When you're done eating, try to get a couple of winks, Mary," Al said. "Gerry, you too."

"Wake me in two hours. I'll take the second shift," Gerry said.

Three and a half hours later Al shook Gerry's shoulder and said, "Wake up, man. Half hour to Bien Hoa."

Gerry opened his eyes and shook his head back and forth to get the cobwebs out of his brain, then said, "Damn it Al. You were supposed to wake me."

"You just looked so damned cute sleeping I couldn't wake you up, you being my son and all."

Gerry lifted his hand, three fingers sticking up and said, "Read between the lines."

"Naughty, naughty, cousin Gerry. What would Aunt Mercy say?" Mary said jokingly.

"Who do you think taught me that," Gerry said, got up and walked back to the cargo area.

"Captain Prem, we're close to Bien Hoa. Can we harness a couple of your men and post them to each of the rear doors. Let them use the M60s. Just a precaution in case the commies take some pot shots," Gerry said.

"Yes. Done," Prem said and barked some orders to his men.

"Wait till I tell you then open the doors and get set up."

Gerry went back to the cockpit and radioed Jerome to do the same.

When they reached 5,000 feet, Gerry told Prem to post his men.

Gerry picked up the microphone and said, "Bien Hoa Controller, come in. This is Air America number 4578 requesting landing."

The radio cracked and a heavy accent voice said, "No land. No land."

Gerry replied making crackling sounds in the middle of his words trying to confuse the controller. "Cannot read you. Repeat. Must land, emergency."

He looked at Al and pointed down. Al pushed the yoke down and the plane began to lose altitude. "Follow us in, Jerome," Gerry said into the mic.

The Bien Hoa controller kept saying, "No land. No land," over the speaker.

At about 1,000 feet, Al heard the M60's rhythmic chant. He looked out the right window and saw a small group of men wearing the uniform of the VC, black pajamas, running into the jungle.

"Oh shit, there's a car in the middle of the runway," Gerry yelled.

The wheels of the plane touched down. The plane barreled down the runway at 100 miles per hour. As they approached the car, three men jumped out and ran to the side of the runway. Al steered the plane as far as he could to the left without hitting the dirt. His right wing passed over the car. Jerome seeing what Al had done did the same. They pulled up at the end of the runway and turned both planes so they pointed back the way they had come.

Gerry ran to the cargo area and pulled the lever to let the cargo door down. One of Prem's men jumped in the driver's seat, while five others ran down the ramp and surrounded the airplane. Tripp loosened the straps and the driver backed down the ramp. Prem's other men immediately started to unload the cans of fuel. Even before they were done unloading, Al was supervising two of the men as they started to refuel the aircraft.

Gerry checked on Jerome in the second plane and saw that he had everything under control. He ran back to Al and said, "If it looks like you're going to get overrun get out of here. Those VC were close."

Before Al could say anything Gerry ran back to the truck and jumped in the passenger seat. Prem was driving and he pulled the now-empty truck to the side of the runway. That's when Gerry saw the car he had almost hit speeding towards them. Prem also saw it, jumped out of the truck and ordered two of his men to point their rifles at the car. Gerry got out of the truck and said, "Prem, stop them but don't kill them. Looks like a South Vietnamese staff car."

Prem said something in Thai and the two men opened fire hitting the runway 100 feet in front of the car. The car stopped, did a u-turn and went back up the runway. Prem and Gerry got back into the truck and started up the runway as well. Jake followed in the second truck. When they reached the airbase exit there were several South Vietnamese soldiers in front of a flimsy wooden gate.

"Go through it," Gerry yelled

Prem accelerated. The South Vietnamese guards seeing the trucks were not stopping, jumped out of the way just before Prem smashed through the wooden barricade. Pieces of the wood hit the windshield and harmlessly bounced off.

Saigon was about an hour, depending on the traffic, from Bien Hoa. The road to the capital city passed through several small villages and acres of raw jungle and farms. At any point, the Viet Cong could attack them. Gerry had read that the North Vietnamese army had taken the key cities of Hue and Da Nang and were rapidly moving south towards Saigon. They hadn't arrived yet and he felt sure the biggest threat was the VC, who were experts at guerrilla warfare, but wouldn't have tanks or heavy artillery.

"Prem, we need to watch out for VC. Have the men stay alert," Gerry said.

Prem barked some commands in his radio. The Thai soldiers in both trucks rolled up the canvas on both sides and took positions with their rifles pointed outward. They had left one M60 machine gun with Al. The other one was positioned on the roof of the cab of the second truck.

Approximately 10 miles outside of Saigon the traffic stopped. Gerry climbed on top of the truck cab to see what was happening. He saw several jeeps blocking the road and at least 10 Army of the Republic of Vietnam soldiers checking various vehicles and carts. Gerry climbed down from the cab and walked back to Jake's truck.

"Hang out here for a minute. I'll check and see what's happening," Gerry said

"Hurry up. I don't like sitting here. I feel like a fish in a barrel," Jake said.

Gerry walked back to his truck and asked Prem to come with him. Prem picked up a rifle and hopped out of the truck. As Gerry and Prem got closer, he noticed that the ARVN soldiers were not just searching the vehicles, they were taking anything they found of value.

An ARVN officer approached them, his pistol drawn from his holster, and asked," Who you?"

"CIA" Gerry answered.

The officer spoke a few commands and three soldiers pointed their rifles at Gerry and Prem. Another soldier took Gerry's .45s and Prem's weapons. They handed the .45s to the officer and placed the other weapons on the hood of a black Citron car that was waiting to get through the barricade.

"You money?" the officer asked and held out his hand.

"Yes. In truck," Gerry said making a sign as if he were using a steering wheel.

"Go money," the officer ordered.

"Prem, go get this officer $10,000 will you," Gerry said and smiled at the officer.

The officer motioned to his men and two of them followed Prem to the truck.

Gerry looked into the Citron and saw an older man and a woman he assumed was the man's wife. He walked over to the car, bent down and asked, "Speak English?"

The man looked at Gerry, thought for a second and answered, "Yes."

"Can you translate for me?" Gerry asked.

The man got out of the car, straightened his tie and stood next to Gerry. The ARVN officer said something to the man in Vietnamese. Gerry didn't understand.

The man replied to the officer and then said to Gerry, "He wants to know what I'm doing. I told him you want me to translate. He said, so translate. What would you like to say?"

"Ask him why he is blocking the road and stealing these people's valuables?"

The man translated. The officer moved closer to Gerry, pointed a pistol at his head and said something in Vietnamese.

"He says, none of your business."

Gerry put his hands in front of him and said, "Tell him okay. None of my business." The man translated. The officer lowered the gun.

The ARVN officer said something to the man. The man translated for Gerry his voice a bit shaky, "He says shut up or he'll kill you, then he'll kill me and my wife for helping you."

"Nice guy," Gerry said.

"Not all soldiers are like this. We have good officers who tried to keep our country free. My son gave his life for that purpose. This, excuse me, piece of shit is not a good officer," the man said then spit on the ground.

The ARVN officer yelled something at the man. The man replied. "What did he say?" Gerry asked.

"He wanted to know what we were talking about."

"What'd you tell him?"

"I told him you asked if we had seen any VC. And I told you, fuck the VC."

Gerry smiled, and asked, "What's your name?

"Tam."

"Mr. Tam, why are you going to Saigon?" Gerry asked.

"I was a professor at a college in Hue. We left before the communist took over. We have nothing left in Hue, so I took some small things and my wife and I came to Saigon to start over. Now this man has taken the little that we had."

The ARVN officer yelled something, hit Tam then walked to the Citron and dragged Tam's wife from the car. He pointed the gun at the woman's head and yelled again.

"He said we are to shut up or he'll kill my wife," the man said his voice shaking.

Five minutes later Prem came back holding a brown paper bag. He gave it to Gerry. The two guards were not with him.

"Tam, tell him I have the money."

Tam said something in Vietnamese and at the same time Gerry reached into the bag, pulled out a small pistol, pointed it at the ARVN officer's head and pulled the trigger. A small hole appeared on the officer's forehead and he collapsed to the ground. Ten of Prem's men came out from the trees and pointed their rifles at the other ARVN soldiers. The soldiers dropped their weapons.

"Tam, please tell those in line that if they had items taken to come retrieve them. Tell everyone if they want to follow us into Saigon to pull over to the side of the road after they pass through the barricade. Then they can follow us," Gerry said.

Tam went off to tell the people in the long line. Gerry had Prem's men strip all insignia from the ARVN soldiers' shirts. Then he pointed back towards Bien Hoa and said, "Di di Mau." The soldiers, relieved they were to live started running.

"Where are the two soldiers who went to the truck with you?" Gerry asked Prem.

Prem ran a finger across his neck and walked after the ARVN soldiers.

When Tam finished talking to the other Vietnamese, he came back to Gerry and said, "Some will follow. Others just want to go. Thank you for being an honorable man."

Gerry looked at Tam for a minute and then said, "What're you and your wife going to do now?"

"We will try to find somewhere to hide in Saigon and when the communist come, maybe they will not find us," Tam said.

"Tam, have you ever considered coming to the U.S.A?" Gerry said.

Tam stammered and said, "No, but everyone talks about how nice it is."

"We're on our way to an orphanage to pick up seventy three children and four nuns. I am bringing them back to my city, Philadelphia," Gerry explained.

"Ahhh yes, the Liberty Bell."

"These kids are going to need a teacher, someone to teach them to speak English and learn our ways. Would you like that job?" Gerry said.

Tam's eyes opened wide in surprise and he said, "May I talk to my wife about this?"

"Sure."

Tam walked over to his wife who had gotten back in the Citron car and spent five minutes speaking to her. He came back and said, "My wife said she will accept your generous offer, with one condition."

"What's that?"

"She wants to help teach the children also. My wife was a teacher in Hue, you see," Tam said.

"Deal," Gerry said and put his hand out. Tam took it and shook it robustly.

"Prem, I'll drive Professor Tam's car."

There was one more checkpoint before they reached the city proper, but they had no problem and the soldiers allowed the convoy through. The streets of Saigon were pretty much the same as Gerry remembered. More crowded, maybe. People were going about their lives with little care about what was to befall them. *Truth was*, Gerry thought *many of these people probably don't know how dire the situation is.*

The Citron and the two trucks pulled up in front of the Hoi Duc Anh Orphanage. Gerry saw that it had not changed much in the years that he was gone. The bar across the street was rebuilt after the VC bombed it and killed his friend Hung. Gerry felt a debt to Hung's family and had sent a telegram a week before telling them to bring anyone in the family that wanted to leave to the orphanage on this day. He hoped they had come.

# Chapter Thirty-Five

Prem deployed his men around the trucks and at the door to the orphanage. When Gerry entered the orphanage a young nun ran up to him, hugged him and said, "Mr. Gerry, me so glad to see you."

When she released her embrace, Gerry looked at her, but didn't recognize the petite nun. He stammered to say something.

The nun saw this, smiled and said, "You have chocolate for children today, Mr. Gerry?"

Gerry blinked then his mind flooded with recognition. "Cam? Little Cam?"

Cam nodded yes, took Gerry's hand and said," Come, Sister Kim waiting for you."

Jake followed Gerry into the orphanage after telling Professor Tam and his wife to wait in the car. Gerry and Jake walked up the stairs and then into the main assembly room. All 73 children were there, holding onto small plastic bags that held all of their short lives' possessions. Sister Kim was sitting at a table with two other sisters. When she saw Gerry, she cried.

Gerry walked over to her and hugged Sister Kim and said, "I'm here now. The children are safe. We're going to America." Then Gerry reached into his pocket, pulled out a can of Spam, handed it to Sister Kim, and said, "And you can have all the Spam that you want."

Sister Kim took Gerry's hand, kissed it and said, "Thank you and thank God."

"Sister, we need to get the children in the trucks. Our planes are waiting in Bien Hoa. The faster we get out of here the better."

Sister Kim rose from her chair, swooned and fell back down.

"Are you ill, Sister?" Gerry asked.

Cam said, "She take care some kids who sick. Now she sick."

"We have a doctor with us. We'll take care of her and the children who are ill. But, now we must go," Gerry said.

Cam said something to the children in Vietnamese and they all stood up and got in line. Young girls took the babies who couldn't walk yet, positioned them on their hips, and waited. Then Cam started walking to the trucks and the children followed.

Sister Kim said something to one of the other nuns, then Kim said, "Mr. Gerry, your friend here. I send Sister Bich go get them."

When Sister Bich returned, four adults and three children followed her. Gerry had never actually met Hung's family in person, but heard Hung talk about them all the time. He especially would praise his daughter Mai's beauty and her kind nature. Gerry had talked to Mai on the phone a number of times over the last couple of years, but he was not prepared when she walked up to him and introduced herself.

Mai was as beautiful as her father had claimed, maybe even more beautiful. She was slender and tall for a Vietnamese. Her almond-shaped brown eyes were bright and clear. Gerry hesitated a minute, then took her hand and said, "Gerry Amato."

"I know," Mai said and bowed.

"Mai, please take the family to the trucks. Tell them to leave their clothing and suitcases and just take what they really need. We're short of space in the trucks. Tell them I'll buy them new clothing in the U.S.," Gerry said.

Mai bowed her head, turned and spoke to her family in Vietnamese. A couple of them seemed to complain about leaving their suitcases, but Mai's mother snapped at them and they did as Gerry wished.

"Uncle Jake, can you help take Sister Kim to Professor Tam's car. I'll see to it that Hung's family is situated," Gerry said.

Jake said, "I'm sure you will." Then he smiled and picked up Sister Kim and started for the truck.

The road back to Bien Hoa was packed with people going in the opposite direction, towards Saigon. It was a small road and the crowds impeded Gerry's convoy, making the trip a lot longer than it should've been. Gerry asked Professor Tam to find out why there were so many more people going to Saigon. Tam stopped several refugees and found out that the city of Xuan Loc was under attack and was expected to fall any day. It was the last outpost to protect an all out attack on Saigon. Bien Hoa, was between Xuan Loc and Saigon, and had no chance for survival once Xuan Loc fell. The question on Gerry's mind was, *when would it fall*?

The convoy was on the road for two hours when they came upon the same roadblock they had encountered when they were going to Saigon. There were three ARVN soldiers holding up traffic. When they saw the familiar trucks, they ran into the jungle.

"That's those same sons of bitches that were there earlier. Prem, Have your men get them," Gerry said.

Prem spoke into the radio and five of his men ran after the soldiers. Several minutes later there were gunshots. A few minutes after that Prem's men came out of the trees with two of the ARVN soldiers.

"Where's the third guy?" Gerry asked

One of Prem's men drew his finger across his throat, and then grinned.

"Ask Professor Tam to write two signs in Vietnamese. They should say I STOLE FROM THE VIETNAMESE PEOPLE," Gerry said and pointed. "I want you to tie them to the post there and put that sign around their necks."

Prem found some paper and did as Gerry asked. As they pulled away, some of the refugees were stopping and spiting on the two ARVN soldiers. *They're getting what they deserve*, Gerry thought.

The two trucks and one Citron automobile arrived at the Bien Hoa Airbase an hour later. It was five o'clock in the evening. Sister Cam, the other sisters and Mai supervised getting the children off the trucks and into the airplanes. Each plane had enough food to feed about fifty people. Al and Paul passed out the food packs to the children then started to prep the airplanes for takeoff.

"It's five fifteen already. By the time we make it back to the airfield in Thailand it'll be nine. Damn it. I was hoping we could get back before dark. We can't land at the field in the dark. They have no lighting," Gerry said.

"So we stay here until daybreak," Jake said.

"I'm worried about the VC. They know that it's only a matter of time before the North Vietnamese get here and take the field. They might start harassing what's left of the ARVN Army," Gerry said.

"We don't have a choice. I'm not trying to land a plane full of children in the pitch dark. It's suicide," Jerome said.

"I know. Okay, we stay until morning. We have to get those kids out of the planes when the sun goes down. It's too hot in there," Gerry said.

"Uncle Jake, can you tell Prem what we're doing? Have him post guards through the night. We'll go tell Paul and Al," Gerry asked.

"Done," Jake said.

Mary Byrne checked out the children and found two that were ill. She moved them and Sister Kim to the Citron, gave them antibiotics and made them eat something.

Sister Cam and the other sisters explained to the other children that they would stay the evening, and then fly to Thailand and on to America. Some of the children had brought small blankets with them. They laid them out for the babies, then the rest of the children lay on the sun warmed tarmac. The women all snuggled close to them and gave some comfort.

When the children settled down and fell asleep, Gerry checked on Prem's men. It was nine in the evening and it was very dark. There was no moon and the stars provided only a small measure of light. It was always amazing to Gerry how many stars there were and how many more you could see when there was no light from the surroundings. In all his years in Philly, he had never seen as many stars as had appeared in that evening. He sat on the tarmac and star gazed.

Gerry's moment of peace ended with several of Prem's men yelling. He jumped up and looked where the men were pointing and saw two small lights coming quickly at them. As the lights became larger, Gerry told Prem to ready his men. The lights stopped approximately 200 feet away. He heard a door shut and then saw four figures walking toward them backlit by the lights. They looked like walking shadows, all with their hands up. There was one large figure, a smaller figure and two even smaller figures. Gerry told Prem to have his men lower their weapons.

Army of the Republic of Vietnam Colonel Nguyen Van Hien stepped up to Gerry and said something in Vietnamese. Gerry put his hand up to stop him and said to Prem, "Get Professor Tam."

When Professor Tam arrived, he asked the colonel what he wanted. The colonel explained that his wife and two children came from Saigon to be with him two weeks before and that he was now afraid for their lives. The VC and the North Vietnamese Army would not treat the family of a senior officer kindly. The officer put his hands together as if he was praying, and pleaded that Gerry take his wife and children to safety.

Tam translated what Colonel Hien had asked. Gerry thought for a few minutes and said, "Okay, we'll take them. The colonel also.

Tam translated what Gerry had said and Colonel Hien bowed and thanked him. He told Professor Tam that he could not go. His duty was to defend Bien Hoa Airbase. Then he kissed his children, embraced his wife and walked off into the two shining headlights. As his car turned and headed back down the runway, his children cried, "Ba, Ba không đi. Ba, Ba không đi." Tam told Gerry they were saying "Father, Father don't go."

After the car was out of sight, Gerry took the colonel's family to where the children from his airplane were sleeping. He asked Professor Tam to get them some food if they were hungry, and show them where to sleep. Before Gerry left, the colonel's wife took his hand and laid three four-ounce gold bracelets in it. Gerry took her hand and gave the bracelets back. He told Tam to tell her that she would need these in America. The wife bowed several times and Gerry walked back to the front of his aircraft. He lay down by the wheel and in a few minutes was asleep.

# Chapter Thirty-Six

There was a loud explosion and Gerry woke with a start. Then another explosion further down the runway got him to his feet. Prem ran up to Gerry and told him that the explosions were probably mortar shells and that they were coming from the left side of the runway.

Gerry took a quick look at his watch. It was five in the morning. If they left now it would be after nine when they landed back in Thailand. He thought, *better to take a chance taking off in the dark then getting creamed by a mortar.* Then he said, "Prem, get everyone on the planes as fast as you can. We're leaving." Prem nodded and ran off.

Al, Jake, Jerome, and Paul Jefferies ran up to Gerry and asked what was happening. Gerry told them and said, "Get the planes ready, we're leaving now. Uncle Jake, be sure Mary's on my plane.

Gerry started his plane's engine; first the left, then the right engine. He asked Al to see if everyone was on the plane. There had been several more explosions since the first two, but they were up the runway. The VC probably didn't know they were there. If they found out that would be the end of them. He picked up the microphone and said, "Jerome, you loaded up?"

Jerome said, "Roger, we're good to go."

A minute later Al came to the cockpit, took the right seat and said, "They're on."

"Here we go," Gerry said as they started to roll down the runway. There were two more explosions a lot closer now. At 1,500 feet, Gerry pulled back on the yoke and the front end of the C-123 started to rise and then they were in the air climbing as fast as he could.

Once Gerry was off, Jerome started down the runway. Soon they were at 500 feet, then 700 feet. As they approached 1,000 feet, a sudden explosion to the right side pushed the C-123 to the left slowing its momentum. Jerome struggled to keep it on the runway and regained speed. There was another explosion behind them. As they approached the 1,500 foot mark Jerome was not up to take-off speed. He pushed the controls for the two jet-assisted engines and the plane lurched forward. At 1,800 feet Jerome left the runway. He put the plane into a steep ascent, assisted by the jet engines.

Once they reached a reasonable altitude, he reduced the climb angle. He heard Gerry's voice over the speaker. "Jerome, take her to 10,000 feet,"

"Roger," Jerome said. Then he turned to Paul and saw blood on his shirt. "What the hell? Are you hurt?"

"Not bad. Something came through the fuselage. Hit me in the arm. I'll get the first aid kit."

"Check on the kids while you're back there. See if everyone's ok," Jerome said.

Paul walked towards the back, checking the passengers as he went. He noticed two children crying and holding a woman. He stopped to see what was wrong and noticed that the woman was not moving. He tapped her shoulder to wake her, but she didn't move. It was then he noticed blood and a small hole on the fuselage behind the woman. He checked her pulse and there was none. He picked up her head, turned it and saw a small hole, blood oozing from it, at the base of her brain.

Paul motioned to the adults next to the children to hold them. Then he picked up the woman and started back towards the cockpit. The sounds of the children crying and calling for their mother broke his heart. Paul laid the woman in an open space between the cockpit and the cargo area, and then tapped Jerome on the shoulder.

"Everything okay back there?" Jerome asked.

"No. No it's not.  One dead. A woman. Looks like a piece of shrapnel hit her in the head."

"Who was she?" Jerome asked.

"Colonel Hien's wife."

Jerome called Gerry on the radio and conveyed the bad news. He also asked Gerry to check the outside of his C-123 for any damage. When his wheels went up he had heard some metal on metal noise. Gerry dropped a few hundred feet lower and slowed down as Jerome caught up. He checked the left side first and then moved over to check the right side of Jerome's plane.

"Take a look at this, Al," Gerry said pointing towards Jerome's plane.

Al leaned over and looked and said, "Shit. That's not good."

"Jerome, hold her steady. I'm going to move closer to check something."

"Roger," Jerome responded.

Gerry moved his plane up to 50 feet from Jerome's plan.

"That's what I thought," Gerry said.

"It's fucked," Al said.

"Jerome, your landing gear door is a tangled mess and you're leaking something. Looks like hydraulic fluid," Gerry said. Jerome didn't answer. "Jerome, come in."

"Roger. Just checking something. I'm going to have to find somewhere to land before I lose control," Jerome said.

"That wheel's probably not going to come down," Gerry said.

"I know. I'll try a two-wheel landing. Nothing else I can do."

Gerry made the sign of the cross and said, "Have you ever done that before?"

"No, but there's a first time for everything. I think I can do it. That is if we find somewhere to land," Jerome said.

"I'll pull off a half mile. You stay on this course. Whoever finds a landing field first wins," Gerry said trying to make light of a serious problem.

"Let's not take too long or else I'll be landing on top of the trees," Jerome said.

A half hour later, they still had not found a place to land.

Gerry picked up the microphone and asked," Jerome, what's the chances you can make it to the landing strip in Thailand?"

"Not very good," Jerome answered.

"We're close to Phnom Penh. We could land at the airport there?" Gerry suggested.

"No, Tripp said Phnom Penh fell to the Khmer Rouge in early April. Not an option," Jerome replied.

Gerry pulled a map of Cambodia from his map case and studied it for several minutes. Then he picked up the mic and said, "Tripp, I need you in the cockpit."

Tripp worked his way through the children to the cockpit and asked, "What's up?"

Gerry explained the situation and pointed to the map and said, "We're here. Do you know of any poppy or pot growers near us?"

Tripp thought for a few minutes and said, "I remember Gabe mentioning an operation south of us. About here I think?" Tripp said and pointed to a place on the map.

"Do you think they would have a landing field?"

"Not sure, but Gabe said it was a pretty big farm. The best way to get the product to the market would be by plane," Tripp said.

Gerry explained the plan and told Jerome to follow him.

"One thing you forgot," Tripp said to Gerry.

"What's that?"

"The commies. What if they took the farm like they did with us?"

"We'll deal with it. We have no choice anyway. Either we find a landing spot or Jerome crashes," Gerry said.

Thirty minutes later Al yelled, "There it is. A runway at eleven o'clock."

"Jerome, you see it," Gerry said.

"Yeah, I see it," Jerome said in a solemn voice.

"You could be a little more excited about it," Gerry said.

"I could be, but now I have to land this baby without killing all of us," Jerome said.

"We have faith in you," Gerry said, crossed himself, and said a pray. Then he said, "I'll do a flyby and check out the field. You stay up here until I tell you. When it's clear you can land and I'll follow you in."

"Roger that," Jerome said.

Gerry put the C-123 into a dive and leveled off at 200 feet as he passed over the landing strip. Then he gained altitude and came around behind Jerome's plane.

"Looks clear. Didn't see any troops. Take her down, Jerome," Gerry said.

"Paul, tell everyone in back to hold onto something and come back here as fast as you can," Jerome said.

When Paul returned Jerome pushed the yoke forward and headed for the field. He cleared his mind and concentrated on only one thing, landing the plane on two wheels. As they hit the dirt, Jerome tilted the wing slightly and prayed it wouldn't hit the ground. The left wheel touched down, then the front wheel. Suddenly, the front wheel collapsed and the plane's front end dug into the dirt. They were sliding down the dirt runway at 100 miles an hour. Then the left wheel collapsed.

Jerome and Paul lost any control they had. All they could do was watch the trees at the end of the runway get closer. The drag on the fuselage began to slow the plane down. The right wing dug into the dirt and the force turned the plane sideways, then backwards. The plane stopped 25 feet from the end of the runway.

"Let's get these kids off the plane," Jerome shouted.

Gerry saw Jerome's plane stop and a few minutes later the children were coming out the side doors. Gerry landed his plane, pulled up near Jerome and turned to face back the way he came.

Tripp dropped the cargo door and started to make room for Jerome's passengers. The C-123 was designed to hold about 50 troops. He had to fit 75 children and over 30 adults into the plane. It was like packing sardines in a can. Jerome and Paul were the last to get aboard. Jerome made his way up to the cockpit.

"Sorry, Gerry. I broke your plane."

"Yeah, well, we have a few more. Sit down, Jerome. Let's get these kids back to the U.S.," Gerry said then paused. "And Jerome, I have never seen anything like that. You're an amazing pilot."

# Chapter Thirty-Seven

The flight back to Thailand was uneventful, other than the playful nature of 75 young children. They touched down at the poppy farm landing strip at 10:00 am. Gerry decided that he would give the children the remainder of the day to rest. Tripp arranged to have four buses arrive in the morning that would take everyone to the Bangkok Airport where a charter airplane was waiting.

Mary had taken the two sick children and Sister Kim to the medical tent and all three were doing much better. Now she was tending to Paul.

"How you doing cuz?" Gerry asked Mary.

"A bit tired, but I feel so..." She paused to find the right word."I don't know how to say it. Euphoric maybe. Certainly more than just happy. We plucked 75 children out of the jaws of possible death."

"I'm glad to hear that and I'm glad you forced your way on this trip," Gerry said and smiled.

"She's amazing." Paul said.

"Mary, looks like you have a fan," Gerry said.

Mary blushed and said, "I'm a fan of Paul. If it wasn't for Jerome and him landing safely, we could have a whole different situation now," Mary said as she finished wrapping Paul's wound.

"Oh, I almost forgot. One of the kids in tent three has diarrhea. Can you go take a look?" Gerry said and walked out of the medical tent. Gerry suddenly felt as if he needed a cup of coffee, so he headed to the mess tent. Before he made it there, Professor Tam and his wife stopped him.

"Could I speak to you, Mr. Gerry?" Professor Tam asked.

"Yes, of course," Gerry answered.

"My wife and I want your permission so we could adopt Colonel Hien's children. They have no one now. We have no one either. I can assure you we will take good care of them," Professor Tam said.

Gerry looked at Tam's wife then back to Tam and said, "Of course. And, you won't have to worry about money. You'll both be working for me and when we get back, I'm going to find you a house."

Tam smiled and translated to his wife. She took Gerry's hand, kissed it, and said something in Vietnamese that Gerry didn't understand. Gerry shook Tam's hand and said, "You and your wife are good people. Those kids are lucky to have you." Then Gerry walked off to get his cup of coffee.

Jerome was sitting with Al Watson, Jake and Tripp, so he poured a cup of strong black coffee and sat down with them.

"How's the plane, Al," Gerry asked.

"Checked it out and it's good. I had the guys refuel her in case we need it," Al said.

"Good, but we won't be needing it again. I told the owner of the farm I was leaving the plane for them in return for his help. Anyway, we're, as you know, moving to jets," Gerry said.

Al, Jake and Jerome looked at Tripp and Al said, "Go ahead, Tripp."

Gerry looked at Tripp and said, "What's up?"

Tripp stumbled for his words and finally said, "I got a favor to ask you." Gerry was about to say something and Tripp held his hand up and said, "Wait till I explain. Something's been eating at me ever since Gabe and I had to fight our way out of his house. I just can't stand the idea that those fucking Khmer Rouge commie bastards will be living in Gabe's house. I hate the idea of it."

Gerry was about to say something when Tripp held his hand up again and said, "Hold on. I want to fly over there and bomb the shit out of that house. The more Khmer Rouge in there the better. So, that's it. I can't fly so I need one of your pilots to do it and I need your C-123."

"Can I talk now?" Gerry asked.

"Yeah, go ahead."

"I was going to say, Gabe deserves retribution. So why don't we fly over to his house and take it out along with as many Khmer Rouge as we can find," Gerry said.

"Really?" Tripp asked.

"Really, "Gerry answered.

"You remember what we did to those VC on the Ho Chi Minh trail?" Tripp said.

"Of course."

"We'll, we can do the same thing again. I was hoping you would agree so I bought a truck and had it loaded with 1,000 lbs of C4. Al already put it in the plane," Jerome said.

"So you guys had this planned all along," Gerry asked.

"Don't blame them. I didn't want to bother you with this until we got back from grabbing those kids. I told them before we left, so they could help convince you when the time came," Tripp said.

Gerry shook his head back and forth and said, "Tripp, you saved my life and you made this," Gerry held his arms out, "all possible. How could you think I might not help you?" Gerry got up and continued, "So let's get out of here and kill some fucking commies."

An hour and a half later the C-123 carrying Gerry, Al, Jake, Tripp and a truck with 1,000 lbs of C4 was flying at 11,000 feet over Gabe Barra's farm.

Tripp strapped himself in and opened the left side back door of the plane. He leaned out and adjusted his binoculars until the image of the farmhouse was clear. He yelled back to Jake, "Looks like they're there. I see some trucks and a couple of cars."

Jake relayed the message to Gerry and Gerry said, "Jake, put the safety harness on and open the left door. Tripp showed you how to use the M60, right?"

"Yeah," Jake said

"Tell Tripp we're going down."

Jake told Tripp then attached his harness to the fuselage and opened the door. The wind almost knocked him down. He regained his balance, picked up the M60, and attached another strap to it.

"Whatever you do, Jake, don't shoot the wing off," Tripp said and smiled so Jake could see.

Jake nodded back and pointed the M60 towards the ground as the plane slowly circled downward. When they were approximately at 2,500 feet, several Khmer Rouge soldiers started to fire at them. Jake and Tripp fired back and with a range of 1,200 yards, the M60 7.62mm bullets created havoc on the ground. Two of the soldiers crumbled to the ground and the other one and several who had been in the trucks ran into the house.

Gerry straightened the plane, flew two miles south and turned to go back to the farmhouse. Jake and Tripp closed the plane's doors, loosed their safety straps, and unstrapped the truck.  Tripp picked up the mic and said, "Tell me when."

"Set the timers for 5 minutes, and then drop the cargo door.

"Roger," Tripp said as he jumped in the back of the truck. When he finished he lowered the cargo door, opened the truck door and got ready to release the truck's parking brake.

As soon as they made the turn Gerry started to lose altitude. By the time they were a half mile away from the house he was flying at 50 feet above the rice paddies. He yelled into the mic, "take the brake off." then asked Al, "Time?"

"Three minutes."

Just before they crossed over the house Gerry pulled the yoke back and Al hit the

jet-assisted engines. The C-123 immediately responded upwards at a steep angle. The truck rolled out onto the cargo door and then into the air. It landed on the roof of the backside of the house and fell inward to the first floor.

"Time?"

Before Al could answer there was a deafening explosion. The plane rocked from the concussion, but Gerry was ready and straightened it out as they continued to ascend. 5,000 feet, Gerry gently leveled out and turned the plane around. Tripp closed the cargo door and he and Jake came to the cockpit. Even far off they could see the large crater that was once the farmhouse. The Khmer Rouge trucks that had been parked outside were a few hundred feet away, overturned and on fire.

Al pulled out five double shot glasses, handed them out and poured Jameson in each glass. Gerry opened the pilot's window and as the air rushed in, he recited a toast, "Death leaves a heartache no one can heal; Love leaves a memory no one can steal."

The four men tapped glasses and drank. Gerry poured the fifth glass out the window and said, "For you, Gabe. You will always be remembered."

# Chapter Thirty-Eight

On April 25, 1975, Bien Hoa Airbase was evacuated. Five days later, on April 30, 1975, the city of Saigon and the country of South Vietnam fell to the combined forces of the Viet Cong and North Vietnamese communists. The 20-year Vietnam War was over.

On May 15, 1975 Professor Tam, his wife and their two adopted children moved into their new house in Northeast Philadelphia. The recued Vietnamese orphans were settled in three different facilities where they were learning to adapt to a new culture. Sister Kim, Sister Cam and the other sisters from the Hoi Duc Anh Orphanage were living in the convent at Saint Hugh's Church and spending their days administering to the children.

Mercy insisted that the Hung family stay with her until Gerry could find them suitable housing. Although busy with Mercy Row Foundation work, Mercy found time to teach Mai and her mother how to cook American food. In return Mai's mother taught Mercy how to make a wonderful beef soup she called Pho and a kind of egg roll the Vietnamese called Cha Gio. One night the whole family gathered for a traditional, but Americanized, Vietnamese meal. Jake was so taken by the Cha Gio he pleaded with Maria to learn how to make them.

"Maria, you ready to make some egg rolls," Mercy asked.

Maria picked up an egg roll Mai's mother had made as an example and said, "I'd rather eat one, but yes I'm ready."

"So you're learning more for you than for Jake," Mercy said and smiled.

Grinning Maria said, "Let's keep that our secret, shall we? You know how men think everything's about them. Speaking of men, where's Gerry today? Normally he's following Mai around like a little puppy," Maria asked.

"He and Al are in Mexico. You think Gerry has a thing for Mai?" Mercy asked.

"Oh my God, yes. He is always…" Maria was interrupted when Mai and her mother came to the kitchen.

Mai and her mother bowed slightly and Mai said, "Good morning, Miss Maria, Miss Mercy."

"Good morning," Mercy said, paused and continued. "We were just admiring your mother's egg rolls."

Mai said. "Thank you," then she said something in Vietnamese to her mother. Her mother replied in Vietnamese. Mai translated, "My mother said please enjoy some."

Mai picked up the platter of egg rolls and held it out to Maria and Mercy. Each took one, took a bite and smiled. Maria said, "These are so, so good." Mai didn't need to translate. The smile on her mother's face said she understood.

"I wish my Mom and Dad were here. They would love these," Mercy said and took another bite.

Jacob and Molly Byrne moved to Fort Lauderdale, Florida during the fall of 1968. Franklin and Catherine followed a couple of weeks later. Every June, they traveled back to Philadelphia, stayed through New Year and then went back to Florida to avoid the cold Philly winter. Having a large Florida home near the beach ensured that you had plenty of guests during the months from January to June. So, they kept busy entertaining friends and family, and that made Molly happy. She enjoyed cooking for people and missed the hubbub of their Sunday family dinners.

Franklin and Jacob bought a 38 foot sport fishing boat a couple months after they arrived in Florida. They often took guests on fishing trips, which were more drinking beer and talking than actual fishing. They kept the boat at a marina on the Stranahan River, which was a short trip away from the Atlantic Ocean.

Jeff Byrne, Jacob's grandson was visiting. He was a senior at Georgia Tech, studying aerospace engineering and was on Spring Break. Jeff was a serious student. Not that he didn't like a good time, but he had a goal of one day working for NASA and they only took the brightest and most educated engineers. So, while his classmates were guzzling beer on the beach and trying to get laid, he was visiting his Grandparents and dreaming of getting his Masters or even a Ph.D. Jacob and Franklin suggested they go for a boat ride.

"Beer, Jeff?" Franklin asked.

"Sure."

"How's school going?" Jacob asked.

"It's good. Hard, but good Grandpop," Jeff answered.

"Well, today you take it easy. Enjoy the sun and the water. We can do some fishing if you like," Jacob said.

"Relaxing is good enough for me. Fishing's too much work," Jeff said smiling.

"Drink up, Jeff," Jacob said and touched his bottle to Jeff's.

"How far out are we going? Jeff asked.

"Mile, mile and a half maybe. It's calm today. We'll just shut off the engines and drift for a while."

"Sounds good to me," Jeff said.

The three men sat in silence for over 15 minutes as they watched the gentle swells of the Atlantic Ocean. Finally, Jeff said, "I was thinking how much Uncle Mike use to love coming out here. I miss him."

"Me too, Jeff. Mike was one of a kind," Jacob said.

"That fucking cancer's a bitch. When I go, I want it to be fast. Here's to Mike," Franklin said and spilled some beer on the deck. The three men took a drink from their bottles.

"You know, Jeff, Uncle Frank and I are the last of the Mohicans," Jacob said.

"What do you mean?" Jeff asked.

"Mike, Grady, Tony Amato. All gone. To Heaven I hope," Jacob said, paused and continued, "We're last of the original gang."

"If I know them, they're raising hell in Heaven," Franklin said and smiled.

"Did you and Uncle Frank really meet in jail," Jeff asked.

Jake looked at Jeff and pondered how he should answer him. He decided to be honest. "We did. I was a kid and Uncle Frank saved me from a pretty bad beating."

"Tell me about it," Jeff asked.

Jacob looked at Franklin. Franklin nodded his head and said, "Go ahead, tell the kid the story."

"Well, I was a snot-nose teenager and I hated the idea that the Italian gangsters from South Philly were coming to North Philly trying to sell their stolen goods. One day I had enough and I smashed one of them in the mouth and took the watches he was trying to sell. Anyway, the cops saw me and took me to jail. Your Uncle Frank was in the same holding cell."

"What did he do to get arrested?" Jeff asked.

"Assault. I didn't know it at the time, but Frank was working for my Father as a construction manger. He had a fight with a contractor. Beat the guy silly. So anyway, some big guy," Jacob paused then asked, "What do you think he weighed, Frank,"

"Had to be 350 lbs and 6'2," Franklin answered.

"I still remember his bad breath. Makes me ill. So this guy tried to steal my money, but the cops had already taken it. So, he decides he'll take his due flesh. Fran…"

Jeff interrupted Jacob and asked, "What's that mean. Was he going to cut you?"

"No. He was going to rape me."

"Whoa, are you kidding?" Jeff said.

"No, it's true and he would have, except Uncle Frank hit him over the head with a stool," Jacob said.

"Did you kill him?" Jeff asked.

"Nah, just knocked him out, I guess. We never saw him again," Frank said.

"After my father got us out of jail, I gave Uncle Frank one of the watches I stole," Jacob said. "Show him the watch, Frank,"

Franklin fished around in his pants pocket and took out an old worn pocket watch and handed it to Jeff.

Jeff looked it over and asked, "How old is this?"

"I don't know. Pretty old. I gave it to Frank 52 years ago. Not sure how old it was then," Jacob said.

"How'd you hear about us meeting in jail?" Franklin asked Jeff.

Jeff handed the watch back to Franklin and answered, "All the grand-kids have heard lots of stories. We don't know if they're real or not."

"Well, let's keep this between us and as far as whatever other stories you've heard, I am sure they're exaggerated," Jacob said.

"I'm going to lie down for a while. I want to suck up some sun and fresh salt air," Franklin said.

"Sounds good to me. Radar's clear. Jeff, close your eyes for a while and enjoy the air. I'll do the same. After, we'll take a run down to Fisher Key and when we get back, we'll all go to dinner. Sound good?" Jacob said.

Jeff nodded yes. Minutes later the rolling motion of the boat, the clear air and the warm sun did their job. All three men were asleep.

The blaring of a ship's horn startled Jeff awake. He jumped up and saw a cruise ship at least a mile to their east and nowhere near them. Relieved they weren't going to be creamed by a ship Jeff sat back down. He looked at his Grandfather, who was still fast asleep and then at Franklin. Something didn't look right. Franklin was breathing heavy and rapidly. Jeff ran over to Franklin and shook him. No response. He shook him again. Again nothing.

Jeff ran back to Jacob and shook him. Jacob opened his eyes and said, "What's the matter."

"Something's wrong with Uncle Frank."

Jacob got up, shook Franklin and said, "Wake up, Frank. Wake up." Frank's chest was heaving. "Jeff, start the boat and head west as fast as you can." Then Jacob opened Franklin's mouth to check his airway. It was clear. He laid Franklin down on the deck and started chest compressions, stopping only to breathe air into Franklin's lungs.

Jeff started the boat's twin diesels and brought the vessel to a west heading. Then he opened her up. The boat lurched, the back dipped and the massive engines pushed her forward faster and faster.

Ten minutes later Jeff yelled out, "I see the beach."

"Drive her right into the sand. The lifeguards will get help," Jacob yelled.

"But there are people in the water," Jeff said.

"Blow the horn. They'll get out of the way," Jacob yelled.

Jeff pushed the horn button and held it.

"We're close, should I slow down?"

"No, stay at this speed. Turn the engines off only when we hit the sand."

Horn blaring, the boat hit the sandy bottom and continued until it was half out of water. It stopped abruptly, almost knocking Jeff to the deck. By the time he got to the front of the boat there were two lifeguards waiting. Jeff yelled, "Get an ambulance. We need help."

One lifeguard ran back to the guard shack and the other one jumped on the boat and ran back to where Jacob was still doing compressions on Franklin. The lifeguard motioned Jacob away and took over.

Jacob sat back. He was in a daze. He put his hands to his face.

When the ambulance arrived, the EMTs tried to stabilize Franklin. As they carried Franklin to the ambulance, Jacob saw one of the EMTs shake his head back and forth.

"I'm going with Frank. Call Molly and Catherine and tell them we're at the Holy Cross Hospital," Jacob said.

# Epilogue

Franklin Garrett was buried at the Resurrection Catholic Cemetery in Cornwell Heights, Pennsylvania. According to his wishes, a memorial was held prior to his burial at his and Catherine's home in Lower Moreland Township. During the memorial, it was announced that Franklin had bequeathed half of his estate to the Mercy Row Foundation.

During the memorial, Catherine Garrett presented Jacob Byrne with a very old and worn pocket watch. Franklin had put in his will that if he died before Jacob, Catherine was to give him the watch. Fifty-two years before Jacob had given Franklin that watch, while both men were in jail. As it turned out it was the beginning of an era and of the K&A Gang of Irish mobsters. During Franklin's wake, Jacob placed the watch back in Franklin's suit pocket and said, "I'll pick it up the next time I see you."

The end of that era was over when on May 1, 1988, Jacob Byrne passed away in his sleep at the age of 82. Molly Byrne followed him a year later at age 87. Jimmy Byrne retired from Byrne Construction a year later and he and Sally moved to his Mother's house in Florida. Jimmy turned the operation over to his son Mark, who worked with him since graduating college.

Catherine Garrett, at age 59 starred in several exercise programs for people over 50. Her VHS tapes were sold on a home shopping channel netting her a considerable sum of money, which she donated to the Mercy Row Foundation.

Mercy Byrne Amato married Al Watson on June 10th, 1977. Al continued to work with Gerry Amato and they have built a sizable airfreight company. The C-123s were retired and the company now flies only jet aircraft. Mercy continues to run Mercy Row Foundation without the aid of the K&A Gang crews, which dissolved in the early 1980s.

Dr. Tam and his wife taught the orphans from the Hoi Duc Anh Orphanage until all were adopted. With the help of Gerry Amato they continued their work with Vietnamese refugees who flooded into Philadelphia for years after the takeover of Vietnam by the communists.

George Byrne was made Rector of the Northeast Catholic High School in 1980. Charlie Byrne retired and turned over all North Philadelphia gambling to the South Philadelphia Mafia. He currently resides with his wife Janet in Fort Lauderdale, Florida near his brother Jimmy's home. Jake Byrne with the assistance of his son, Joey continues to provide protection services to various criminal organizations in and around Philadelphia.

Jeff Byrne received his Ph.D in Aerospace Engineering and after two years working on research projects, he earned a position with NASA. In November of 1985, he was on the crew of the Challenger shuttle's visit to the Space Station. He is married and has two sons Martin and Barry. Alicia and Bella Byrne work with Mercy at the Mercy Row Foundation. Bella handles investments and Alicia is in charge of issuing grants. Both are married with one child each.

Dr. Mary Byrne married Paul Jefferies on Valentine's Day 1978. Mary remained with the free clinic, eventually building a string of clinics that serve Philadelphia's needy residents. Paul died in a fiery aircraft accident in January of 1988, along with Tripp Edwards and Jerome Washington. The plane went down shortly after takeoff crashing into the Neshaminy Mall's parking lot. The FAA ruled that the aircraft was downed by an explosion in the cargo area.

Gerry Byrne Amato married Nguyen Thi Mai on May 4, 1977. They have two children, Anthony and Lois. As the FAA continues to investigate the cause of the crash of the Byrne Airfreight jet that killed three of his closest friends, Gerry faces a threat far more lethal than the family has ever experienced.

◆ ◆ ◆

## Reflections of Growing Up in North Philadelphia

As I wrote Mercy Row Retribution and the other books in the Mercy Row series, I would often remember various aspects from my childhood in North Philly. I started to post short stories on Facebook of some of the adventures my friends and I had growing up in North Philly. I thought I would take this opportunity to share some of those stories with you.

While the Byrne family and their activities are pure fiction, much of the surroundings and normal life events actually happened. I did eat potato chip sandwiches, Tastykakes, scrapple and soft pretzels when growing up. The streets I mention in the stories are real. The hospitals and buildings are real as well. Even some of the actual events are real.

For instance, when Gerry first met Hung, the taxi driver in Saigon, he was with a group of pilots who were throwing money at Hung to make him drive faster. This results in a crash. That actually happened to me. My friends weren't pilots, but airmen like myself. Another true event in my stories was when Gerry, Sean and Mike visit the Circle Billiards Hall. Harry was my father and he did own that poolroom. There was a backroom where they played cards and, my father was a champion pool player. The trick I explain was actually one he could do and did many times.

I hope you enjoy my stories of growing up in North Philly as much as I did remembering them.

## The Slingshot from Hell

There was a time when my friends and I were into shooting construction staples (pretty heavy with two pointed ends) at each other from slingshots. It's a miracle that none of us were hurt or lost an eye.

One day we bought a couple boxes of rubber bands and a box of heavy construction staples. Our goal was to build the largest slingshot to ever have been made. We strung the rubber bands together and stretched them from my house to the house across the street. I would say it was 30 feet or so. We then proceeded to try to break windows in the Bell Telephone factory three blocks away by shooting construction staples at them.

We never knew if we reached the building. I am pretty sure we didn't. I have no idea what happened to any cars or people that might have been in the path of our staples from hell.

You say, "Where were the parents?" They were working their asses off at factories or similar jobs. Some moms were washing clothes without a washing machine, cooking actual meals, which we had at home always, and cleaning the houses. They didn't have time to oversee every little thing we did. And, we did some crazy stuff.

## Everyone was a Bookie

When I was a kid the greatest thing about growing up in Kensington in North Philly was the people. There were people from all over the world living just on my street. You could hear several languages being spoken and smell foods cooking from numerous countries.

Mickey the milkman drove a horse-drawn milk wagon and delivered dairy products to your door. I later learned he had a side business as well. He was a numbers runner, a bookie if you will. Mrs. Milky lived down the street. She was the nicest lady. I later found out she also was a bookie (took bets on numbers and horses). I used to buy great hoagies and other sandwiches at Charlie's around the corner. Turns out, he was a bookie as well. Joe the pretzel man, who had cerebral palsy, made his living selling one and five penny soft pretzels. He owned several houses and had a driver. You guessed it. Joe was a bookie as well. My own father was a bookie during the depression and early 40s. He stopped when the Feds cracked down on gambling. My mother said it was the best we ever had it.

I have been wondering how such a blue-collar (translation not rich) neighborhood could have so many bookies.

## Fabulous Sundays

My father's father died when my Dad was only 11 years old. The family was poor and as the youngest child, he was able to stay in school only a couple years more. He quit school in the eighth grade and got a job to help his mother. He worked on an ice truck helping to deliver ice to homes that had iceboxes (which was all of them) and he also worked in a factory that made baseballs. He, as I mentioned, became a bookie sometime in the 1930s after he married my Mom.

He was a hard drinker in those days (he stopped drinking and smoking in the late 1940s) and my mother's father would often go with him to the bars and recover the money my Dad left on the bar counters. During the war he worked at BUDDs, a factory that made planes. I believe he was shearer of metal. During this time he was able to bend a half dollar with his fingers. Did my father get in fights, do things maybe he shouldn't have done? I don't know. It was never discussed.

I lay this groundwork so you better understand what happened when my brother and I were old enough to hang out with our Dad. During the week, we didn't see Dad much. He worked at his poolroom late and left before we got home from school. He did come home for dinner at 5 o'clock and then would leave to go to his poolroom where he oversaw 10 tables and a backroom where high rollers (well as high rollers as possible in Kensington) played poker.  On Sundays everything changed.

From the time I could remember till I was about 13 (more interested in hanging out with the guys then) our father had a ritual.  He would load my brother and me in his Hudson car, and the first thing we did was drive to one of Philly's many cultural attractions. We went to the Philadelphia Art Museum, the Franklin Institute, The Rodan Museum, The Japanese Pavilion, the Aquarium, and The Museum of Natural History. You name it we went.

After getting some culture we drove to center city Philly where we went to Horn & Hardart Automat put a nickel in the slot and pulled out a piece of pie. Then we went through the line and got a cup of coffee. Yeah, you heard right. Kids drank coffee back then, at least with my dad. After our repast, we walked around the corner to the Nut House and he would buy each of us a bag of candy. We were not allowed to touch it until we got to the movie theater, generally on Chestnut or Market Street. Oh, and we had to eat the candy while we waited for the movie to start. No eating during the movie as it made too much noise.

After the movie we would drive north on Fifth Street and back to the house, where my mother and grandmother had roasted something and made our special Sunday meal. After dinner, Dad went to the poolroom.

I often think about how my father had a very limited education, but had math skills I couldn't believe. He also read a lot, mostly science fiction that I remember, but also other books as well.

He knew a lot, before it became popular. When he was older, he started eating oatmeal everyday for breakfast. We laughed at him when he told us why. Some doctor who came to the poolroom told him it was healthy for your heart. He also started drinking orange juice with vinegar. Again we laughed. Of course, today both are considered healthy foods. Dad was called the Gentleman by the folks who frequented the various poolrooms around Philly. He was a champion player and a pool hustler as well. Dad was like an M&M candy; hard on the outside, but soft in the middle.

I said goodbye to my father when he was 77. He, my mother, sister and brother-in-law visited us in Atlanta. I got to play pool with him one last time, at a place I found in Sandy Springs, GA. That evening my mother woke us up at 2 AM and said something was wrong with my father. My brother-in-law Dave and I rushed to his room and found him lying on the floor. Dave gave chest compressions while I gave mouth to mouth. The EMTs came and took him to the hospital. Bill, Nancy, Duoc, my sister Roberta, Dave, my Mother and I followed. Fifteen minutes after he entered the hospital, the doctor informed us that Harry Mark Hallman, Sr. had passed away.

What won't pass away are my memories of those fabulous Sundays we spent with him and those special Sunday dinners my Mother and Grandmother made.

## School Daze

I went to the same grade school as my mother, my sister and my brother - William Cramp Elementary. Now when I say I wasn't the best student what I really mean is that I was not the best student. I was more interested in the social aspects of school. I passed but sometimes by the skin of my teeth. I was kicked out of kindergarten for a day and had my mother come to get me because I lifted a little girl's dress up to see what was there. At five I had no idea. At seventy-one I'm forgetting.

Later I somehow became a patrolman safety, then a sergeant and finally the captain of the William Cramp Safety Patrol. That was my last year in grade school. I was suspended as captain for two weeks and was made to attend a second grade class for a few weeks for getting into trouble in school.

I went to Stetson Junior High School just as my mother, sister and brother did. I still had the habit of talking too much in class and had a teacher tell my mother they thought I might become a politician because I talked so much. (God forbid) Truth is Jr. High was a scary place. It was common for kids to carry knives. I even knew those who brought guns to school. In my Jr. High you never wanted to be caught in the halls between classes or you could be robbed of your lunch money.

Teachers often were as tough as the kids. I will never forget Mr. S., a science teacher. Once a student called him a mother'fer. In a second he was on that kid (kid was big and tough), threw him to the front of the room, bashed him against the wall several times and threw him out the door. Same teacher did a similar thing to another student who broke in the class with a message without knocking. Mr. S., we found out, was a black belt in Judo. Our Drafting teacher brought a kid up to the front for talking in class and gave him a lecture. The kid held his book up in front of his face and said, "Your breath sinks." The teacher punched the book, which hit the kid's mouth, and then he threw him out of class.

The kids were tough also. I once saw the toughest boy in the school fight a girl. I will never forget her name, Freda (I'll leave the last name out just in case she reads this ☺). She beat the toughest boy in school.

Fridays were reserved for racial tensions. After school (more times than I can remember) African American kids would take one side of Allegheny Avenue and the white kids (Irish American, German American, British American, Slavic American) took the other side. Often the police were in the middle. Some fights occurred, but nothing serious. It was over when most of the kids got to their homes.

High school was better, but I wasn't. I was very surprised when I enlisted in the Air Force that I did so well on the tests. I went to two schools for photography and did well. Even got student of the month. How did that happen?

## Games People Play

Imagine a world without computers, smart phones, any mobile phones, electronic games, and no TV or TV with 3 channels. Horrifying, right? What would kids do?

Well, that's the world I grew up in.  Believe me I am happy to have all those electronics now, but when I was a kid the first transistor radio was just invented. We had a party line on our phone; that's where two or more households share the same telephone connection. I was 5 years old when my family bought our first TV, a 12 inch black and white RCA. If you were lucky enough to have a record player, it was probably a 45 RPM.

Wait, I'm not saying, "Oh poor me, I didn't have these things." Nobody did and we didn't miss them one bit (I would now). Instead, we either made up games or did what kids from North Philly did for generations; we played traditional street games.

I loved playing STEP BALL. We would take a pimple ball and toss it at our doorway steps. The idea was to catch it as it returned. You got extra points if you could hit the edge of the step and catch the ball. Using that same pimple ball we would play WALL BALL, a game that could be played by two or more people. You hit the ball with your open hand against the side of a building. We generally used the house on the corner of the row. (Mercy Row of course ☺)The other guy had to return it and so on and so on. If you missed you got a point. Too many points and you lost.

Again using the pimple ball we would separate into teams of three or four and play HAND BALL. We used the whole street for this. The four corners, that generally had a sewer were the bases. A pitcher would bounce a ball to the hitter who used his fist to hit the ball. Standard baseball rules applied, except you could hit the base runner with the ball to get him out. WIRE BALL was another favorite game. The idea was to hit the electric wires with the pimple ball and the other guy had to catch it. Sometimes it was difficult because there were many pairs of sneakers hanging from the wires.

When the pimple ball split open it wasn't discarded. We cut it in half and played HALF BALL. It is similar to stick ball but with a pimple ball cut in half. This required two factory walls across from each other. We had no shortage of those. The pitcher threw the half ball and the batter using a broom stick hit it. If it was caught you were out. If it hit the wall and no one caught it, that was a home run.

Now if there was no pimple ball or half pimple balls, which was often, we just cut up an old hose and played HOSE BALL. It was a little harder but it didn't stop us. Another favorite game of mine did not involve the pimple ball. We would get a used tin can from the gas station and played a game called TIN CAN EDDY. One person would be it. They threw the can as far as they could, counted to 30 with their back to everyone. Everyone would hide. The person who was it then had to find someone, run to the can and get there before the person they had found and toss the can again. And on and on it went. If you see me sometime, ask me to show you the scar I got when my finger got caught in the jagged opening in the can when I threw it.

My least favorite game that also did not use the ubiquitous pimple ball, was ROUGH AND TUMBLE. We took newspaper and tied it with string. Generally it was small enough to hold in one hand. If you were holding that bound newspaper, it was fair game for other players to tackle and hit you. If you threw it to someone they had to catch it and then they had to avoid the other players.

As you can imagine the PIMPLE BALL was a key status symbol in our neighborhood. We didn't always have the nickel to buy one, so anyone who had climbing skills and could get on the row house roofs was a kind of pimple ball hero. We would also hold other "heroes" by their feet to get the balls that went in the sewers. Disgusting? Yeah, but effective.

I am glad my kids or grandkid did not have to hang upside down in a Philadelphia sewer to get pimple balls. That being said, I am a little sad that they didn't get to play street games as I did.

**North Philly Adventures**

Growing up in Philly was one adventure after another. We were free to roam the neighborhood and even beyond if we had the courage. We had a railroad line a couple blocks away that was the source of many adventures. For the most part we stayed away from the tracks, but not always. Kids are, contrary to belief, fairly smart. One or two stories about a kid losing his legs or having his head chopped off by a train was enough for us to stay on the sidelines most of the time. But, we had plenty of other places to find our adventures.

*Sneaking into the Movies*

The Wishart Movie Theater was one block away from us. The entrance was on Alleghany Avenue but the emergency exits were on Wishart Street and in an alleyway between the theater and a furniture store. We didn't always have the 15 cents admission to go see a movie, and even if we did we wouldn't have enough for a box of Good and Plenty candy or popcorn.

We solved the problem using an age old strategy; find a way sneak in and not be caught. We sent one person to pay and get in the theater, and he would make sure the usher wasn't around. Then our Trojan horse, so to speak, would crack the door open a bit and we would crawl through and take a seat. It didn't work all the time. If we got caught they just kicked us out and told us not to do it anymore. Today you probably would end up in jail for six months.

*The Construction Staple Caper*

One day after school a bunch of our ten-year-old gang members decided they wanted to go to the railroad and shoot "whatever" with their slingshots. You might remember I told you that we used construction staples as ammunition. I sensed this might not be a good idea so I made up an excuse that I had to do homework and didn't go.

The next day I found out they went to a railroad bridge and started shooting staples at some workers. They ended up in police custody and had to go to juvenile court. Seems they actually hit one of the workers. Nothing really happened. The judge told them not to do it again and let them go. It was one adventure I was happy not to be part of.

## The Battle of Wishart Street - North vs South

One summer it became in fashion to save your money to buy a civil war army hat. This was after the Davy Crockett Coon Skin hat craze. You could get a northern hat or a rebel hat. The idea was if you saw someone wearing an enemy hat you could beat them up and vice versa. The craze didn't last that long and we didn't need excuses to get into fights.

## Bombs Away

Another summer, we learned how to make bombs from our toy pistol caps. I remember it involved some nuts and bolts but that is the extent of my memory about that. We would make the bombs then go to our mother and father's bedroom on the second floor and toss the cap bombs out the window. If we saw someone walking our way, we waited and it was "bombs away" as they walked by. For some reason our neighbors didn't like that and it was a short-lived adventure.

## The Monster of Fifth Street

One year a rumor went around about a MONSTER being loose in the neighborhood. We were both scared and intrigued over this unusual happening. Of course, we believed in monsters. After all, most of the movies we saw had monsters in them so what's not to believe. Anyway, we went all over the neighborhood, as far as Fifth Street (5 blocks away) searching for the monster. We never found it, but we had fun looking.

## The Night the Sewers Came Alive

There were actual monsters in the neighborhood. They were called cockroaches and rats. Rats were more rare but roaches were prevalent. Every house had them at some point and they certainly walked the streets at night. Oh, did I tell you that these roaches were mammoth, and some could fly. Oh yes, thanks to our factories that imported cotton from the south, we had an overabundance of big black flying roaches. Most of us kids hated them but we learned to share the streets with them to a point.

One night we were all hanging out on Westmoreland Street, probably sneaking drags from cigarettes and BSing about whatever kids back then BSed about. We started to notice that there were more roaches than normal, but we kept our distance and dispatched to roach heaven those that came too close. It got so bad that we had to go investigate. We found that the roaches were coming from the sewer covers in the middle of the street. I guess we were not the only ones who noticed and the city sent some men to check it out. They opened the lid to the sewer and these monstrous large flying roaches swarmed out. It was a nightmare. For a month every time I felt any sensations on my legs or arms I thought it was roaches; a couple of times I was right.

## Growing Up With Phil

August 31 is my childhood best friend Phil Gormley's birthday. He would have been 72 (2015) years old.   Unfortunately, he passed away a few years ago. I met Phil when he moved into our neighborhood when I was about 11 or 12 years old. Despite the fact that when he met me he felt like punching me in the face (that's North Philly for you) we became best buddies. We did all the kid things together like learning to smoke, drink whiskey, and curse. Because of Phil and his family, I decided to convert to Catholicism. My dad, who was already Catholic, started to go to church after 25 years and my mom converted as well.

After a year or so of being Catholic I did what all (okay most) North Philly boys did. I played hooky from church on Sunday with Phil and his older brother Bob. We went to the Greek restaurant and ate French fries and PRAYED our mothers didn't find out.

Phil and I had many adventures together and I loved his family. I have always looked up to his mother, who took care of seven kids and didn't have much support from her ex-husband. A very strong woman she was. His mother had a good friend that owned a new Ford car, the one that had a hard top convertible. Anyway one rainy day Phil decided to "borrow the car" and he, his brother and me went for a ride. Now some of this history may be blurry and it might have been Bob who was driving, but whoever it was it didn't turn out good. Back then Philly was full of trolley tracks and they were slippery in the rain. Of course, we slipped and hit another car. The friend forgave Phil and Bob and I never mentioned this to my mother. Sorry, mom.

Phil and his brother Bob met two Irish sisters when Phil was about 14 (a guess here); Emily and Eileen Hannigan, both beautiful girls in flesh and spirit. After a few years, Bob broke up with Eileen but Phil had found his true love, Emily. Many nights, so many I cannot count, Emily, Phil, and the third wheel ME, would sit on her or his steps and talk about anything and everything. I am guessing this was 1958-61 or so. For some reason we got talking about the future and the year 2000 and the change of the millennium. We pretty much felt that by then we would have passed on to heaven (if we were lucky). After all, I would be 56 then and Phil 57. Not saying how old Emily would be. ☺

Well, Phil, you certainly passed the milestone by many years. Today I am going to pour myself a drink and pour a little on the ground for you.

## Blacktop Education

Philadelphia and especially the neighborhood I grew up in is mostly cement, bricks and blacktop (asphalt streets). The closest we came to having a lawn was the moss growing between the cracks in the sidewalk. What we lacked in greenery was made up by the education we received on those asphalt streets of Kensington.

There were four things a boy in North Philly had to learn and learn fast: Sex, how to smoke, how to drink and the best curse words to use. There was other curriculum as well, but these were the most important.

### Sex

The earliest I can remember hearing about sex was when I was about eight years old. My sister got married and one of my friends was taunting me saying my sister was going to have sex with her husband. I was so mad we got into a fight. I had no idea what sex was then, but I knew it was BAD. As the years flowed by I learned more, but never did I know of anyone whose parents sat them down to discuss the birds and the bees. You learned everything from the street or you didn't learn.

*Cursing*

At Sunday school we were taught cursing was wrong and in some cases using the wrong curse would get you a one way ticket to hell. Of course, we paid no attention to that. After all, hell would be overflowing with people from the neighborhood. Men generally didn't curse in front of women or children, but a stroll down the street was enough to get you a Ph.D in improper language.

My first lesson in cursing came from my mother. They were mild curses such as hell, damn and sh*t. She did say freaking also but that was an acceptable substitute for the most diabolical four-letter word ever invented.

Cursing education is important in North Philly, so we could not leave it up to our parents to teach us. We learned from each other. I could fill a book with just curse words I learned in the asphalt jungle. I did that. You can find many of them in my first Mercy Row novel.

*Smoking*

I remember the exact time I learned to smoke cigarettes. Oh, I smoked before that but it was just silly things like filling a pipe with Tetley Tea and smoking it. We saw Arthur Godfrey do that on television.

I was 13 years old when I first tired a cigarette in earnest. Hell, everyone else was doing it so why not and anyway it looked cool. I lit up and took a puff, inhaled and almost choked to death. You would think that would be enough to stop you, but not a North Philly boy. It took ten years and a surgeon general's report to knock some sense into my head.

*Drinking*

The first time I got high drinking was when I was eight years old. My sister got married and we had the reception in our 18 x 30 foot house. The house was packed with friends and family. I found out if I would elbow my way through the crowds and get drinks for my uncles they would give me MONEY. I could buy a lot of pimple balls with that money. Every time I got a highball for them, I sipped some from the glass so it wouldn't spill. They found me in my room asleep with thirty or more coats on top of me. I must not have been the only kid sipping drinks because my mom's friend's 8-year-old daughter, Joan, was in the bed passed out with me.

I gave up drinking for a few years and when I was about 14 I started again. Beer was our preference at first, because it was easy to get. Later we tried whiskey, and even wine. "What's the word? Thunderbird! What's the price? Thirty thrice!" seems to roll around my head even now. It was a reference to Thunderbird Wine, which I cannot believe cost as much as 90 cents back then.

We never had any problems getting sprits. A promise to buy a Bum (our name for a homeless drunken guy) a bottle was enough to get some State Store hard stuff. Beer was easier. In the early years we had friends that looked 17 or 18 and they had no problem buying quarts from the bar or even cases from the beer suppliers. Keep in mind the legal drinking age in Philly was 21. By the time we were 16 or so we were able to buy drinks ourselves. There wasn't a lot of ID checking back then, at least in Kensington. We could even buy beer in bars that were open illegally on Sunday. No one, by law, was supposed to sell booze on Sundays. But laws were for the people on the main line not us in Kensington.

## The Night We Invaded South Philly

Even in the 50s when I was a teenager, Philadelphia was a city of gangs. Stories abounded about what this gang did or what another gang did to them. One story was that a North Philly gang had a machine gun mounted in a van. Farfetched were most of these stories, but not all.

Our "gang" was mostly peaceful. We were just a small group of guys wanting to only smoke, drink, make fun of each other, and, of course, meet girls. We hung out mostly between two factories where there were few neighbors to complain. Later we moved to a sandwich shop across the street from the 25th District police station. Probably not the best choice as we ended up in that station a number of times for doing nothing more than hanging out. But, that's another story.

The gang at 10th and Ontario had a reputation for being the toughest gang in North Philly. That is other than the K&A Gang which was a real criminal gang. The 10th and O guys were mostly Italian. Somehow they got into a beef with some South Philly Italian gangs. One day the guys from the 10th and O gang came to other gangs and groups like us and told us that we were to be at 10th and Ontario on Saturday night. If we weren't then we would be considered an enemy and we all know what that meant or at least we thought we did.

So Saturday night we got in our car, with several metal pipes and one chain and drove to the specified streets. Sure enough there were many cars full of kids waiting. I have to tell you I was very uneasy about this. Fighting was not my forte. Anyway, at a certain time (can't remember exactly) we got the word that we would convoy to South Philly and seek out and destroy (beat up) any gang members (and how we were to know who was a gang member I don't know) we saw.

Our car was towards the back of a pretty long line of vehicles (nobody f***s with North Philly Yo!). I sensed apprehension from the others in our "gang" even though a couple of the guys were pretty tough. By the way, I have vague memories of searching for pieces of pipe and putting lead into them. I should say that back then it was rare that anyone would have a gun. I'm not sure if that was because we wanted to be fair and only use pipes and knives or more likely no one could afford a gun.

As we drove through the streets of North Philly, the cars in front of us started turning down side streets. We stayed straight until we learned why. We ran smack into a roadblock of Philly's finest. The police asked us what we were doing and where we were going. We told them we were just driving around and hanging out. They asked if we had any weapons and we, of course said no. I'm sure they were busy (lots of cars behind us) because they didn't search the car. They asked us where we were from. We told them Front and Allegheny. They said we didn't belong in this neighborhood and we were to go back to Front and Allegheny.

I was never so relieved and I am sure the others were as well, not that anyone would admit it. We couldn't find the convoy and so we went home. A couple days later stories of how some gangs from North Philly came to South Philly and beat up some guy started making the rounds.

I used adaptations of this story in my first Mercy Row novel. Of course, the outcome in the book is much more violent than the actual event it is based on.

## Jail Bird

"I'm not really a juvenile delinquent. I just play one in my books."

Truth be told, I never actually broke any laws that mattered when I was a kid (or after), but still I was taken to the 25th District police station by police officers at least three times.

### First Time

My friends and I used to hang out at a luncheonette that was located directly across the street from the 25th District police station. We were told to move on a number of times before one fateful night. A group, and when I say group, I mean quite a few boys and girls were hanging outside the luncheonette. For a change, we were not drinking (we weren't that stupid). We were having fun as teenagers will, especially when girls were around. Hey, if you can't try to show off what good is it to have girls hanging with you.

All of the sudden several officers came to the corner and had all of us stand against the wall. Then they marched the whole lot of us across the street and put us in two small rooms. One for girls, one for boys (they're also not that stupid). One smart-ass boy asked if we could smoke and the officer laughed and said yes.

We all lit up and in minutes we were choking on the smoke. There was no ventilation in the room. Ha Ha. They took each of us, one at a time to the desk and got our home phone numbers. They were set on making us sweat by calling our parents. What they forgot was these were North Philly parents. The luncheonette owner was the first to arrive, and she was one of the mothers as well. She read the riot act to the police.

One by one the parents started to show up and they were angry at us at first, until they asked what we did. The police said loitering. Then they were mad at the police. I thought some of the parents were going to get arrested. It all worked out. After a couple of hours they let us out.

*Second Time – Scary*
It was the dead of winter and we were all in my 1950 Ford that I paid 30 dollars for. We had the car running and the heater on. Mind you now, we were parked. All of the sudden the police flashers go off in my rearview mirror. Two police cars and several officers, including a very rare (at the time) policewoman got us out of the car. They got our IDs and said that we should follow them to the 25th District police station. Of course, we knew where it was. It was just around the corner.

When we got there they lined up all the boys, there was one girl with us, in the small magistrate's courtroom. We had no idea why and what for. We saw the woman police officer bring a small girl to the hallway and had her look at us through the glass door. Finally, the little girl shook her head no. They let us go but told us that the reason they were picking up teenagers was that the girl was molested. We all said no problem and we hope you find the bastard.

*Time Three*
Okay I was 17 and my friend was also 17. It had snowed a lot and we had no school or work so we went to our luncheonette across from the police station. We were the only ones there and the owner was happy to see us. At least she might make a buck or two. After a sandwich and a Pepsi (oh, get over it, Atlanta) we went outside. Three ten-year-old boys

started chugging snowballs at us. So we did the only thing we could do, we chased after them while trying to hit them with our snowballs.

Of course, we all ran through the police parking lot several times. Then a couple of officers came out and took us into custody. Now keep in mind they were probably bored as crime tends to go down when it's cold and snowy. They took the ten year olds and threatened them with jail time. They tried that on us, but we were veterans of police intervention and we knew better. So, they told us to stay in our own neighborhood, which was two blocks south.

Our innocent run-ins were just that, but the police did have their hands full with kids in the 25th. No one in our crowd ever got arrested for real, but I would have to use all my fingers, all my toes and those of two other people's to count those that I knew of that went to prison for one thing or another.

## The Days the Streets Collapsed

The neighborhood I grew up in and my childhood house were built around 1920, but some of the places near it dated back to before the turn of the century. This meant that a lot of sewer systems were very old. Add to that the fact that the area, at one time, had various streams running through it. We never thought about that until the streets started to cave in.

In 1951 the street at 2nd and Lippincott (just a couple blocks from my house) caved in. In 1959 a tragic collapse at 5th and Clearfield Streets took the life of a 25-year-old police officer. He wasn't found for eight days. When his body was recovered, he was only a couple blocks from being washed into the river and possibly taken out to sea.

Sometime in the 1960s (my family is fuzzy on the date) the 100 West block of Lippincott sewer and street was totally replaced. They had found signs that this street would also collapse if not fixed.

It seemed to me, as a kid, that the city was always doing something to the streets around us. I remember one large hole on Howard Street. We used to play army around it. Of course, I fell into a deep hole they had made. I wasn't hurt and got out easily, and never mentioned that to my mother. If it hadn't been for the city digging I would have never known there was soil under the asphalt and concrete.

## Circle Billiards Parlor

I've already mentioned that my father was a champion pool player, a pool hustler and a gambler of sorts. During the early 1950s he opened a poolroom with a partner. As I remember it had 8 to 10 tables. A couple of tables were tournament size and the rest were regular size.

Circle Billiards was located at Allegheny Ave and Lee Street in the Kensington section of Philadelphia. At some point in the building's history someone had combined four standard row homes and opened a bar on the lower level. Maybe it was even a speakeasy. Anyway, the poolroom was on the second floor of this bar. When I was a kid the bar became Nino's Nightclub and we all thought it might be "connected" to the mob. I went to school with the owner's kid and when he was sixteen he was driving a new car. An unheard of thing in our neighborhood.

Anyway, to get to the poolroom you had to walk up a long, dark and dank stairway. You could smell the cigarette smoke mixed with hot dog odor from the rotary cooker as soon as you opened the door. As you walked into the main area the noise of pool balls hitting other balls, men cursing at missed shots or having fun assailed your ears. There were lots of dollars on the tables as the men gambled to see who the best player was.

From age 8 to about 12, I frequented the poolroom, almost every day after school. So did my brother. If it was slow, Dad would teach us how to play pool or even play a game with us. That was always boring because we would break the rack of balls and he would then sink two or three racks until he finally took pity on us and missed a ball.

If you have read my Mercy Row books you would have experienced some of the influence the poolroom had on me. The new book Mercy Row Retribution has a scene that takes place in the poolroom. My father was very good at trick pool as well as regular pool. He showed us many tricks. The one I remember most I have put in the new book.

## A Long Walk to "Nowheresville"

Where is Nowheresville you ask? I can tell you that it's not near "Clarksville" and there are no "Last Trains" going there. Sorry I had to fit in a connection to the Monkee's song of 1966. Like the meaning of the Monkee's song, Nowheresville is a place you might not come back from if you ever get there in the first place.

When you grow up in the blue-collar area of North Philly the expectations are that you will aspire to get a job in a factory or, if you're lucky, learn a trade such as plumbing. You could also get a job in construction or become a roofer. Lots of roofers in the 1950-60s North Philly. Now that's fine if that's what you want. All are respectable jobs and some of them can provide a very good living.

For me, I wanted something else. Maybe being a Pool Shark like my dad would have been fun, but I wasn't a good enough player for that. Problem was I didn't know what I wanted. I hadn't found myself yet. Go to college, you say. Nice thought but back then there was no expectation that a guy or girl from our neighborhood would go to college. Most parents didn't have the money to pay for college. I don't remember any government-sponsored high interest college loans either.

So at 17 I took a job as an apprentice plumber. Hey, plumbers were making 5 bucks an hour back then. I started off making $1 an hour and often worked 50 - 60 hours with no overtime pay. It was a good job but, a hard job. I dug ditches in 100 degree weather, helped plug outdoor leaks in 5 degree weather, carried bathtubs up 4 floors and a lot more. It was okay and some day, after 4 years or so, I could make that $5 an hour. Something was missing, but I had no idea what. I felt as if I was on A Long Walk to Nowheresville.

So I did the only thing I thought I could do. I quit my job, joined the Air Force and hoped I would find a career I loved that would carry with me my whole life. The Air Force had another idea. They enrolled me in a school to learn how to handle and load bombs on air planes. Yikes!!!

I finished basic training and was put on a train to Denver, Colorado. Lowery Airbase was a school base. They taught lots of different skills, many of which translated to good careers when you left the military. Loading bombs on planes was not one of them. Again, the nagging feeling came over me. I felt as if I was still on A Long Walk to Nowheresville.

Sometimes crap happens and puts you back on course without you even knowing it. Call it God's intervention or providence, after a month of kitchen duty and shoveling coal waiting for our bomb class to start, me and several others were pulled out of line and told to see the master sergeant. He asked me if I had studied Physics in high school.

I said, "No, Mastbaum was a trade school."

He said, "If you didn't study Physics then you can't load bombs on airplanes.

I asked, "Then what can I do?" I was hiding my joy about losing the coveted load bombs job.

He handed me a book and said, "Pick anyone, expect Intelligence school. That's for brainiacs."

I looked and I didn't see anything that interested me. Fortunately, I had met a guy at the local beer hangout who said he was going to Photo School. That stayed with me and I asked the sergeant about it.

He said, "Yeah, they teach that on the other side of the base."

I didn't know it then, but I guessed later it was as far away from the "normal" schools as they could get it. You know how those creative types are? Wouldn't want them contaminating regular military.

Anyway I asked how long the school was. He told me it was 17 weeks. I thought about it for a second, realizing the other schools were mostly 6 months or longer.

I said, "I'll take it."

I hated the first week in photo school. *Why did I do this*? I thought. But that passed and I soon started to love it. What I didn't realize then was it wasn't photography in general that I loved, it was being a communicator. And, so this led me on a path from being a photographer to being a marketing executive to now being a writer. How funny life can be.

The moral of the story is - yes for Christ's sake there is a moral- don't settle for what is expected of you. Experience things until you find something you love.

One last thing. I was in my late 40s when my mother finally stopped telling me she wished I had stayed a plumber.

## Scariest Night of the Year

From about age 4 to 12 years old, Halloween was as important a holiday as Thanksgiving for us. Kids dressed up like ghouls, monsters and fiends and roamed the streets in search of candy and pennies. Even so, Halloween wasn't the scariest night of the year, Mischief Night was and it was the neighbors who were scared, not us kids.

We celebrated Halloween for four days: Mischief night on the 29th of October, Soap night on the 30th, Halloween on the 31st, and All Saints day on November 1st. Mischief Night started by us sneaking into the refrigerator (yes, by then we had a fridge, not an icebox) and taking as many eggs as we could hold. We would also grab a bar of soap and maybe a small brown paper bag or two. Then we would meet up with our gang and prowl the streets looking for suitable targets.

There were years that some kids took Mischief Night to extremes, throwing rocks through factory windows or committing vandalism in some fashion or another. I just want to say we were not those kids. The worst our neighbors would have to do after Mischief Night was to clean egg or soap off their windows and cars. Sometimes they would have to clean their shoes.

Yes, we threw eggs at people's houses and we soaped windows, mostly stores, and a few times we put dog crap in bags, lit them and placed them on someone's step. We rang the bell, ran and hoped they would try to stamp the fire out. It worked 50% of the time.

Soap Night, I think was made up by the grownups hoping we would forget about Mischief Night and only soap their windows. Eventually there was only Soap Night but the fiendish adult plan backfired and we just combined both into Soap Night.

On Halloween, we would get our costumes. Now at that time, we never saw readymade costumes in the store. Even if we had, we wouldn't have been able to buy them. Some kids took an old sheet and cut arm-holes in it. Just like that, they were ghosts. I would find some old clothes with holes in them (Today they pay a lot of money for clothing like that J). Then I would find an old stick, probably the same as we used for stickball, and made a cloth bag to go on the end. The piece de resistance was to find an old cork and burn the end. Then I rubbed it on my face to make me look dirty. We called that the BUM, but today I believe the correct term is Urban Outdoors Man.

My brother Bill, who is four years older than me, had collecting candy down to a science. He would grab a pillowcase, as we all did, and started his quest to get as much candy as possible. He and his friend started at 6 PM and stayed out until midnight, methodically visiting every row home in a two-mile radius. Some he went back to if they were giving out pennies. Bill would collect two full pillowcases of goodies on that one night. I wasn't as aggressive as he was and would come home with only one pillowcase full of wrapped and unwrapped candy, apples, loose cookies and pennies. The best fun was sorting them out and eating the candy.

The funny thing was we would eat all that candy in about two weeks. I never remember anyone saying we were hyper because we ate too much sugar. Then again, we were out on the street playing every day of the week from after school until bedtime (Okay, we had a break for dinner for half an hour). On weekends, we were out from the time we woke up until our parents dragged us in to eat or go to bed. So, I guess no one noticed how hyper we were.

**Thank You, Thanksgiving Day**
Thank you for all the wonderful memories of feasting with the family at my grandparents' house, then my parents' house in Kensington, North Philly.

Thank you for telling the teachers to have me draw turkeys, pilgrims and autumn leaves so my parents could put them on the refrigerator.

And, thank for having the trees near school shed their acorns so we could throw them at each other.

Thank you, Thanksgiving for being in late November when the weather was cold and my mother could stuff us into the snowsuits so we could run or hardly walk. And, thank you for the turkey sweater that made me look more dorky than I already was.

Thank you for the Gimbels Thanksgiving Day parade with all the local stars, floats and the school bands playing music. And, thank you for having the crowd be so loud we couldn't hear the school bands. No really, thank you.

Thank you for the El and the trolley cars that took us downtown with all the families that were stuffed like sardines in a can. I was hoping to see Howdy Doody, Buffalo Bob, Dilly Dally, Carabell the Clown and especially Princess Summerfallwinterspring, but I was usually disappointed because they were busy at the Macy's New York Parade. That disappointment, however, quickly faded, when I spied Sally Star, Wee Willy Weber, Pixanne and Bertie the Bunyip.

Thank you for the crowds of people that battled the cold and sometimes snow and lined the streets every year to get a glimpse of Santa. And, thank you for the small children who were perched on their Dad's shoulders so they could see the parade and blocked my view.

Thank you for having Santa climb up the fire truck ladder to the fourth floor of Gimbels. Thank you also for having Santa scared the hell out of me when I was very small.

Thank you for having those Santa's helpers that dressed just like him on every street corner in downtown Philly and Kensington Avenue the day after Thanksgiving. And, thank you for being sure they were much taller than me, so I didn't have to smell the whiskey on their breath.

Thank you, Thanksgiving for making merchants wait until your holiday was over to start the Christmas Season. Maybe you could talk to them now about going back to that tradition.

Thank you for the wonderful smell of roasting turkey that permeated our 16 x 40 foot two-story row home. And, thank you for allowing us to drink and eat until we would burst, and for us having only one bathroom in the house when we had 15 guests.

Thank you for the mashed potatoes, the stuffing, cranberry sauce and the wonderful pies. I loved the apple pie, minced meat pie and of course, pumpkin pie. In addition, double thank you for the time the bar of soap fell in the mashed potatoes and I learned about it the hard way.

Most of all, thank you for grandparents and parents that understood the value of holiday family gatherings. It was a time when all the cousins, brothers, sisters, aunts and uncles, especially those who were living like a million miles away in southern New Jersey, got together and enjoyed each other's company. I never have understood when people say they have to endure another Thanksgiving dinner with family. I feel sorry for them. I wouldn't change a thing about my memories.

So again, thank you, Thanksgiving. See you next year. I would give anything to have just one more Thanksgiving dinner with my Grandparents and Parents. Maybe, someday I will.

Growing Up North Philly With Mom

My mother's birthday is October 16th. She would have been 101 years old (2015). We had her around for 87 of those years and I am very grateful for that. I have spoken a lot about my Dad in my previous Growing Up North Philly posts. Now it's Mom's turn.

My Dad's birthday is October 20th. When I was a young child I couldn't understand how my Dad could be older than her when his birthday was after her birthday. I think I mentioned I wasn't the best of students. I figured it out later. Mom was the glue that held the family together. She never forgot a birthday, never missed an opportunity to hug us and, when needed slap us in the face.

As I look back on it, I'm sure we tortured her. My sister was 10 years older than me so she was probably helping out by the time I was born. I do remember a story my mother told me about my sister. She was just seven or eight or so and it was Christmas time, so my sister went shopping on Front Street. She had about 25 cents. She came back with gifts for the entire family, which when my mother saw them she knew Roberta (Berta) could not have bought them. When she asked, Berta admitted she just took the gifts. Mom made a big thing out of it, marched her back to the store and made her return everything. A lesson well learned, as my sis never did that again.

Berta probably did some other stuff, but I think it was my brother Bill and me that gave our Mom the most trouble. First of all, my brother and I fought like alley cats. He would hit me on the head (not so lightly) every time he passed me. I would be sure to do things he hated like, smack my lips, eat pretzels making a loud noise, chew gum or breathe. This gave my Mom lots of opportunities to say, "Will you two shut the hell up" and to administer a slap on the cheek. This was a mild irritation for my mother. Believe me we did worse.

Back then, we had a party line on our phone, which meant we were not the only household to share the same number. Sometimes you would pick the phone up and hear the other family talking. My Mom was addicted to talking to her friends on the phone so she was on it all the time. I'm sure the other family was livid about that. We had a small hassock she sat on near the phone. Once she got up to stretch and I pulled the hassock away as a joke. Give me a break, I was just six or seven. Anyway, when she sat back down the hassock wasn't there. To say the least, she was not happy.

My brother Bill did me one better. Once again, my mother was sitting on the hassock and on the phone. She sent my brother to the candy store to buy some bubble gum. You know those small hard rectangular-shaped pink chewing gums that pull fillings out of your teeth. She gave him a nickel and he ran over to the store. He bought five pieces. When he came back, he was in a hurry to get out and play. So, in typical Bill fashion, he yelled "Here, Mom," and threw the bag to her from 20 feet away. My Mom turned and the bag of rock-like gum hit her in the eye. Yes, she got a black eye from it.

Mom's addiction to bubble gum only lasted until she became enamored with maple taffy. She made it herself. She boiled maple syrup and put it in a flat pan. When it cooled, she would break it up and it was ready to eat. She did this for a number of years until finally her addiction centered on chocolate. My mother and her mother ate ice cream every night. I mean every night. My mother also ate chocolate every night. I once bought her Godiva Chocolate thinking a high quality chocolate would be tastier for her. She ate it but said she preferred Hersey's kisses. My mother and her mother were not overweight and my mother, remember she ate chocolate and ice cream every night, lived to be 87. My mother had a Toy Poodle who she also gave chocolate to every night. That dog lived to be 20 years old. I'm just saying.

When I joined the Air Force, I know she probably was upset, but she didn't let me know. I was off to an adventure and she was losing her youngest child. When I told her I was going to Vietnam, then came home and told her I volunteered for a second tour, I know she was upset, but she didn't show it. I am sure all the bad memories she had during WW2 of sending her two brothers off to war came flooding back. She never made me feel bad about it.

When I told her in a letter I was getting married to a Vietnamese girl and later sent her a letter addressed Grandmom Hallman to announce we were having a baby she was nothing but supportive. God, I sound like an asshole. She and the whole family accepted my choice of a wife, even though it was uncommon back then for a North Philly boy to marry an Asian.

Mom, I am so grateful that I was lucky enough to have you for a mother and to have the family I had.

**Twas The Night Before Christmas In Philly**
When I watch the movie The Christmas Story it's like watching a replay of my childhood Christmases. I'm not sure I should tell you this, but hey, it was 63 years ago. Do you remember the scene in the movie where the kid sticks his tongue on a freezing cold flagpole? Well, that was me, but it was a light pole not a flag pole. It took awhile for me to free my tongue and no one called the firemen.

For us, Christmas started the day after Thanksgiving. The merchants on Front Street as well as Kensington Avenue had wonderfully colored Christmas lights streaming up and down the street. All the decorations came out as well. A week or so later all the houses started to light up. Santa was in his big chair at Gimbels, Lit Brothers and Wanamaker's Department Stores just waiting for us to show up. We didn't have malls back then, so department stores were the center of Christmas activities.

My mom loved to decorate for Christmas. Colorful Santas, elves, snowmen, and wreathes all adorned our house. On Christmas Eve she always burned a Bayberry candle, which was supposed to bring you good luck all year. The candle had to burn all night or it wouldn't work and you would be, God forbid, at the mercy of chance. One year my grandfather saw the candle burning after everyone went to bed, thought it was a fire hazard and put it out. To say my mother was upset is an understatement.

Speaking of my grandfather, for a number of years when I was a kid he sold Christmas trees. Each year, he made an arrangement with Nan Scott, the lady who owned a small candy shop on the corner of Wishart and Front Streets, and she allowed him to set up his trees. He used the whole sidewalk and if you were going shopping on Front Street, you had to pass by his trees. No officials asked for a business license, no sales tax, no credit card swipe machines and no one complained. It was just a guy trying to make an extra buck. Unfortunately, today he probably couldn't do that.

I have vivid memories of my mother and sister making wreaths from the broken pine tree branches. They tied a red ribbon on them and he sold those as well. Speaking of Christmas trees, people generally bought them a week or more early and put them in their back yards. When I say yard I mean a patch of concrete 8 x 16 feet. Anyway, when it came time to bring them in the house to decorate they smelled like cat pee. One thing about urban living in those days was the numerous alley cats and tomcats. At night, you could hear the loud "screams" of the cats as they looked for a mate. It sounded like babies crying. Since the green trees were the only vegetation available, the cats thought we put them there for them to pee on. The smell went away eventually, usually by New Year's Day.

Sometime in the 1950s my mother got tired of the cat pee smell and bought a silver artificial tree. It came with a color wheel that reflected different rotating colors off the silver. It was cool but I missed the cat pee smell. Later when I came home from Nam and Duoc and I got our first apartment my mother gave us that tree. She upgraded to an artificial green tree. The silver tree lasted a couple years more and brought some pleasure to my kids and a couple of photo ops for me.

Like the movie, we all wanted a Red Ryder BB gun: Unlike the movie I never got one. But, my mother was sure we all received lots of toys from Santa. She would start saving in her bank-sponsored Christmas savings fund in January, just to be sure she could get all the presents. She also made sure she pasted all her S&H Green Stamps in the books.

My brother was a kind of rambunctious kid and got a lot more slaps than I did. One year my Grandfather, always the jokester, put coal in my brother's Christmas stocking. Needless to say, there was pandemonium for a few minutes until my mother gave him the real stocking. One year I got a Shmoo doll from the comic strip Li'l Abner (Look it up on Google). The Shmoo was said to have magical powers and every morning it would leave something special, like an apple, an egg or a piece of candy. One morning I ran down the steps wide-eyed and anxious to see what the Shmoo had left me. The magical gift was always under him, he laid the gifts as a chicken would lay an egg. I pulled off the Shmoo with anticipation and reeled back in horror. The Shmoo hadleft me several cat turds. My Grandfather at work again.

Christmas Eve was always crazy. The tree needed to be decorated and my mother would supervise my grandfather and brother as they placed the bulbs and tinsel in just the right places. This often required my grandfather to get on a ladder to put the star or angel on the top of the tree. I'll never forget the year my grandfather was leaning to place a decoration and fell into the tree. Down came the tree, my grandfather and my brother, who was handing him the decoration. No one was hurt, but it remained the source of much laughing for years.

Of course, we never wanted to go to sleep Christmas Eve. We were too excited, but after much pleading and hollering, we ended up tramping up the steps to our 10 x 8 foot room with a single bed we shared until Bill joined the Navy and I left for the Air Force a year later. How can anyone forget getting up early on Christmas morning, running down the steps and seeing the blazing Christmas tree on a train platform and the American Flyer engine pulling a caboose chugging around the tree. Surrounding the tree were the whole family's presents. My Mother was sure to put them in the same place each year. I was on the left and my brother's gifts were on the right. The adult's gifts were in the middle. One year my mother reversed that order. When I came down the steps I saw that I had no gifts. I cried for five minutes until my mother convinced me that my gifts were just in a different place.

My Dad was always home for Christmas day. He closed the poolroom and spent time with us. Once again, the house would fill with the wonderful scent of baking turkey. We would have bacon and eggs and sometimes Scrapple for breakfast and always we had breakfast cakes and rolls from the German bakery around the corner. Lunch was generally a sandwich and my brother and my favorite was the potato chip, Lebanon boloney and American cheese sandwich.

In my early years, we always had the whole family, uncles, aunts, cousins at my Grandmother's house. She had a dining room table and the adults crowded around it while the kids were in the kitchen. Later, after my Grandmother and Grandfather moved in with us it was just the immediate family. The cousins would come over during Christmas week. My father would take his seat at the table a full ten minutes before my Mother and Grandmother were ready to serve. I think it was his way of saying, "Hurry up."

Remember the American Flyer train set I mentioned? When we got it my brother assumed it was his only and we had many arguments about that. Because he was four years older than I was he won most of the time.

After we laid our mother to rest in 2002 at the Resurrection Cemetery in Bensalem, PA., we found two baby books my mother had written, one for Bill and one for me. Talk about a tearjerker. I still tear up when I read it. Anyway, amongst the comments about our weight at different ages and comments about how we had grown up to be wonderful children was an entry that brought terror to my brother's heart.

My mother had written in one of the baby books, and I quote her, "Today we bought Billy and Buddy (my childhood name) an American Flyer train set." Once again, Mom solved a dispute between my brother and me.

## New Year's Eve and Day

The time between Christmas Eve and New Year's Day was the gold standard (Summer was the Diamond standard) for time off of school. You had the toys you received for Christmas and there were always leftover pies, cakes and candy that had to be eaten. The day after our Christmas bounty.

The first time I remember feeling sorry for someone happened during this time when I was about eight years old. My friends and I were playing Tin Can Eddy and a kid from a few blocks away asked if you could join in. We had seen him around, but he wasn't one of our regular gang. Still we let him play. Somehow, the conversation got around to each of use telling what treasures we had received for Christmas. Remember, I mentioned that my Mom saved all year just to be sure her children got many cool presents. When it came to Joe to tell us what he received from Santa (I'll call him Joe because I don't remember his name), he lifted his hands and said, "Gloves." We quickly asked what else he got and he said, "Just these gloves. They're cool right?" Joe said. I said, "Yeah, they are cool," but in my heart I felt sorry for him and more appreciative of what I had. That feeling passed quickly and "Joe" joined in and had a great time. Afterwards he went home and we never saw him again. Maybe Joe was really an angel come to teach me a lesson. Nah?

In the mid-1950s my sister and brother-in-law moved into my grandmother's house and my Grandfather and Grandmother moved in with us. My sister (ten years older than me) started having New Year's Eve parties in her new house, which was around the corner from us. She invited our family and family friends and it was always a great time. The adults drank beer and highballs, and kids got to drink sodas (soda in Philadelphia is any carbonated soft drink). It was a fun time and I wonder now how so many people fit into such a small home. At ten o'clock or so, the chips and pretzels were replaced with hot dogs and sauerkraut and roast beef on Kaiser roll sandwiches. It was torture for us kids as we had to smell the food cooking all night before we could get some. It was always worth the wait.

At midnight, all the kids and some of the adults got pots and pans and large spoons and made as much noise as we could. The entire neighborhood did the same and for the first fifteen minutes of the New Year, it was bedlam.

After the noise making I always went back around to my house to say Happy New Year to my Grandmother. She didn't like parties and instead at midnight simply heated up a coffee cake she bought at the German bakery. I can see her now sitting at the front of our small kitchen table drinking her coffee and eating her cake. I would kiss her on the cheek and she would give me a piece of cake. My father normally didn't go to these parties either. He worked at the poolroom late, came home, and was in bed before the midnight.

On New Year's Day we would wake up, have a good breakfast and get ready to see the Mummers Parade on TV. Several times my Dad did take us to see them in person, but I think that may have been before we had a television set. To be honest it was much easier and you saw at lot more on TV than in person. One thing I do remember about being at the New Year's Day Parade was the men selling roasted chestnuts. They smelled great and anything hot on a cold January day was welcomed.

Soon the house would fill with the aroma of baked ham with cloves. This was our traditional New Year's Day meal. Come to think of it, that was our traditional Easter meal as well. There were pies again and all the fixings that went with baked ham. Just like Christmas and Thanksgiving after the meal, everyone laid around half-comatose from eating too much. When my head cleared, I would remember that I had school the next day. The thought would hit me like a ton of bricks. We would have to wait until February to get another day off from school.

## The Old Man in the Bay

My Grandfather, Harry Hird, was a consummate angler. As long as I can remember, he would drive two hours to Wildwood, New Jersey to a boat rental place called Otto's. Otto rented small boats, with or without motors, which people used to fish in the bay. Pop (My Grandfather) mostly rented the boat without the motor because he didn't have enough money. That was the same reason he always used the Tacony Palmyra Bridge since it was a 5 cents instead of 25 cents toll. He would make this trip three or four times a week during the summer. I have to tell you the cars Pop owned were not in the best of shape, but they got him there.

Pop always caught fish, flounder mostly. In fact, he was so prevalent in the Wildwood bay, the tour boats would point him out as the "Old Man in the Bay". They would ask him over the loud speaker to hold up the fish he caught. A few times, he held up a couple of minnows he used for bait. He liked to be funny. People coming to Otto's to fish would ask him what bait he used to catch so many flounders. He would say gumdrops. Off the would-be anglers would go to find some gumdrops.

More than once, I received a fish in my face when I would watch him clean his catch. It was never a hard hit, but enough to make you cringe at the fishy smell and slimy wetness on your cheek. My mother told me a story of the one time she went fishing with her father. They started early in the morning and after a few hours, my mother asked him to go back to the dock so she could take a pee. He told her to do what the men do and pee off the back of the boat. That was the last time my mother went fishing.

My brother was his fishing partner from the time he was old enough to go on the boat. Pop and Bill would jump into the Model T or the 39 Chrysler and head to the "shore". Shore is Philly speak for the land by the Atlantic Ocean. Actually, any ocean I guess. They would get up at 3 am and fish from 5 am to late in the afternoon. My brother has a not-so-fond memory of doing this one day and not eating. Pop refused to take the boat back so Bill could get a sandwich. When they finally did dock, Bill insisted he had to eat something. Mind you, he was about 11 or 12 at the time. Pop asked Otto's wife to make Bill a hamburger. Bill claims to this day "it was the best damn meal I ever ate."

I also went fishing with Pop and Bill, but Pop wasn't thrilled with my presence. He would complain to Bill that I talked so much I scared the fish away. It didn't break my heart not to go fishing, mainly because of a fish I caught when I was about eight years old. It had the biggest teeth I have ever seen. I believe it was called an Oyster Cracker. Pop told me that it could bite your finger off. What I lacked in fishing enthusiasm my brother made up for. He has been a lifelong fisherman and has been fishing in places Pop could only dream about.

When Pop couldn't go to Wildwood to fish, he went to one of many fresh water spots in and around Philly. The canal at New Hope was good for carp and catfish, as was a small pond near Willow Grove Amusement Park in Willow Grove, PA. That pond didn't start out as a great fishing spot, it got that way because Pop would catch carp and catfish and release them in the pond. He did this so he would always have a place to fish that was closer than New Hope. When in his early seventies Pop started caddying at a couple of golf courses. As I remember, there were no golf carts then and he carried the bags himself. After a hard day at caddying and instructing people how to play golf even if they didn't want instructions, he would fish in ponds on the premise. First, he had to stock them.

Nothing it seemed could stop Pop from fishing. One day something did. He was coming home from fishing and his car swerved and hit a parked car on 5th Street. Later the doctors determined he had a stroke. After that, he couldn't drive any longer and his beloved fishing became a thing of the past. Within six months Pop passed away. The docs said it was from lung cancer, but I believe it was because he couldn't fish any longer.

I fantasize that Pop is fishing in paradise's ponds and restocking them when they need it. He would laugh at me if I could tell him that. He wasn't much of a believer. He once told me that "When I die just stick a bone up my ass, throw me in the back alley and let the dogs drag me away." I used his quote in my first Mercy Row book.

# Author's Biography

*Harry Hallman*

Hallman was born in 1944 and raised in the Kensington section of North Philadelphia. Hallman's father was Harry Hallman, Sr., a champion pool player who also owned a poolroom called Circle Billiards, located at Allegheny Avenue and Lee Street in Philadelphia. The younger Hallman spent many hours after school at his father's poolroom and watching his father play in other poolrooms in Philadelphia and New Jersey. The people he met, some belonging to the real K&A Gang, influenced his writing of the Mercy Row series.

After a year of being an apprentice plumber he served four years in the U.S. Air Force, including two tours in South Vietnam as a photographer. His first tour was at Ton Son Nhat Airbase where he processed film shot by U2 Aircraft over North Vietnam and China. He returned to the same place for his second tour, but processed film shot by U.S. fighter recon aircraft. He is married to Duoc Hallman, whom he met in Vietnam, and has two children, Bill and Nancy, and one grandchild, Ava.

Hallman is a serial entrepreneur who has created several marketing services and digital media companies and continues to work as a marketing consultant.

Email Hallman at harry@mercyrow.com. Keep informed at www.mercyrow.com or on Facebook at www.facebook.com/mercyrownovel.

42845543R00165

Made in the USA
Middletown, DE
23 April 2017